Praise for Heather Morrison-Tapl

"*I was blown away by the ease with which I fell into this story, it took me through many emotions and also mirrored my own love of healing herbs... I hope to read this many times and recommend it to all ... Amazing.*"

— Amazon Review

"*I loved this story and the author's style of writing. It is not easy for a novel to hold my attention. This one definitely did! For me, this was a real page-turner. I sure hope there are more books on the horizon!*"

— Amazon Review

"*What a wonderful book! I just had a good feeling all the way through the book that I wished would never end! Thank you for writing such a wonderful story. Keep 'em coming!!!!*"

— Amazon Review

HIGHLAND MAGIC

Heather Morrison-Tapley

ISBN 979-8-218-28303-2

Also by Heather Morrison-Tapley
The Herbalist

To Mummy the English rose,
Daddy the Scottish thistle,
and David the knight.

And to my Great Aunt Sybil,
whose incredible true story
inspired this book

CHAPTER 1

It was Maren Philip's thirty-fifth birthday. She sat at an old wooden table, set unevenly on the ground of an outdoor restaurant just outside New Orleans. Lights were strung among the tree branches, tables full of happy customers, and in the distance the sun set over swampy water, out of which grew tall trees with swaths of Spanish moss blowing in the breeze.

Water full of God knows what, she thought. Snakes and alligators and danger. Little did she know the real danger was coming later that night. Life-threatening danger. Life changing.

But the restaurant was lively and the food delicious. They were having shrimp gumbo, crawfish, and jambalaya. And wine. Lots of wine. She was celebrating her birthday doing what she did best, having fun and keeping things light.

One of the revelers, a cheerful young woman in her twenties named Maddy, stood and raised her glass. "I have an announcement," she said. Maren sat up and smiled, expecting a birthday toast. "I got a job in Berlin! I'm going to be teaching English at the American School!"

Everyone cheered and raised their glasses and the conversation turned to Germany and moving and Maddy's plans. Maren sank back in her chair. She looked over at Trey. Handsome, funny, Trey. She met him in Montana and they had been together for almost a year, a record in Maren's current life of quick adventures, no ties, and constant moving. She and Trey were celebrating her birthday with a small group of friends.

Were they friends? Maren wondered as she sat on the creaky wooden chair on the damp grass. She had known them for about a month.

There were always groups of twenty-somethings wandering the globe, some American, others from every corner of the world, working for a few weeks or months, then moving on. They were always friendly, adventurous, and temporary.

Maren pulled off a piece of fresh, crusty bread. She dipped it in the spicy sauce of the gumbo, took a big sip of the cold white wine, and sighed. *Thirty-five.* Looking at the fresh faces of the others, right out of high school or college, having a quick adventure before heading home, she suddenly felt very tired.

Trey filled his wine glass and put the bottle down. Maren picked it up to fill her own. Chivalrous he was not. Trey was on his fourth glass of wine, finding everything hilarious, especially himself.

"Ok listen to this one," Maddy said. "I spent two days living on a nude beach in Brazil, camping with this super-hot guy named Benjamin. Man, he was cute. Anyway, at the end of the weekend, we packed up to go and found someone had stolen all our clothes! We had to walk into the village stark naked and buy clothes at the outdoor market, we almost got arrested!" The partiers all burst into laughter. Everyone told tales of their adventures and mishaps around the world. The same types of stories told by all the travelers she had met over the years. *Were they always the same stories?* They had seemed so much more interesting in the past.

Maybe she'd had too much to drink. She was getting melancholy. She probably had. She told herself to snap out of it. This was her birthday. She should be happy. *Should* be.

So, she downed her wine and said, "Let's go dancing!"

Half and hour later, she jumped on the back of Trey's motorcycle and they sped off toward a New Orleans nightclub. The roads were winding and the gravel loose. She hugged Trey as they leaned into corners and glided along the road back toward the French Quarter.

Maren was belting out the Beatles' *Birthday* song when they leaned a little too low and took a corner a little too fast. She felt the tires slide out from under them, and then her world went black.

***

When Maren woke up, she didn't know where she was. Slowly, as her eyes focused, she realized she was in the hospital. She went to sit up and winced in pain. Her left arm was bandaged and stung like it was on fire. So did her left leg, which also had a white bandage wrapping it from knee to toe.

With her right arm, she scooted herself and sat up. Across the room was another bed with a very old man asleep in it.

"Ahh, you're awake," a nurse said, walking in with a small computer on wheels. "Good.".

"Where am I?" Maren asked.

"University Medical Center. You had a motorcycle accident," she said, with a smile that hid something else. Maybe a drop of judgment?

Maren thought back to the last thing she remembered. Trey had been drinking before they left the restaurant, and they got on the bike. She felt ashamed.

Suddenly, her heart seized, where was Trey?

"My friend? Where is he? His name is Trey Hillman. Was he hurt?" she asked in rapid succession.

"I don't know, honey. He's not here," the nurse said, finishing taking her blood pressure and punching numbers into the computer.

Not here? Where the heck is he?

He had crashed their motorcycle, and she had been unconscious in the hospital. Where on earth would he be that was more important than being there?

"What happened to me?" Maren asked, looking at her bandages.

"You were very lucky. Just a bad road rash on your arm and leg and a concussion. It could have been much worse. Apparently, you weren't wearing a helmet," the nurse said as she packed up her cart and left the room.

Maren suddenly had a flashback. She was eighteen and there were two policemen at the door. Her parents, both alcoholics, had driven their car into a tree. *What was I thinking?* She had almost just done the same thing. A thing she had judged them so harshly for her whole life.

Just then, the old man in the bed across the room woke up. He smiled at her, but before he could say anything, a crowd of people rushed in, speaking rapidly, hugging and kissing him, producing bowls of delicious-smelling food, sitting him up, and plumping pillows behind him to make him comfortable. Everyone talked at once, smiling and doting on the man.

Maren looked around again. Maybe Trey had just gone to the bathroom. Or the cafeteria. He'd probably stayed up all night by her bedside and needed a coffee. But no one appeared in the doorway for her.

The man across the room must have seen her looking hopefully at the door. He whispered something to one of his visitors and a kind-looking middle-aged woman put some food into a bowl and carried it over to her. With a smile, the old man made the gesture for her to eat it.

"Thank you," Maren said to the woman, then nodded to the man in thanks too.

Maren's phone had been smashed in the accident and she felt helpless, scared, and completely isolated, alone in the hospital with no phone. Though, worse still, who would she call anyway, other than Trey? She had no family. No roots. She was floating in the wind. Which had been her goal for years now. No attachments, no hurt feelings. Although, in the quiet hours in the middle of the night, she sometimes admitted to herself that her feelings hurt more than they ever had, trying to stay light and unattached. To some people, it seemed to come naturally. To her, it did not. But it was marginally better than having her heart shattered over and over, so she would shut her mind off and jump in a car or on a plane and take off to another city, another adventure. Another fling.

But sitting alone in the hospital, in pain and scared, her heart hurt. The one thing she tried so hard to avoid. Where were the "friends" from her party? Not one person had shown up to visit her in over twenty-four hours.

As she sat there, she realized she had the answer to the question she'd asked herself at her party…they weren't friends. They were people whose paths had crossed in a party city. They weren't people looking for complications or heavy things, like injuries and hospitals. Most of all, they weren't people who wanted someone to need them.

She felt angry and rejected, until she realized she had been the exact same way all these years, picking up and moving on as soon as anything even hinted at complication.

Finally, on Maren's second day in the hospital, Trey showed up. By then Maren was furious. Or was it hurt? Weren't they the same thing?

He walked toward her bed with a big smile, casual, like he hadn't almost killed her in a motorcycle accident, and then abandoned her. Casual like they hadn't lived together for almost a year.

"Babe!" he said. He leaned over and kissed her. "How are you? Oh my God, that was intense, right?"

"Intense?" Maren replied. "Trey, we could have been killed. I've been in the hospital for almost two days with no sign of you. Where the hell have you been?" Angry tears welled up in her eyes.

"Dude, I'm so sorry. I had to deal with the crazy motorcycle rental people. They wanted me to pay for the damned bike, and I was like, no way, you jerk, I had insurance. It was a whole thing. Then the gang was worried about you, so I had to tell them all you were banged up but okay. Sorry, I just was really busy. And you haven't even asked how I am. I had to get seven stitches in my arm, dude!"

She could smell the alcohol on his breath. Unbelievable. He'd been out drinking while she sat alone in the hospital. And just like that, without planning it, she said, "I need you to get out, *dude*"

"Oh." Trey looked confused. "Yeah, you're tired, I get it. Okay, I'll come back another time." She sensed his relief at having done his duty. Now he'd be able to go back to whatever bar he had been at.

"No. Get out. I mean, go away. We're done," she said.

"What?" he said, clearly shocked. "What are you talking about? I was just a little late. Jeez, don't be so dramatic."

It must have been the near-death experience, coupled with her birthday, and the loneliness in that hospital bed, staring at the door for a whole day. But it was also *every* day they'd been together: fun, light, no strings. What was she doing? She didn't really care about this guy who had the emotional depth of a puddle. And she was sure he didn't care about her, other than as a fun travel buddy, and someone to go to bed with at night.

She suddenly had total clarity. She was done. Done with him, done with this nomadic existence, partying and pretending that adventure was all she wanted out of life. She had crossed a line. . She had been drunk, and she knew Trey had been too, and she had gotten on the bike with him. She was thirty-five and acting like a teenager. A reckless, irresponsible teenager. They could have killed someone. Or themselves. She was doing exactly what she had hated watching her parents do her whole childhood.

Maybe she didn't want a life of constant heartache thinking about the past, but she didn't want this meaningless, reckless life either.

"Trey, you're not a bad guy. But this is over. This is not what I want. I need someone who actually cares about me. I sat here alone and in pain for a day and a half all by myself. Please just go away."

"Wow, that's ridiculous," he said, instantly defensive. "One freaking late hospital visit and we're over? Well, fine by me. Not like I wanted anything serious anyway." He turned to walk away, with no hint of fighting for her or wanting things to change. It was confirmation of everything she had been thinking. "Good luck!" he said, with spite in his voice, before marching out.

Maren looked over at the old man in the bed opposite. His wise, watery eyes crinkled as he smiled and nodded at her.

Later that day, Maren was released from the hospital, scabbed and sore, but miraculously, no more hurt than that. She returned to the cheap motel, where she had been staying with Trey. He had moved all his things out. He was probably in Bali, or New York, or Timbuktu by now. None of the birthday party friends had come to visit her.

She felt almost embarrassed that she was thirty-five and found herself with nothing. No real life. Not a soul on earth who cared about her. No family. Not even any friends. Wasn't that what she'd been going for all these years? No ties?

"Be careful what you create," a wise person somewhere along her path had said to her.

She had created exactly what she had set out to—a total lack of dependence on anyone.

But now she just felt sad. And incredibly alone in the world.

She sat on the creaky hotel bed and cried. She felt like a little girl. She had been sad and alone then too. She felt a deep longing for something she had almost never had. She longed for a sense of place, a connection to something bigger than herself. She longed to belong. She longed to go home.

The problem was, she didn't have one. And she wasn't sure where to start.

So, she decided to start at the only place that had ever felt like home in her life.

CHAPTER 2

Maren stood in the pouring rain, everything she owned in the bag on her back, staring at the craggy, mist-covered Scottish mountains rising in the distance. She was exhausted, cold, soaking wet, and happy.

She adjusted her bag and started the half-mile walk down the muddy dirt driveway from the spot on the paved road where the Highland bus had dropped her in the middle of nowhere. She could have called and had someone pick her up, she supposed. Though she didn't know anyone to ask. Could have arranged a taxi maybe. Could have asked for help. But if Maren Phillips was the most capable woman in the world in almost every aspect, the one thing she did not know how to do was ask for help. So, there she was, trudging down the dirt road with her heavy burden, with a smile on her face so wide it almost hurt.

When she rounded the final bend of the driveway, it came into sight. The little white cottage of her childhood summers. Her refuge from a home that was filled with drunkenness and disorder. The cottage meant safety and warm meals and adventure.

Her heart quickened to see it now. Her beloved Uncle Gordon, the provider of all the good memories of her childhood, was gone. And the cottage itself was in near ruins. *Like me,* she thought. A tear rolled down her cheek.

"What is within is without," a spiritual teacher had once taught her in Santa Fe. Or was that one in California?

I am this cottage, she thought.

She dropped her backpack and ran to the door like a child.

Hidden Stone Farm was Maren's favorite place on Earth. The cottage had been built in the late 1800s. It was whitewashed stone, and the bright white stood out against the rocky hills that jutted up behind it.

The roof was made of slate tiles, some coming loose, she noticed. There was the main cottage, a smaller cottage behind a grove of oak trees, and, off to the right, a large stone stable. The stable had been her uncle's pride and joy. Behind the cottages lay her uncle's enormous vegetable garden, several fruit trees, and then walking and riding paths leading up into the hills. Her uncle always described the hills in summer, carpeted in purple heather. But to Maren the hills were gray in summer or winter. Maren was profoundly colorblind and as an adult, she mourned all the colors around the world that she had not seen. But, as a child, it had seemed normal that the world was white and grey and black. Somehow it seemed to fit her life. And she loved the farm whether it was purple or green or black.

Maren opened the cottage door and stepped inside. She felt a home-coming so profound it shocked her. She saw herself as a child, sitting by the big stone fireplace, fire cheerfully crackling inside, her Uncle Gordon in a chair, reading to her, while she smiled up at him.

Then that image faded, and she stepped from the small entranceway into the living room and saw the cottage as it really was. The fireplace was intact, and some furniture was still there, but the window was broken and there were damp leaves and dirt all throughout. The living room was large and had beautiful wood-paneled walls. There were built-in book-shelves, soft, cushy armchairs, and a sofa. Her uncle told her the room was colorful, with a red chair and blue sofa and spines of hundreds of books. She couldn't see the color, but she could feel the comfort and the love in the room.

She turned and walked back through the entryway and to the other side of the cottage, into the kitchen with its woodstove, big wooden table, and deep stone sink. There was a hole in the roof where the wooden timbers had rotted, the roof falling in at one spot. Slate roof shingles lay on the stone floor of the kitchen, some intact, some smashed to pieces.

She was shocked to find herself staring straight up at the sky, rain falling on her face. The kitchen was a mess of leaves and slate and mud.

Out of the corner of her eye, something moved, and she jumped back as a small bird flew out from the top of the kitchen cupboard and soared straight up into the air. Maren laughed. Her uncle, never married, and with no children of his own, had left Maren the cottage when he died. But, back then, she had had no intention of moving to a remote village in the Scottish Highlands. She'd been busy waiting tables in Santa Fe, New Mexico, hiking, taking painting classes, and dating a very handsome yoga instructor. But that was two years ago.

Softly, but steadily, the cottage had called to her during that time. Mostly when she felt lost and alone. Often in her dreams. It was always a comfort knowing it was here. And when the fun had finally run out of all the running, it had called to her one more time. And now she was facing the consequences of her choices. The ruin of the parts of her life she had left abandoned and untended. And she knew she was right where she was meant to be.

Upstairs were a bathroom and three bedrooms: her uncle's bedroom, another which had been used to store things, which was always full of boxes back then and still was, and a third room which had been hers every summer when her parents had shipped her off. Although she had been more of a parent to them than they had been to her, Maren's parents were always eager to get rid of her and had sent her to her Uncle Gordon's as soon as school let out. To Maren it was heaven, her uncle was kind and loving and funny and it was the only time all year she had home-cooked meals and was read to and taught things and taken care of. It was the only time she ever felt safe and loved.

At the end of the hall, Maren squeezed the black metal handle and the latch lifted. She pushed open the door and there was her room. Her bed against the wall, a little table with a big mirror on it, a chair set in front of a window overlooking the front lawn. And then she smiled. Her paintings, childhood watercolors, still hung on the wall, curled at the edges, but still there, held up by tacks in the whitewashed cob walls. Even her little doll still sat on the tiny child's rocking chair in the corner of the room.

The room was musty, but it was solid, with windows intact and no leaks. It was just as she had walked out of it all those years ago.

It was winter, cold and wet. Maren stood back in the kitchen as the sun began to go down at only 3:30 p.m. The winter Highland days were short. She heard something scurry across the floor. Mice, no doubt. The rain still fell, but it was lighter now. She had brought a sandwich, a bag of chips, and two bottles of water in her bag, realizing there would be nothing to eat in the cottage. She wished she'd thought to bring some tea bags.

Her fingers hurt from the cold as she sat at the wooden table and pulled the sandwich out of her backpack.

Rain fell on her head, so she got up and dragged the heavy wooden table to a corner of the large kitchen, where there was still a decent roof. At least she'd stay dry, if not warm. Perhaps there might still be wood in her uncle's woodshed out back. It was funny how quickly one's needs went primal. The thought of fire on this cold, wet night, alone in a ruined house, suddenly felt thrilling.

She walked out behind the cottage to the shed where her uncle stored his gardening tools and wood. Her heart leaped when she saw a large pile of firewood neatly stacked and bone dry. Tears unexpectedly stung her eyes. Her uncle was still taking care of her. Even from the grave. The only person who ever had.

She took a hammer and nails and a plastic tarp she also found in the shed, and nailed the tarp over the livingroom window to keep out the rain and some of the cold. Maren went back to the kitchen to get her sandwich. She looked on the table, but there was nothing there. *Did I take it out back? No. Upstairs? No.*

Then she saw the paper sandwich wrapper on the floor and realized, with slight panic, that something had taken it. Some critter sharing the house with her, and really, who was much more established as a resident than she was, had taken her sandwich in the fifteen minutes it had taken her to collect firewood and start a fire. She should have been horrified, but she was charmed.

"Hello there. Whoever you are. Raccoon? Do they have raccoons in the Highlands? Fox? Ghost? I hope you like egg salad!" she called out into the dark house.

She decided she wouldn't allow her imagination to wander into images of the animal ending up on her chest as she slept. Maren was a champion at shutting off thoughts, or feelings for that matter, that she didn't want to have. An Olympic-level survival skill many children of neglect developed. Of course, those feelings usually welled up into a tsunami that crashed over her at random times, for seemingly small reasons. But that wasn't something to think about tonight either.

Maren hadn't slept and had barely eaten in twenty-four hours. At least she had the chips from her bag. Then she had another memory, her uncle kept bottles of wine in the dining room. She doubted there would be any after all this time. But it was worth a try. She opened the carved wooden sideboard next to the table in the small dining room and actually jumped up and down when she saw four bottles of wine. A few minutes later Maren had beaten the sofa with a long stick to remove the worst of the dust and make sure any squatters got out, thankfully nothing ran out when she did so, and she was seated on it with chips in one hand, a glass of merlot in the other and a huge, warm fire dancing in front of her.

*****

The morning after her rainy arrival in Scotland, Maren woke to bright skies and cold sun. She stepped outside. The air was fresh, and Maren's heart felt a strange stirring…happiness. She decided to start by exploring the garden. She went to the shed and got the basket and clippers, hoping there would be something still useful there after two years of neglect. There were stalks of beans, peas, tomatoes, chard, broccoli, peppers, and more, withered and limp in the hard ground. The beds ran in six straight, long rectangular rows, three rows on either side of a path with smaller paths between the beds. The plants were, like all things that grew in the Highlands, resilient.

Next to the rows of vegetables was a big circular herb garden full of sage, rosemary, thyme and mint, chives, and many others. She went to take a closer look at what was salvageable to be dried in the kitchen and used during the winter. Her hands stung with cold, and she pulled her uncle's wool cardigan closer around her. The sage looked fine, and the rosemary. She remembered their sharp, aromatic smell from her childhood, and when she touched them, the aroma was still there. *I'll cook myself a real dinner tonight.*

Maren knelt and held the tops of several stalks of rosemary. She cut them, and as she did so her hands tingled wildly. She looked down, and her eyes grew wide and her mouth fell open.

Slowly, something started to move up the leaves. She wasn't sure what she was seeing, but she felt small sparks in her head, like electricity.

Then she realized, in awe, she was seeing color. At least she assumed it must be color, this strange shade appearing like a mist. She was seeing green! Or at least this must be what green was. She knew people said herbs were green. She was half thrilled and half terrified.

She placed the stalks in the basket softly, like they were holy relics, then reached for more. Each time she cut, it happened again. Green rose like a small wave up the leaves. Her heart pounded as she moved over to the carrot bed and pulled hard on a bunch of the wilted tops sticking out of the ground. Up came a big clump of long, slightly withered carrots, and as she shook the dirt off them, it happened again. This time a bright, surprising wave came up the carrots. *This must be orange!*

Tears streamed down her face as she stared at the miracle in her hands: color. *Color.* Something she had never seen in her life. It was so beautiful, so glorious, that she wept as she stroked the carrots, then looked back at the herbs, feeling like she had just finally been let into a spectacular club the rest of the world had always belonged to, but to which she had been unfairly denied access her whole life.

She pulled some parsnips with bated breath, only to feel huge disappointment when no color flowed up the root, but then she remembered, parsnips were white. *Okay, white I know.* She smiled. Then she looked around wildly, but to her disappointment the rest of the world was still black and white and gray. The mountains rising behind the cottage, the stables, her clothes. But the disappointment didn't last long. She was still thrilled looking back at the miraculous harvest.

Maren walked back to the kitchen, put the basket on the table and sat down, staring at, and slowly touching, the vegetables. What on earth is happening? She couldn't make sense of it. Especially because only the food from the garden had color. Nothing else. She sat at the table for ages, in awe. Finally, she got up. She was starving and desperate for a hot cup of tea, so the first order of business was to go into town to get some things in the house. She could wonder about this strange magic and shop at the same time, she thought.

Maren walked out back and lifted the garage door. She prayed her uncle's little car would start. If it didn't, she'd have to walk the half mile to the main road and wait for the bus. To her delight, the engine turned over, coughing a bit, but then purring like the reliable old thing it always had been. She put it in reverse, heard a horrible metal screeching as she lurched backward, then slowly backed out and headed down the bumpy drive into town.

Maren not only needed to do a big food shop, but the cottage needed a deep clean, even in its state of disrepair. She wasn't sure how she was going to fix the roof, and she needed to get the electricity back on, but those were issues for another day. One thing at a time, she told herself.

Two hours later, all her errands run, she drove home. Home. She smiled. She already thought of the cottage as home, even though she'd only been there a day.

As she bumped back down the road to the cottage, her eyes grew wide. There, standing on the front step of the house, was a sheep. Beautiful, white fleeced, with a patch of paint on its hind flank to identify which farm owned her. It looked at her with that sweet smile that sheep always had, that probably wasn't a smile, but was endearing anyway.

She stepped out of the car. "And who are you?" she asked, walking slowly toward the sheep. "Or who are ewe? Get it, ewe?" She laughed out loud at her stupid joke.

"That's one o' mine, I'm afraid," said a man's voice from behind her.

She spun around to see a tall, broad-shouldered, extremely handsome man standing just feet away. He looked about her age, had slightly wavy hair, sparkling bright eyes, and a muscular frame. He wore a plaid shirt, oilskin jacket, and jeans. At his heels sat a black-and-white border collie, perfectly behaved.

Maren was mortified that the handsome stranger had heard her laughing at her five-year-old ewe joke.

He spoke again, "I'm Alexander Campbell, and I'm afraid this sheep is a Houdini, I dinnae ken where he squeezes out o' the fence, but the wee beast wanders over here from time to time. Finn and I will get him out o' here." He patted his dog's head. Finn's tail thumped on the grass. "Sorry to trouble ye."

Maren, recovering from the shock of finding both a sheep and a handsome man on her doorstep, said, "It's no trouble at all. I guess you know you don't live in the city when you come home to a sheep on the doorstep." She smiled. "I'm Maren Phillips," she said, holding out her hand. "I'm Gordon McGlashan's niece. I've just moved here."

"Aye, I heard you were here. I'm so sorry fer yer loss, while ago as it was," he said, shaking her hand. "Gordon was a great man. He's missed."

"You knew my uncle?"

"Aye, I did. I bought the farm next to this property a few years ago, sheep farm, in case ye couldna tell," he said with a smile that made Maren's heart skip a beat. "I grew up in the village, but now I live on the farm with my dad, Hugh. He and Gordon were fast friends and spent many a night having a wee dram together." He paused, then said, "We'll be on our way then. I'm right over that hill there. If ye ever need anything, come right over."

Maren felt ridiculously sad that he was leaving, considering she'd only known him for two minutes. "Okay, thanks, I'll do that," she replied, finding it was a comfort to know someone who lived nearby and was willing to help in an emergency.

Alex called, "Away!" and Finn bolted toward the sheep, who jumped at the sudden movement and trotted off up the hill, Finn on its heels. Alex smiled and walked behind the animals, over the hill and home.

Hmm…I might need to have an emergency soon, she thought.

Remembering her groceries, she gathered the bags from the trunk of the car and headed inside to put things away. The next thing she did was open every window in the cottage. The cold air blew through the thin cotton curtains on the sides of the windows, and the light fell in shafts into the rooms, lighting up a million sparkles of dust. Maren gathered a bucket, mop, rags, lemon oil, and vinegar and headed upstairs. After a deep clean, the bedrooms were transformed, airy, clean, and smelling deliciously of lemon.

Downstairs, she did the same to the living room.

The kitchen, however, was a disaster. The kitchen had been an addition to the cottage decades ago, and there was no second floor above it. With the huge hole in the roof, icy air blew in, and the leaves on the floor danced in a circle on top of a layer of mud and dead branches. Time for a break. She'd grabbed a sandwich in town and gone straight to work when she got back, but she was hungry and tired, and the kitchen was daunting.

She took the old metal kettle off the stove and washed it in the deep stone sink, filled it with water, and remembered she didn't have electricity for the stove. So she went into the living room, threw a few more logs on the fire and went back to the kitchen. She found a thick cast iron pot, washed that out, and poured the water into it. But she couldn't put the pot on the bumpy logs, which adjusted and moved as they burned. She marveled at how many things she took for granted in her life, like the ability to quickly make a simple cup of tea.

Just then, two tiny field mice appeared next to her. Probably drawn by the delicious warmth of the fire. She didn't jump or scream. She smiled.

"Hello there," she said, and the mice didn't seem scared either, strangely.

They stared up at her and sat like two guests arrived for tea. One mouse looked toward the corner of the large fireplace, and there she saw a grill. It was a metal grill with legs on either side, exactly designed for cooking over a fire. Then a vague memory rose from the dust of her mind of her uncle cooking sausages over the fire one evening.

"Well, thank you, little mouse!" she said, certain the critters had come to give her that message.

She had spent enough time, deep in deserts and on the top of mountains, with wise women and men, to know that the world was full of magic. Of this, she was sure. And animals were often the doorway to help us lost humans remember how to find it. In stories, it was often the wolf or the eagle, or a more impressive creature than a mouse, but you didn't get to pick the messenger, and all of them were sacred.

She returned to the kitchen and pulled a corner off a piece of bread. When she came back, the mice were still sitting there. She slowly put the crust near them. They scurried over, sniffed it, grabbed it, and disappeared back toward the kitchen.

Maren laughed and carefully placed the grill over the flames, setting the iron pot on top. A few minutes later, she had a steaming mug of tea in her hand. She added milk and sugar and took the first sip and let out a blissful sigh. Was there anything better on earth when you were cold and tired than a hot cup of sweet, milky tea?

***

The next day Maren was ready to explore. She was excited to see how the rest of the farm had held up over the years. The hills around the cottage had provided all the adventure Maren had experienced in her childhood. Unless you counted trying to survive without functioning parents since birth as an adventure. The hills had provided the only *happy* adventure of her childhood, anyway. Maren had been an adult since the age of five. With two parents with soft hearts, who meant well, but who were blind drunk by noon every day of their lives. Maren had raised herself. She got up on her own, her parents passed out on the sofa or in bed, or occasionally on the floor. She would stand on a little stool to reach the countertop in the kitchen, make herself toast, pour a glass of milk, pack a sandwich containing whatever food was in the house or in the little shop downstairs that her parents ran. She would put on her backpack the school fund had given her after she kept arriving at school with her things in a plastic bag, and she would walk the half mile to school every day. No one helped her tie her shoes or brush her hair. No one hoped she had a good day. No one kissed her goodbye. But she remembered summers racing around the little worn paths up into the hills, picking apples and pears from the old trees in the orchard, and feeling a connection to the earth that soothed her tired little child's soul. And now, as she pulled her jacket tight against the cold and wandered the beautiful farm, it was soothing her tired grown woman's soul.

CHAPTER 3

Alex Campbell woke early, as he did every day. Finn bounded up from the dog bed on the floor by the foot of his bed, and the two went to the kitchen. He fed Finn and, a mug of steaming tea in hand, he donned his thick oilskin jacket and went out to check on his farm.

There was a bitter wind, and a dusting of snow had fallen in the night. His large gray stone farmhouse had a cobblestone yard with a stone barn on the other side. He walked to the barn, looking up at the Highland hills, and smiled. As he had smiled in heat and rain and fog ever since he left London, and then Inverness, and the bright lights, traffic, glamour, and money, and moved to Samach Farm.

Alex opened the large wooden barn door and stepped inside. He was hit with a wave of warmth and the sweet smell of hay. A huge pen of sheep looked up as he entered.

"Morning all," he said, looking with satisfaction at the sheep who had come in from the pasture during the night.

Some of the Scottish breed sheep in his herd liked to come in out of the snow, though they were bred for the Highland climate and many stayed toasty warm in their thick winter wool coats out in the fields. His ewes had been tupped in November. If you tupped your sheep on Bonfire Night, they'd be born around the start of April, which led to the saying, "In with a bang, out like a fool." He had hired several promising rams from a neigh-boring farm to cover his ewes, and soon he'd have Charlie come and do ultrasound scans to see who was pregnant and who wasn't. He'd learned the hard way his first year as a sheep farmer that not knowing can lead to problems, pregnant ewes needed a very different diet than ones that weren't. Plus, it was a great excuse for his friend to come over for the day.

But, for now, he looked over his sheep and went about his chores. There were several fields, surrounded by ancient stone walls that still worked to keep the sheep in, except, sometimes, Houdini. Alex loaded hay onto a trailer attached to a four-wheeler and drove out into the field to deliver breakfast to the rest of his flock.

After that, hands stinging from cold, he went back into the blissful warmth of the kitchen. His large glass greenhouse wouldn't need his atten-tion for another few weeks. Planting season was far enough away that he could happily skip tending to that in this cold. Inside, the fire was crackling in the woodstove in the huge farm kitchen. His father was up, and the de-licious smell of sausage and eggs greeted him as he took off his coat and sank into one of the two ancient armchairs by the fire.

"Mornin', Dad," Alex said.

"Mornin', son," his dad returned, poking at the sausages that spit on the hot pan.

"Sleep well?" he asked his father.

"Aye. You?"

"Aye."

And that was the end of their morning conversation. It was the beau-ty of living with his father, Alex thought. They loved each other dearly and enjoyed living together and the easy companionship it offered. And the quiet.

In fact, after all the noise and commotion of London, Alex had bought this eighty-acre property and named it Samach Farm, Samach being the Scottish Gallic word for quiet. The blissful quiet was probably Alex's favorite thing about living there.

"What's on today, then?" his father asked after they'd finished their breakfast in companionable silence.

"Not a lot, really," Alex replied. "Soaking up a wee bit of quiet before all hell breaks loose here in a few weeks."

"Aye, that it will." His father knew that, come April, lambing season would be on them, and neither of them would sleep for weeks with the sudden flurry of activity making sure the ewes all lambed safely. And at the same time, Alex would be starting up seedlings for the farm's vegetables for summer. "Enjoy it while ye can."

"How about you? What's on for you today?" Alex asked.

"Heading ta village. Going to stop with Mike fer a bit. He's had that knee replacement and set to lose his mind fer boredom stuck at home."

"Give him my best." Alex rose to go upstairs and put on his warmest clothes. He might not have had a lot to do that day, but work on a farm was never done, and there were some parts of the stone wall around the fields that needed repair.

A few minutes later, he came out in thick layers of wool sweaters, lined jeans, and heavy work gloves.

"See you tonight, Dad." Alex braced his shoulders and headed out into the stabbing wind. When he stepped outside, he was greeted by a Range Rover careening into the yard. Finn had to race to get out of the way.

Alex scowled with irritation at the presumptuousness of the driver. But he wasn't surprised.

A tall, beautiful woman, with thick red hair falling around her shoulders, stepped out of the car. "Alex!" she said with a big smile. She walked toward him quickly, her high heels clicking on the cobbles.

"Hello, Portia," he replied, hoping this wasn't going to throw off his plans for the morning. "What brings you up here?" *At a hundred miles an hour*, he wanted to add, but didn't.

"I just thought you'd like to try some new wines," she said, as if it were the most normal thing to need wine at eight a.m. on a Tuesday morning. Portia worked at a wine shop in a large town ten miles away. She sold wine to local restaurants, including the restaurant Alex's brother, Ian, owned in Inverness.

"Och, that's kind of you," he said, torn as he always was between wanting to cut the conversation short, and being struck by how beautiful she was. *Stupid man*, Alex thought.

Portia Highflint was the daughter of the owners of a huge country estate. She'd gone to all the best schools. After ending up in London, and in a "spot of trouble" last year—which actually was more than a spot, as she'd been arrested for shoplifting in Harvey Nicks, which made no sense as she had been spoiled rotten her whole life and could afford to buy anything she wanted —she had come home to "regroup." That was the word they were using.

Still, everyone had their troubles. And he couldn't be judgmental. He'd certainly had his own. Not only that, he had also found himself in bed with the pretentious, but beautiful, Portia on more than one occasion after a lively night in the pub. Though he apparently wasn't the only one in the village who had had that honor. Which was absolutely her right, to enjoy herself. And in a way, a good thing, as it helped keep things casual.

Though, for some reason, it didn't seem casual lately, as she showed up at his farm more and more often, with excuses to be there. It made him nervous. After his divorce seven years earlier, he hadn't met anyone who made him want to risk his heart again, and he didn't want to give her the wrong idea.

"I've got a lovely Malbec here for you. It's all the rage right now. Cab is very five minutes ago," she said shoving a bottle toward him

"So kind of you. Thank you, Portia," he said, peeling off his thick gloves and taking the bottle from her. They stood there in awkward silence.

Alex was surprised to find his mind suddenly turn to Maren. There had been something both endearing and sexy seeing her caught off guard, making the silly joke about the sheep. She had long, dark brown hair. Not red or blond like some Scots, but dark. Pictish, maybe, he thought. The darker, original line of Celts. The pagans. The nature-worshipping, fire-dancing pagans. She had beautiful, large, bright green eyes, and her figure was fit but curvy. She moved almost like an animal, gently, confidently, and smoothly, he thought.

"Hello?" Portia snapped.

Alex realized he'd been lost in thoughts of Maren. Portia was standing with her hand on her hip looking annoyed.

Alex shook his head to clear it. He wanted to get to work on his stone walls, but he was enough of a gentleman to know she was hoping for an invitation inside. Just as he was starting to say, "Would you like a cup of tea," another truck came up the road and into the farmyard, parking next to Portia's car.

Saved by the truck, he thought. He recognized the vehicle as belonging to his best friend.

Charlie jumped out of the truck, which was hauling a horse trailer. "Alex, I've got a problem."

Alex politely excused himself and told Portia he'd have to see her another time. He thanked her again for the wine and watched her stomp grumpily back to her car like a toddler who hadn't gotten what she wanted. Charlie widened his eyes as she peeled out of the farmyard.

***

Maren made a cup of tea and strolled out the front door to sit on the weathered teak bench in the garden. She tipped her face up and smiled. The thin, watery Highland sun gave off little warmth, but in the sheltered spot by the cottage, it was enough to feel wonderful.

On the agenda for the day was to go into the village and try and get the electricity hooked back up and hire someone to fix the living room window. And she'd have a look at the roof over the kitchen if she had time and see how she could fix that up too. Snow had fallen in the kitchen in the night and, though one part of her liked the adventure of living half wild, the other part of her was cold and sensible and figured she'd be able to fix it at least enough to keep the snow out.

After a few minutes, she got up and wandered to the barn. This had been the reason her uncle had bought the farm. The cottage was sweet and served him well. But it was the horse barn that was his love. He had boarded and trained horses and given riding lessons to supplement his income. . And he had taught Maren everything he knew about horses, starting from when she was a very little girl. She had been lunging and riding and wandering he fields with the horses for as long as she could remember, and she shared her uncle's deep affection for the beautiful, sensitive animals.

In fact, on one of her endless adventures, this one in Sedona, Arizona, Maren had taken a course on horse whispering—working with horses as therapy. Though having worked double shifts as a waitress for two months to pay for the course, she'd been a bit disappointed. Between her uncle teaching her, and her own innate connection to the beasts, she had known almost everything they taught: how to feel the energy of the horse, how a horse will always reflect back to you, not what you want or you think, but what your energy is saying. How if you are stressed, and you walk over to a horse, pretending to be calm, the horse will have none of it and will react to your stress, not your words.

It was a great way to help people truly get grounded and in their bodies. Most people, Maren had come to learn, didn't even know what their own energy was doing, and it took the horse acting it out for them to be able to see it and change it, slowly getting calmer and more relaxed as they tried to get the horse calmer and relaxed. It was miraculous when it worked. Which it always did for the horse. And often did for the humans, unless they were too impatient or skeptical.

Maren slid the giant wooden door to the side and stepped inside the barn. It was bitterly cold, and she shoved her hands in the pockets of her bathrobe. She smiled wistfully, remembering long, happy days there as a child. She saw the barn full of beautiful horses, heads poking over their half doors, eager for breakfast. She saw her uncle smiling and filling their net bags with hay.

Then, that faded, leaving the barn empty and echoing her footsteps as she walked the length of it. It was sad to see it empty. She had a vague idea of trying to board horses there as income, as her uncle had done. She had what was left of the money from the sale of the little apartment back in Massachusetts years ago. It was something, but it wasn't a fortune. Seeing the stables were in great shape made boarding horses for some income seem not only logical but exciting.

There were two long lines of horse stalls on either side of a flagstone corridor that ran down the center. Twelve stalls on each side. At the front of the barn, right when you walked in the door, was the feed room on one side and the tack room on the other. The tack room held several harnesses, lead ropes, and buckets still hung on the pegs. A saddle hung over a long wooden peg jutting out from the wall. Her uncle's saddle. She was moved to see it still there. As if waiting for him.

Just then, she heard a voice call out, "Allo!"

She jumped. She wasn't expecting anyone. In fact, she had her thick dressing gown over her nightgown, feet in Wellington boots, and hair in a messy ponytail. She definitely hadn't been expecting anyone.

She looked out the barn door. A tall, broad-shouldered man stood outside the cottage. She walked toward the house, and as she got closer she saw it was Alex Campbell. In Alex's hand was a lead, tied to a halter, on the skinniest horse Maren had ever seen.

"Hi," she said, acutely aware of how handsome he was and how ridiculous she looked. "This showing up here with animals is becoming a habit." She smiled. She hoped this wasn't Alex's horse, because if it was, her fluttery schoolgirl feeling around him would be gone instantly. This horse had clearly been mistreated.

"I ken. I'm sorry, lass. I dinnae ken where to go with the poor thing. A friend o' mine, he's a vet in town, a neighbor called him out to an old croft way up in the hills. There were dogs and cats everywhere, and this wee lad, all in a terrible state. My friend took the dogs and cats to the rescue in Lormond, but horses are harder. We called the horse rescue folks, but they're full. There's another one a few hours from here I might be able to take him to tomorrow, but with the storm rolling in soon, I dinnae want to drive there today. The poor lad, look at him. How do ye let a horse get like this?" Alex said, softly scratching between the horse's eyes. "I cannae keep him. I've just the one barn, and it's full o' pregnant sheep. He may be sick, and I just can't risk it. I know it's a lot to ask, but I told my friend you might be able to keep him just fer tonight…I know yer uncle had this barn and that it's probably empty…" He trailed off, looking apologetic for having asked a stranger for a big favor.

Maren was relieved this wasn't his horse, but she felt anger rising looking at the sad animal. He wasn't thrashing around or aggressive, even after being mistreated. Instead, his head hung down, as if he'd given up. As if he didn't have the energy to fight anymore, or even to care.

Maren felt a lump in her throat. She recognized that feeling. She'd had it often as a child, the feeling of having lost the will to fight, of hanging her head and giving up. The horse's coat was caked in mud and dust. He had clumps of hair missing from his legs. Mites, she guessed. As if to confirm the diagnosis, the horse raised one hoof and rubbed it against the opposite leg. Mites itched terribly, like lice.

Poor thing, he must be miserable. His ribs poked through his skin so much that you could count them from several feet away, and his spine stuck up in a bony ridge along his back.

"Of course, he can stay here," she said. "My gosh, the poor thing. You leave him with me, I'll put him in a stall for now. Would you ask your friend to come give him a full checkup tomorrow and treat him for, what I'm guessing are, mites?" she asked.

"Of course, I'll do that! My friend, his name is Charlie, said he'd drop some hay and straw and more feed off later today. Fer now I took some feed from him and put it in here," he said, laying a small sack on the ground with a smile. "It's so verra kind of you to take him. Nothing like arriving here and having this dumped on you very first thing. You're a good woman to take the poor lad."

As he smiled, Maren was suddenly very aware of her own body, the cold on her neck, the flush on her chest. She felt the warmth and aliveness of it just a few feet from the large, strong frame of the handsome man. She was so nervous she was afraid it was visible.

Embarrassed, she looked at the ground and mumbled, "Of course." She took the lead. "I didn't know we were getting a storm. I'd better get the horse in and closed up. Would you like to come in for a cup of tea?" she asked, but as she said it, a red sports car pulled into her driveway. *Who on earth is that?*

A tall, thin, blonde woman unfolded herself from the car and stood beautiful and cheerful looking. Alex smiled at her.

"That's my ride. I walked this poor beast here, as my friend had an emergency call so he took off. I hope it's all right I had her meet me here. I'm headed into the village."

Maren's heart sank. She had spoken to the man for a total of ten minutes in her life, so she felt doubly embarrassed that she was so disappointed that he was going to climb into the flashy car with the gorgeous blonde.

Looking at her ancient, rusty car, the plastic tarp nailed across the front of her house, standing there wearing an old bathrobe, and the scraggly, starving horse on the end of her lead, she felt ridiculous being there at all. For a moment she wanted to run back to the safety of her parents' shop. To stand behind the counter and simply ring people up, not be out in the Highlands on her own, trying to make a life out of someone else's life that had been left behind.

She looked over at the horse, though, and her heart lifted again. She felt her companion understood. Understood how hard it is to try once you've been hurt over and over. Looking at the terrible state of her new charge, she stopped feeling sorry for herself.

"Let's get you some dinner, Laddie. Laddie," she repeated, and the horse lifted his head very slightly. "Yes, that'll do." She grinned with satisfaction.

As the first drops of rain fell and the wind picked up, Maren grabbed the bag of food and walked the mangy horse into the stable and opened the door to a stall. She was desperate to get him food and water. She took two plastic buckets off the pegs in the feed room and filled one with feed pellets. She approached Laddie's stall slowly, speaking softly and gently as she did, making sure her own energy was calm and grounded.

"Hello, my lovely," she said, slowly pulling the latch back on his door.

He had been subdued outside, but any horse person knew that it took a while to get to know a horse, and one that had been mistreated might try to kick or bite. He didn't seem to give any sign of that as she carefully entered the enclosed space with him. She hung a water bucket on the wall and filled it with the hose, then the bucket with grain, and hung that on another hook. He looked pathetic standing there. Tomorrow, she'd have the vet check him out, and she'd get a proper look at him.

Before she even got the door closed, he was devouring the food, nose-deep in the bucket. She wondered when the last time was that someone fed this horse and looked after him in any way. He certainly hadn't been fed properly.

Once he emptied his food bucket, he turned and took long pulls of the clean, cold water. When he lifted his head, she could almost feel him sigh with contentment. The unfamiliar feeling of a full belly and a dry stall made him instantly sleepy. He hung his head and his eyes slowly closed.

Maren looked back up the length of the stables, the storm now starting to blow outside, but the horse snug and safe inside. It was one of the best feelings Maren ever had, when animals were safe and loved and cared for. Funny, she had wanted to bring life back into the barn, and suddenly it had happened. Though, of course, this wasn't her horse. But it was a sign. And a good one.

She pulled an old mac coat off a peg by the door, opened the door just wide enough to slip out, closed it behind her, and ran through the pouring rain, back to the cottage.

***

"Teatime, dear," Penny, the nursing home aide said. The old woman heard the aide place the teacup in front of her, and she carefully felt around on the little tray table in front of her for the handle.

"Thank you," she said, and she smiled.

"It's a lovely day out. Maybe you'd like to walk in the garden later?" Penny said.

"That would be nice," she replied. *And that will be all that happens to-day.* As it had been all that had happened for years and years. For decades. No one would visit. No one on earth knew that she was alive outside these walls. Hidden away in the Highlands of Scotland like a dirty secret. So she would sip her tea, and listen to the television in the background, and stare into the darkness. And later she would walk in the garden.

Sometimes she wondered at the fact that she was still alive after all they had put her through. This nursing home was like heaven compared to where they'd put her before. She thanked God for the one thing no one had been able to take from her, and that comforted her even now in her dark and lonely world. She thanked God for the gift. Second sight. The knowing.

The *sight* that hadn't left her, even when the sight in her eyes slowly stopped working and showed her only black. She may have been trapped in an old body, behind blind eyes, but inside, the old woman felt the energy of the standing stones on the other side of the mountain. And of the trees, and the ocean, and the souls that had been before. They all kept her company in her dark and isolated world. But she knew now not to talk about them. Not after everything that had happened.

So, she would walk in the garden and feel the energy of the stag and the hare and the heather, and she would smile, and she imagined that the kind nurses looked at one another with sympathetic smiles, thinking she was a simpleton.

But the elk and the hare and the heather were smiling back, and the old woman felt sympathy for the nurses who were missing out on a whole other world.

After tea, the old woman held onto Penny's arm while Penny told her what she could see as they strolled.

"Nothing blooming in the garden, of course," she said.. "But the hills are stunning, as always," she added. "There's snow atop o' Craig Phadrig today, all white and bright under a blue sky."

"Yes, I see it. Well, in my mind," the old woman added. But her vision was more than imagination. She saw the energy of it, which was almost the same as actually seeing it. "I love the clearness of winter energy." Then, catching herself, she added, "I mean winter weather." Even that didn't really make sense, but no one expected her to make sense, so the nurse simply patted her arm.

Just then a wind picked up. It swirled, grabbed a few dead leaves from the ground, and whirled in a circle just around them.

"Och, getting cold, dear. Let's go inside for a wee cup o' tea," Penny said.

"Wait," the old woman said. This wasn't just wind. This was a message. She felt it in her bones.

The wind blew harder around and around them, and the old woman heard it whisper to her. Not out loud. It was never out loud. It was simply a transference of information, from the wind to her mind, or maybe her soul. Or sometimes from stones to her soul, or the earth, or often an animal. They were all messengers. Most people just didn't know how to hear the messages.

She almost replied out loud but caught herself. But her heart did a little flutter, something it hadn't done in many, many years. Someone was coming. It was impossible, she thought. No one in the world knew she was alive. But she knew better than to trust her thoughts. They weren't nearly as reliable as the messages. Someone was coming. She didn't know if they were coming for her or someone else there. Sometimes the messages were frustratingly vague. And she didn't know when. But soon.

After nearly seventy years locked first in an insane asylum, and now in a nursing home, she could barely believe what the wind was telling her. But she did believe it. Somehow, someone was finally coming.

CHAPTER 4

Maren woke up cold. She pulled on thick wool socks and a sweater and headed to the kitchen. When she walked in her eyes grew wide, and she stopped in her tracks. There, in the middle of the kitchen, was a beautiful fox. He looked up at her and cocked his head to one side. Then continued to sniff around the floor. How on earth had he gotten in? It was winter, he must be hungry.

"Hello, beautiful," Maren whispered, and she sat down where she was in the doorway.

The fox walked toward her, then sat down facing her, and the two stared at one another until Maren had tears running down her cheeks. She wasn't even sure why. She felt completely at one with this gorgeous animal. With the sky visible straight above her, with the cold, with the craggy mountains standing guard behind the cottage. It was the cottage, and the fox, and the horse, and the wildness of the Highlands all coming together. And for the first time in as long as she could remember, she didn't feel lonely.

As if the fox understood this, it crouched and cautiously walked toward her. Logic told her she should be scared, but she felt only a sense of joy, a connection with this animal and this place that filled every inch of her. The fox stretched its long nose toward her and sniffed. She wished she could see him in color. She had been told foxes were a beautiful burnt orange.

Maren slowly held out her hand. He edged forward again and sniffed it. Then, to her surprise, he lay down right next to her. She felt the warmth of his body through her nightgown. She reached down and stroked his fur. It was softer than she imagined it would be. An energy like a small frizzle of electricity ran up her arm. She smiled and stroked him again.

And, so, they sat and lay together for a long time. She wasn't sure how long. Maybe ten minutes. Maybe more.

Maybe he had been lonely too. She knew foxes were cautious, solitary animals. But everyone needs to feel the warmth of a body next to them now and again. She certainly did. And there was a delicious surety in relationships with animals. A horse might kick you, and this fox could snap at her any minute. But they weren't dubious. They didn't trick you. They didn't lie to you. And after a childhood filled with so many lies and so much gaslighting, Maren still struggled to know what was real and what wasn't with humans. But this warm fox, lying against her leg, felt like love.

After a while, the animal rose and stretched, gently touched its nose to Maren's hand. She was sure she heard him say thank you. *Even the* foxes *in Britain are polite.* She laughed at her own joke.

She watched as the animal, in one nimble, swift move, jumped from the floor to the kitchen table to the top of the cupboard and out the hole in the roof.

"Ahh, that explains it!"

She ran to the back door to see where it went and stepped outside just in time to see the fox squeeze under a shrub and into a hole at the very back of the garden. She was happy to know he lived so nearby.

"Bye, Mr. Fox. Come again soon!" she called out, and she pictured him in his den, sitting in an armchair by a fire, having a cup of tea, like some image she was sure she'd seen in a children's book.

Maren made her own tea on the fire and had bread with Marmite, that British spread that you had to be raised on to enjoy—a black, salty yeast extract that she had loved since her first visits to her uncle's place. She took her bread and tea out to the garden and looked over at the stables.

Oh my God, I have a horse in there! She'd completely forgotten Laddie.

She quickly ran upstairs and changed into jeans and a sweater. Pulled on her wellies and headed out to the barn. Inside, the horse stood in his stall, head hanging over the wooden half door, looking skinny and dirty as yesterday. There were two bales of straw, two of hay and a big bag of horse food in the feed room. Alex's friend must have dropped them off at some point.

"Good morning sweet boy," Maren said.

She pulled the latch, opened the door, and eased herself inside to get the food and water buckets. She filled them both and rehung them on their pegs, and the horse immediately had his nose in first one, then the other, until they were both empty. Then he looked up and seemed surprised to find someone feeding him again so soon. Maren wanted to let him out into the huge, enclosed paddock behind the barn, but the vet was supposed to come that day and check him out, so she kept him in his stall. She scratched his long gray nose, and he leaned toward her, ears forward, and closed his eyes in pleasure.

"Don't worry, Laddie," she said. "We are going to make you feel all better, and then…" She trailed off. She wasn't sure what the "and then" would lead to. But, for now, she would take care of him and show him that the world wasn't such a harsh place as it had been.

As if on cue, Maren heard a truck pull into the drive. She was glad she'd remembered this time and hadn't been caught in her nightgown, or sitting on the floor snuggling with a fox. She really was half crazy, she thought with a laugh. This time, she was dressed and ready.

Alex got out of the truck with his friend, Charlie.

"Good mornin'," Charlie said, as he grabbed his bag of instruments and walked toward the barn.

"Good morning," Maren replied with a smile.

Alex introduced his friend, and he and Maren shook hands. Charlie was like a caricature of a Scot, thick curly hair and freckles. But rather than a fierce Scottish warrior, he looked sweet and harmless. He had a huge smile and a cheerful energy about him.

Alex, on the other hand, *did* look like a warrior. He, too, was friendly, and had a ready smile, but there was something behind it too. Something that said, if needed, he'd grab his broadsword and run, wild and screaming, at his enemy.

Maren shook her head. Picturing Alex as a character in *Braveheart* was making her flustered, and she wondered how it had suddenly gotten so hot.

"He's in here," she said, walking toward the barn to regain her composure.

Maren went to the stall, and Laddie bobbed his head up and down, a kind of horse greeting, and Maren felt touched.

"Well, hello to you, too, Laddie!" she said with a big smile, scratching his nose.

"Laddie, is it?" Alex said with a smile that was both genuine and seemed to be making fun of her at the same time.

"Oh, yeah," Maren said. "It just seemed to fit."

"That it does," Alex said, the gentle mocking look gone and now just a kind smile.

"Let's have a look at ye then, wee lad," Charlie said opening the stall door and slowly walking in. Alex stayed just outside the barn. Charlie examined the sad horse from head to hoof, listening to his lungs and taking his temperature. Then he expertly took a blood sample from a vein in the horse's neck, a procedure to which the animal had no reaction at all, which Charlie said was a good sign in terms of the horse's temperament. Then he took scrapings from the skin on the horse's legs.

"Yer a good man, Laddie. You've not had a good go of it, have ye?" he said, running his hand down the horse's bony flank.

He left the stall and pulled a carrot out of his pocket. Turning and holding his hand out flat, he offered it to the horse. Laddie looked at it for a moment, and sniffed it, unsure of what it was. This was a horse not accustomed to treats. Then he nimbly took it from Charlie's hand and devoured it.

"I'll send the bloodwork off and get results in a few days, but I can look at the scrapings from his legs on my travel microscope in the car. I'll be back in a few minutes, and we can chat," he said.

Charlie walked to the car. Alex and Maren stood in the cool, hay-scented barn.

"Oo, you're a farmer?" Maren asked, wanting to break the silence.

"Aye, I am now. Sheep and vegetables. I supply vegetables to a lot of local restaurants, including my brother's in Inverness. All the rage now it seems, 'locally sourced,' 'farm to table,' and all that."

"That's so cool!" Maren said. "That's big in so many places now. And for good reason. Local food tastes so much better. That's definitely some-thing I've found in my travels. Local means it'll taste like real vegetables, instead of something picked two thousand miles away, before it was ripe, and then shipped all over. Environmentally friendly and supports local farmers. I think that's great!"

"I do too. Keeps the wolf from the door, and I'm my own boss. Days outside, with the sheep and the farm, does a soul good," he said.

"I bet it does. I'll have to check out your brother's restaurant. I'm a terrible cook, but I'm an excellent eater!" she said with a laugh.

Alex's expression softened and he tilted his head very slightly and looked at her in a way that made her flustered.

"Have you always been a farmer?" Maren asked.

"Och no. I'm a software engineer actually. Worked for several years in that. Two of them in California, then a couple more in London. Finally, started my own business and sold it for a pretty penny a few years ago. I had to get out of the craziness of it, working twelve hours a day, never seeing the outside of my office. I cashed out, eventually bought the farm, and I've never been happier!"

This guy just gets more and more interesting, Maren thought. Then she remembered the blonde and the sports car, and she felt her heart sink, before chastising herself. *You don't even know the man. Plus, there will be plenty of adventures to be had here, let this one go. Plenty of fish and all that.*

And really, being here wasn't about finding a lover. She'd had those in many ports. This was about setting up her life. Being a grown-up, whatever that meant.

But the image had left her tongue tied and the two stood in awkward silence.

"Allo, there. I've got some results," Charlie called, as he walked back from his car with several items in his hands. "You were right, Maren. Ye know yer horses. Mites. Worst case of them I've ever seen. He's absolutely teeming with them. The poor thing must be being tortured; they itch like the devil. I'm going to give him two injections now, and there's a shampoo that will kill them, too, and some ointment can be rubbed onto his legs. He'll feel so much better. But the thing is, I still haven't found a placement for him, and to be honest, it'll be near impossible to find someone who'll take him so infested with mites. They spread like wildfire and could infest a whole farm. Even sheep will get them, which is probably why you've kept your distance today, Alex."

"Aye, once I heard that word mites, I knew I'd have to stay away and let ye do all the work," Alex said.

Charlie nodded and looked back at Maren. "I don't suppose there's any way you'd keep him a wee bit longer till we can sort him out."

Maren thought for a moment. She tended to say yes to everything and often lived to regret it. Part of this practicing being a grown-up business was to have boundaries. To think things through. She exhaled slowly and felt her energy connect to the horse as she had done in the summers here as a child. The moment when words fall away and there is an unexplainable direct flow of energy and thoughts between human and animal.

Laddie looked up just as she felt it. She knew why. She knew he felt it too. She heard through that energy pathway, actually *heard* him thank her.

Maybe thinking is overrated, Maren thought. She might not know a lot, but she knew herself, and this is how she made decisions. Not by thinking, but by listening.

"He can stay," she finally said. "Absolutely. I will take care of the poor boy and am glad to do it."

Both men smiled at her.

"Wonderful!" Charlie said. "If yer up for it, here's what you do. Give him an oral dose of this ivermectin, shampoo his legs with this anti-parasitic shampoo." He handed her a bottle. "Then rub this anti-parasitic ointment on his legs. It'll need to be repeated in fourteen days, but hopefully by then we'll have found him a home. Oh, and once you shampoo him today, he'll need to go into a new stall, I'm afraid. You'll want to take your clothes off and wash 'em too. It's a lot to ask! I'll leave you all the medicine, and we'll pay for his food and straw, of course. Alex, you can drop more by soon, can't ye?"

"Aye, certainly I can," he said.

"Are you sure yer up fer it?" Charlie asked, having now told her how much work was involved.

"This poor horse has been treated so badly. He's had no love, no care. You couldn't stop me from helping him get better if you tried!" she said with a mix of determination and anger toward his previous owners.

"Yer a good lass," Alex said. "Fer an American," he added. He winked at her, and her heart started doing flips, so much she was afraid he could see it through her shirt.

Stop it, Maren, she said to herself firmly.

And she replied, in her best made-up, grown-up voice, "Not a problem at all." She turned from the men to prepare a new stall.

After the men left, Maren put on the oldest clothes she'd brought with her, jeans and a sweatshirt, and went back to the barn. She walked Laddie out into the sun and tied him to the ring on the barn wall. She got out the hose and proceeded to shampoo the horse head to tail, first with a regular shampoo to get him clean. The water that came off the horse was almost black with dirt. She rinsed him until the water finally ran clear. Mites bite, and as the dirt and crud fell off with the washing, she could see little sores all over his legs. What a misery it must have been to live like that for…for how long? No one knew.

Then she used the anti-parasitic shampoo, which seemed to hurt a bit, as Laddie stomped his feet while it remained on for the instructed amount of time. She rinsed off the shampoo and left him to dry in the sun while she put two new buckets in a fresh stall, filled them with food and water, spread clean straw on the floor, then went back out front to gently rub the ointment on his legs.

As she did so, the horse turned his head and gently nuzzled Maren on the shoulder.

"You're welcome," she whispered to him, a tear rolling down her cheek, his head right next to hers.

She then led Laddie the length of the stable and let him out into the huge, fenced field. He was still skin and bones, but the transformation of the bath was stunning, she wished so much she could tell what color he was. He didn't quite have the energy to gallop, though she sensed he wanted to. But he trotted with tail perked up and ears pointed forward, causing Maren to smile ear to ear before going to strip off and wash her clothes.

That afternoon, Maren continued to tidy the cottage, finally using her uncle's ladder to climb on the roof over the kitchen and nail a large tarp over the hole. The following morning, as she stepped outside with her mug of tea, a van pulled up. It was the electrician. Maren was thrilled he was there to reestablish service.

She led him inside, and when she stepped back outside, another van pulled up…the oil man, this time. His work was swift. He filled the tank, swiped Maren's credit card, and was off.

Just then a third van pulled in, and Maren laughed. "It's like Grand Central Station," she said to the electrician. He smiled but looked confused. Maybe he didn't know what that was.

Was it the man to fix the window? she wondered. But it wasn't. It was a minivan, and out of it poured five women, who looked to be in their sixties and seventies. Several wore long flowing tops, all of them with beautiful necklaces and bracelets with large stones in them. *They must be lost.*

"Hallo," one woman called out, waving as the group walked toward her. "Are ye the owner of this place?" She smiled and reached out her hand, "Isobel Frazer."

Maren shook her hand. "Maren Phillips. And, yes, I am. Can I help you?"

"We hope so," Isobel said as the other women gathered around. "We're the Sisters of the Stones. Well, we're some o' them. We're a group who visit as many of the stone circles in Scotland as we can. We've been, of course, to all the well-known ones, Callanish Stones and those. But we love to find the wee ones, too, ones forgotten about over time."

"That's so interesting," Maren said. She knew about the powerful and mysterious stone circles and standing stones of Scotland, thousands of years old, some older than the Pyramids of Egypt, and still shrouded in mystery. But she wasn't sure why these women were in her driveway telling her this.

Isobel turned and stretched an arm toward the other women and said, "This is Clara, Fiona, Janet and Phillipa." The women nodded their heads and said hello.

"Hello," Maren said to the group. "Nice to meet you."

Isobel went on, "We practice the old ways and keep the traditions alive. We found an old map tucked away in a book at the Inverness historical society ages ago, a medieval map, in fact, and it showed an ancient stone circle somewhere near here. But we havena been able to find it. We've been searching on and off fer years, but when we came here last there wasna anyone here ta ask."

"My uncle died two years ago. I've just moved here. But I'm afraid I don't think there's a stone circle on the land here. I spent all my summers here as a child. I've explored all over, and my uncle surely would have known if there was one. I'm sorry to disappoint you."

"American, are ye?"

"Yes," Maren replied.

"Americans love a good stone circle. You've almost as many pagans as we have it seems," she said with a laugh. "But those of us who still follow the old ways, we can feel when there are stones about, and they're here.

Somewhere. Once we found them on that map, we dug deeper and found a few mentions of them in old books. It's a healing circle, this one is. Powerful energy. You can feel it, too, if you try."

Maren was intrigued, but she had planned on spending the day fixing up the cottage, and it had started to rain again.

"Well, if you'd like to come back and have a wander around some time, that would be fine with me," she said. She ran to the cottage for a piece of paper and jotted down her cell phone number, handing it to Isobel.

"Thank ye, me dear," said Clara. "That's kind of ye. And welcome! There's Highland magic here. You've landed in a special place."

"I couldn't agree more," Maren said. "Thank you so much for stopping by, I'm sure I'll see you soon."

And with that, the heavens opened, and the women ran back to their minivan and Maren ran inside.

***

Thrilled to have electricity, Maren made herself a cup of tea on the Aga stove. She'd still need to get the roof fixed, but after nailing up the tarp she'd cleaned out the mud and leaves and it was now a cozy room. And she'd finally be able to make a real dinner tonight. She was going to vacuum and wash some linens, now that she could use the washing machine, but her mind kept coming back to the women and the stone circle.

She decided to have a look in the room her uncle used to store old papers and books upstairs. Maybe she'd find something in there. She'd just take a quick look around, she told herself. She took down a box and opened it. It contained old bank statements, old cards, and letters he'd thought worth keeping, nothing related to stone circles. She went through another. A box of books, but just novels, nothing historic. The third box she opened was full of photos. She decided to take this box down to the living room. She had no sense of a family and was hoping to see photos of the grandparents she hadn't known or maybe of her mother as a child.

She lit the fire, poured herself a glass of red wine, sat cross-legged on the floor, and slowly took each photo out. Most of them had things written on the back. One was, in fact, of her Uncle Gordon and her mother as small children in Massachusetts. Her grandfather had been an only child and, a widower, had emigrated to America from Scotland with her mother and Gordon when he decided he'd had enough of the cold, isolated Highlands. He thought everyone in America was rich and had swimming pools and sunbathed all day. He'd seen it in a magazine, apparently. There were lots of more recent photos of Gordon and his life, his friends, at concerts, on the farm, pictures of horses and favorite clients. Then there was a small bundle of photos tied together.

Maren untied the ribbon and looked at them. It was a photo of her grandfather as a small child. She knew this because it was written on the back. He was clearly in Scotland in the photo. There was a little girl next to him, slightly younger. On the back, it said "Fergus and Sybil." The two were dressed up, as if going to a party, he in a gorgeous small boy's sailor's suit and she in a ruffled dress.

Maren shuffled to the next photo and read, "Fergus and Sybil, Sybil's fifth birthday." The two were holding hands and smiling. *Sybil?* Maren had never heard of a relative named Sybil. Or maybe she was just a little friend of her grandfather's.

Then, there was another photo, this one of them standing in a kitchen, in school uniforms, "Fergus and Sybil ready for school." The children looked about ten years old. Why would this Sybil be going to school with her grandfather? She looked more closely. Sybil looked remarkably like her grandfather. But her grandfather was an only child.

In another photo was Maren's great-grandmother, Joan, her husband Thomas, her grandfather...and Sybil. On the back, it said "Family Vacation. Dorset."

Maren sat back, and her mind raced, trying to make sense of this. She knew what she was seeing, she just couldn't understand it. Her grandfather had a *sister*. Her mother and uncle's father had a sister. *She* had a great-aunt. A woman Maren had never heard about in her life. She had been told her grandfather was an only child. Her own mother had told her that. Who was Sybil? Had she died as a child, and it was so traumatic no one talked about it? That sounded like the kind of reaction her family would have. Or could she be alive?

Maren did some math in her head. Estimating the child's ages by the photos, she would be in her eighties now. Of course, anything could have happened to her, but it wasn't impossible she might still be alive. Except, if she was, how had no one ever mentioned her? And why? Her mother had been emotionally shut down, but her uncle wasn't, and he'd never mentioned his father having a sister.

Maren went back upstairs, and in the end, never did make that full dinner she'd meant to cook. She stayed up half the night, putting logs on the fire and wine in her glass, and looking through box after box of papers and photos until she'd been through everything in the room. No mention of a stone circle. And no other evidence of this Sybil girl.

Then Maren had an idea. She got her uncle's family Bible off the shelf in the living room and opened it. It had been his grandfather's and had all the births and deaths of the family listed in the back.

And there she was, Sybil. Born December 21, 1936. There was a dash after the birth date and no date of death. Her uncle hadn't been religious at all, so he'd probably never paid much attention to the Bible, other than telling Maren about it as he'd leave it to her one day. So Sybil could be dead, and Uncle Gordon probably wouldn't have updated the Bible. But if she'd died as a child, her great-grandmother would have put that in there.

Maren had a funny feeling all of a sudden, a stirring. She suddenly knew, on some powerful level, that this woman was alive. And that she was meant to find her.

CHAPTER 5

Maren woke the next day with a headache and a terrible taste in her mouth. She'd had stayed up half the night and had too much wine. Even so, she woke up motivated. But there were suddenly so many things pulling at her attention. First and foremost was Sybil. Sybil McGlashan must be her name. Unless she'd married. The mysterious woman needed to be found, dead or alive. But there was a man coming to fix the window that morning, and Laddie needed to be taken care of.

And more than that, Maren needed to get truly settled in. Between all the damage to the house and then the arrival of the horse, she hadn't really done that. She had her savings but it wasn't enough to fund her life there forever. It had helped pay for travel, but she'd waited tables and lived cheaply in other countries. Britain was expensive. So, she'd have to sort out some kind of income. She wanted to dive head-first into researching this mystery relative. But she knew she needed to be practical.

She started by doing the thing that always helped her feel calm...she organized things. In the kitchen, she was met by the mice who had become roommates by now.

"Morning, guys," Maren said, and they all lined up waiting for her to throw them a crust of bread, which she did.

She put the kettle on, made some toast and took inventory of the roof. She'd need someone to come to fix the beams and plaster the ceiling as well as retile it. She'd ask Charlie or Alex whom to call for that. Upstairs, she folded and put away all her clothes, put the framed picture of herself and her uncle on the dresser, and put the few books she always traveled with on the bookshelf in her room. She finished organizing her things in about half an hour because she had next to nothing. Which suited her just fine.

Next, she went to have a look at Laddie. She slid the barn door open, and he immediately stuck his head out over his stall door and nodded it up and down. Maren had returned him to his stall after his run in the field the night before, wanting him to feel safe, and also wanting to be able to treat him again first thing in the morning.

"You're much perkier already aren't you, Laddie?" she said, thrilled to see a bit of spirit in the animal. His coat was clean, and his legs already looked better. She opened the door to let him back out into the field. He walked out cautiously, then took off in a happy prance.

Maren smiled as she stood watching him, her mind working. She looked back at the stables. If her uncle could do it, then why couldn't she? She could give the stables a deep clean and then advertise to board horses. She could even give lessons. She was an accomplished horsewoman and had occasionally given lessons to tourists in places like Costa Rica and Belize, where visitors liked to feel rustic and ride old nags to visit waterfalls and dormant volcanoes.

Her heart leaped with excitement. A project! She was good at projects. Good at starting things. Building things. Changing things. Staying and sticking with them afterward was another story, but she'd cross that bridge when she got to it. For now, she suddenly had a plan, and it felt right. She would scrub the stables from top to bottom, wait till Laddie was definitely not contagious with anything, then start advertising.

With a huge smile, Maren ran back to the cottage. She had a lot to do.

Two hours later, having returned from a trip to the animal center two towns over, Maren was in work coveralls she'd bought, with a bucket of soapy water and a scrub brush. A van pulled in the driveway and she was happy to see it was the window repairmen. She got them set up in the living room. Unfortunately, the tarp had blown off the hole in the kitchen roof during the night so she felt like she was trading one problem for another. But it would all get done eventually. She headed to the stables. She first swept out each stall, then she brushed the walls, the floor of and washed the floor of each stall, finishing by rinsing everything out with the hose. It wasn't done, but it was a start. She met the window men on her way back from the stables. There was a big, beautiful window installed in the living room and Maren was happy to see the cottage slowly coming together. She thanked the workmen profusely and then, filthy and tired, she went inside and filled the bathtub. She added a few drops of lavender oil she'd bought, thrilled at the luxury of hot water, and soaked until her toes were pruned.

She got out and dressed in yoga pants and an oversized sweatshirt. *Okay, tonight I'll make that nice dinner!* She had been grabbing things quickly all week, running from task to task.

But before she could get started, there was a knock on the door. She opened it to find Alex. He wasn't in farming clothes and a dirty oilskin jacket as he'd been the last time she saw him. He was in nice jeans and a sweater that fit tightly enough to show his muscular arms beneath.

"Hi," Maren said, peering outside to see if Charlie was with him. He wasn't. She was glad.

"Hi," Alex said. "Charlie wanted to be here, but a call just came in and he had to go."

Ahh, so this was an Alex-and-Charlie visit. Or it had been meant to be. Her heart sank a bit, but then she remembered the blonde and the sportscar and silently reprimanded herself again for caring.

"Are you busy?" Alex asked, looking at her with a half-smile that made him seem permanently amused by some mysterious joke.

"Umm, no. I just got to work on a new project I'm excited about, and I was going to do some things on my computer. But nothing at all pressing. So, no, not busy," she said, thinking she was blathering.

"Great, grab yer coat. I'm takin ye out!" he said, grinning.

"You are?" Maren said. Her face brightened, even though she didn't know what he was talking about.

"Charlie and I wanted to take you to the pub fer dinner. To thank ye for taking on a mangy half-dead horse when you'd barely arrived and didn't know us at all. It was kind of you. And you haven't been to the pub yet, as far as we can tell, so…you're goin'!"

Maren had been meaning to go to the pub, the center of all village life in Scotland. She just hadn't managed to get there yet. She would have been more excited about it if he hadn't added the "Charlie and" to the "I" in the invitation, but she was excited, nonetheless.

"Give me two minutes," she said, and she ran upstairs.

Maren checked herself in the mirror before heading back downstairs. Not bad on no notice, she thought. Her thick, dark hair fell to her mid-back in waves. She had large almond shaped eyes and high cheekbones. She had the face of a classical sculpture, one Greek man had said to her, trying, unsuccessfully, to seduce her. She put on a small amount of eyeliner and mascara, pulled on her best jeans and a form-fitting ivory blouse, buttons undone just far enough to be interesting, but not tacky. She added some ornate hanging earrings she had gotten for pennies at a market in Thailand, black ankle boots, and she was ready. She was back downstairs in less than five minutes.

"Wow," Alex said, his eyes widening. His reaction was instant and honest, and it made her heart do a flip.

"Thank you," she said, with an amused half smile.

She grabbed her jacket off a peg by the front door, and they headed out into the cold evening.

Maren sat in the passenger seat of Alex's old Range Rover. She watched as the road from Hidden Stone Farm turned a corner and the village of Glenmuir came into sight. The village was cozy and inviting, nestled among the dramatic hills, a welcome sight of community and comfort against the wild backdrop of the Highlands. She imagined how very inviting the sight must have been hundreds of years ago, to cold, tired travelers living a tough Highland life. Though a Scot would never call living there tough. Wild and rugged, yes, but not tough. It was a source of pride to a Scot to live among the stunning lochs and mountains of the Highlands. And as the checkout clerk had said to her when she was buying a new oilskin coat, "In Scotland there's nae bad weather. Just bad clothes." Meaning if you dressed right, even the biting wind, rain, and snow of a Highland winter wasn't so bad.

The first thing you saw as you approached Glenmuir, as with most villages, was the church. A low, solid church made of stone, mostly dark grey in Maren's eyes, blackened with time and soot and age. It had a sharp spire pointing toward the heavens and an ancient graveyard. It was reassuring in its longevity, disinterest in temporal concerns, and its silent invitation to come inside and be quiet.

Beyond that was a pretty row of cottages, all attached to one another, made of stone of some sort. The cottages formed an arc as the road curved toward the center of the village. The village itself was set around a green. A large flat area of grass where, her uncle had once told her, hundreds of years ago, the villagers would communally graze their livestock. Now it was used for soccer matches, Highland games, and walking dogs.

As they drove by the green, there was the village shop, with baskets on the sidewalk filled with the heartier fare that could stand the weather outdoors: potatoes, turnips and onions. The window of the shop glowed with light in the evening darkness, and inside the grocer stood behind the counter, handing a loaf of bread to a shopper with a basket.

Alex turned the car, and on that side of the green, ran the main road through the village. Right on the edge of this road was The Red Stag Pub, a whitewashed building, this one short and squat with a thick thatch roof, shiny black window frames and door and window boxes that, Maren assumed, would be colorful in summer. It looked like it had originally been a small house, standing on that spot on the road through the village, headed to Inverness, calling to cold and weary travelers, for hundreds of years.

Alex parked and jumped out and ran around to open her car door. Maren stared at him in shock. It was a simple act of chivalry and touched her deeply. *I really am unused to kindness*, she thought, but with a little silent laugh rather than sadness.

The cold wind whipped at them as they ran to the door. Alex opened it, and they were greeted by a blissful wave of warmth and light.

"Alex," a few farmers called. Others nodded their heads slightly in acknowledgment.

"Evening," he said back to the room.

He led her to a wooden table next to a cheerful fire burning in the big fireplace. There were two black dogs sound asleep by the fire, and Maren smiled. Sometimes a person would try to bring a dog into the bar near the apartment where she grew up, the bar she'd often have to go into to find her parents and drag them, drunk and protesting, home. It was depressing and had plastic chairs and a linoleum floor and it always smelled of stale beer. This was another world. Of course, she'd been in some nice bars in all her travels. But nothing that felt like this.

It was that strange feeling in her heart again. It felt like home. Like she belonged. The low ceilings had dark wooden beams—you could still see the marks from where the tools had cut them centuries ago. The bar itself was dark wood, surrounded by wooden benches. Long wooden handles stood atop part of the bar, used to pull a pint, which was more like pumping a pint as the barman lifted and lowered the handle over and over to expertly fill the glasses. Behind him, shelves of harder spirits were lined up under a light. There were more types of whisky in that tiny pub than Maren had known existed in the world.

"What'll ye have, lass?" Alex asked her with a smile.

She wished he wouldn't call her lass. It made her head spin and made it hard for her not to imagine all kinds of Highland adventures with the broad-shouldered Scot. And she had already seen his girlfriend. The last thing she needed was a hair-pulling brawl in Glenmuir.

"Well, I guess I'm in the Highlands, so I should have a shot of whisky,"

"A shot?" a gravelly voice from a bar stool said with a laugh. A stranger in The Red Stag was a rare event, so everyone appeared to be listening. "Ye dinnae order a shot here, lass," he said and several men laughed. "Yer no' in Texas." More laughter.

Maren flushed.

"Haud yer wheesht," Alex said in a stern voice, but with a big smile. "She's fae Boston, no' Texas. Give 'er a welcome, Donald, no' a ribbin'."

Maren had no idea what Alex had just said, but he was clearly defending her.

The man at the bar burst into good-natured laughter. "Och, lass, I was jokin'. Yer welcome here!"

Maren returned his laugh, definitely feeling welcomed.

"So, that'll be a *dram* o' whisky, will it?" Alex asked with a wink.

"Och aye," Maren replied loudly, setting off another round of laughter.

"Though I have no idea which one to get, so I'll let you decide."

Alex stood at the bar, ordering, when the door opened and Charlie came in, accompanied by a blast of cold air. He was greeted with the same nods and grunts as Alex had been, and he crossed the room to the bar.

"Emergency is all settled. Dog was choking on a ball, quick fix. One big squeeze and out it popped." Charlie said, as he and Alex sat down at their table with the drinks. "So, mystery woman, tell us yer story. How'd you end up in wee Glenmuir, of all places?"

Maren said, "My uncle lived here. Alex probably told you that part. He owned the cottage I live in now. He left it to me when he died."

"Good man," Charlie said.

"He was. The best. I spent all my summers here growing up. It was the only place that ever felt like home to me. After my parents died in a car accident—"

"Och, I'm sorry, lass," Alex interjected.

"Thanks," Maren said with a weak smile. Not wanting to go into the whole story of how it hadn't been the tragedy it might have for someone from an actual functional home, she continued instead. "After they died, I sort of launched myself out into the world. I decided that I just wanted some adventure. No strings. Just fun and new places and new experiences. It's been amazing. I've lived all over the place for, oh, forever it feels like," she said wearily. "Then I got in an accident recently and, long story short, it made me realize I wanted more. I wanted a place to call home. And this is the only place that felt like home so…here I am!" She ended with a perky tone at the end, to hopefully cut off any deeper conversation. She still wasn't a fan of deep conversations, at least not with strangers.

"Well," Alex said, pushing back his chair and looking at her with a curious expression. "Yer a gypsy, clearly. Gypsy blood, no doubt about it. Always moving, no ties…lots o' gypsy blood in Scotland. Next, you'll be peerin' in a crystal ball or skree," he said. "You've the look of it, too, dark hair and all."

"Funny," Maren said, "there is a family story of someone way back, who ran off with a traveler and returned to bear a child. There were never any details, and we all were sure it was made up. But, who knows, maybe it's true. I like that idea. When I lived in Santa Fe my therapist said my constant need to move was a fear of intimacy and unresolved childhood issues. I *much* prefer the explanation that I'm a gypsy." Both men laughed loudly, and Maren joined them.

After her whisky, Maren had a delicious meal of mince, meat with onion and spices, on mashed potatoes, with a glass of merlot. It warmed her and made her sleepy. She would need to start cooking real meals for herself, she thought again. It was amazing how nurturing a good meal was. The three enjoyed their dinner and drinks, and after the men had thanked her several times again for jumping to the rescue with the horse, Alex drove Maren back to the cottage.

In the driveway, Alex put the car in park. Maren's heart pounded. She felt like a teenager on a first date. There was an awkward silence as they sat there for several long seconds, then Alex said, "Yer brave to move here on yer own, miles from where yer from. I did it years ago, and it's no' easy. Yer uncle'd be proud."

"Thank you, Alex," she said, wondering if her uncle *would* be proud. "He worried about me, bouncing all over the place. Never having any real ties or anything that lasted more than a few months. He was so settled here, you know. He never even took a vacation. He said he was living in heaven on earth and why would he ever want to go anywhere else. I always envied him that feeling. But now I get it. I'm starting to feel that too. And it feels so good. So maybe you're right, maybe he'd be proud of me moving here and keeping his farm alive. I hope so anyway," she said wistfully, looking out into the darkness as if he might be standing there.

"I know he is, lass," Alex said gently.

Maren, remembering Alex's girlfriend, suddenly pulled herself together and flipped the lighthearted voice back on. "Thanks again for dinner. Let's do it again some time!"

And with that, she hopped out of the car and went straight to the barn to check on Laddie before bed.

Alex turned his car around and headed home.

As Maren got to the barn, she noticed the light on. She hadn't left it on. As she slid open the barn door, there, sitting outside Laddie's stall, was a young girl.

"Hello?" The girl looked to be about seven or eight years old. "Are you okay?" Maren asked gently, moving slowly toward her.

The girl looked up, as if surprised someone would be there, as if surprised she wouldn't be left alone forever in the barn. "Yes," she said in a small voice.

Maren waited, but the little girl didn't say anything else.

"I'm Maren Phillips. I live here. What's your name?" She bent down to be closer to the child's eye level.

"I'm Sally," the girl said, wiping her runny nose on the back of her sleeve.

Laddie stuck his head out of his stall and slowly lowered it until he was gently snuffling and nudging the girl's head. When she felt that, the little girl smiled. Her face was transformed, as if sunlight had actually come into the dark barn.

"You like horses, Sally?" Maren asked.

"Yes," she said. Nothing more.

It was freezing in the barn and the little girl didn't even have a coat on. The girl looked like a spooked horse, like one sudden move and she might bolt, and Maren definitely didn't want the poor child running off into the cold night.

"Do you live near here?" she asked the girl.

"Yes," was her reply.

"Where do you live?" Maren asked. "I should take you home, your parents will be worried."

"My mum works a lot. It's okay," she replied.

Maren wasn't sure how to proceed. Should she ask the girl to come inside the cottage with her? That seemed almost inappropriate, the girl had probably been told not to go anywhere with strangers. Then again, she was already in Maren's barn, and she was shaking with cold. Maren decided she had to get her warm.

"I'm a friend of Alex Campbell, does your family know him?" she asked.

Her face brightened. "Aye! He brings food from his farm to the café where my mum is a waitress. He's nice."

Okay, that's my in, Maren thought. "Yes, he is nice. Well, I know him, and if your family knows him, maybe it would be okay for you to come inside my cottage so I can get you warmed up and call your mum or dad."

The girl thought for a moment. "Okay."

Maren stood up and held out her hand. The girl put her small fingers—which were like ice—into Maren's palm, and she helped her stand up. Laddie snuffled her again.

Sally smiled and turned to the horse, laying her forehead against his nose. The two stood like that for a long moment, and Maren felt a pulse of something, like a deep distant drum, or a heartbeat. Something was moving between girl and horse. She knew all three of them were feeling it.

After a moment, Sally lifted her head, scratched Laddie's nose, and said, "What's yer horse's name?"

"Laddie," Maren replied with a smile.

"I like him. He told me not to worry."

Maren's eyes widened. "Did he?" But then she realized *that* was what she'd been feeling, the deep pulse was the animal communicating with the girl. She'd seen it, felt it, and experienced it countless times during her summers here as a child. The magic. She smiled and led the girl to the cottage.

Inside, Maren lit the fire and made a cup of hot chocolate for Sally. Settled in front of the warm flames, mug in hand, Maren tried again to unravel the mystery of where the girl had come from.

"Do you know your mum's phone number? Or your dad's?" Maren asked.

"Umm…" The girl looked off into the distance. "No," she finally said.

"Okay, well, do you know where you live?"

"Aye!" she said triumphantly, like she'd won some kind of game they'd been playing.

"Can you tell me where that is?" Maren asked.

"In the village. Number eight."

It was slow going, but they were getting somewhere, Maren thought.

"Great, thank you, Sally!" Maren said. "Number eight. Do you know what road?"

"The big one. The village road," she answered.

"Okay, well let's get you home then. I'm sure your parents are very worried. It's late. Did you walk here?" she asked, suddenly wondering how the child had ended up in her barn over a mile from the village.

"Yes," she said. "Your horse wanted to meet me."

Maren frowned, confused. She wasn't sure what to make of that. She'd felt the exchange of energy with horses. She knew their magic and their healing powers. But she'd never heard of a horse telepathically calling a little girl over for a play date. But in the Highlands, anything seemed possible.

"Are you hungry?" she asked.

"Aye."

Maren went to the cupboard and got out a tin of baked beans, poured them into a pan and warmed them up on the Aga while she made toast. After a few minutes, she put the beans on toast on the table in the kitchen.

"Come on in and have a bite, and then we'll get you home," she said.

The girl walked in the kitchen, and her eyes grew wide as her mouth fell open. She looked up straight at the starry night sky. Maren had forgotten how strange her kitchen was with a gaping hole in the roof. She laughed.

"Oh, yes, well as you can see, I have a little work to do here," she said and Sally laughed too.

"I like it," she said.

"I kind of like it too," Maren whispered, like they were co-conspirators in a world that most people wouldn't understand.

After the snack, the two got in Maren's car, and she drove to the village, looking for number eight on the main road. Maren drove slowly in the dark, peering at row houses and cottages as the numbers went up.

"There it is!" Sally said proudly.

Maren slowed and parked in the little driveway next to a small cottage just on the edge of the village green. It wasn't fancy, but it looked cozy. The two went to the door, and Maren was about to ring the door when Sally walked straight in.

"Mummy, I made a friend," Sally announced as she strode into the small living room right inside the door.

"Oh my God, Sally, I was worried sick. Ye have to stop wandering off like that!" her mother said, stopping when she saw Maren in the doorway.

"Did you bring her home?" she asked, walking toward Maren, wiping her hand on a tea towel and extending it. "Thank you so much. She tends to wander off. I'm Gillian."

"I'm Maren," she said, taking her hand and shaking it. "It was no problem at all. I'm sorry you were worried. I came home and found her at my cottage."

Gillian turned to her daughter. "I'm verra glad to have met your new friend, but the next time you do this to me, you'll be in trouble, and no mistake."

"Oh, she's not my new friend," Sally said with an innocent smile. "My new friend's name is Laddie. He's really nice."

Gillian looked embarrassed, but Maren smiled, understanding Sally perfectly.

Gillian's brow furrowed and she knelt down in front of her daughter. "Who is Laddie? Is he a man you met?" she asked, clearly trying get information without alarming her daughter.

"No, silly," Sally replied. "Laddie is a horse."

Gillian let out a relieved breath and said to Maren, "I think maybe you'd better come in. If you can. Would you like a cup of tea?"

Maren said she'd love a cup of tea and followed Gillian through the living room into the kitchen at the back of the house. As they drank their tea together, Maren explained who she was, where she lived, and who Laddie was. Gillian told Maren that Sally was wonderful with animals, but had a harder time making friends with humans, so she would often wander off in search of any neighborhood animal she could find. She wasn't sure how she'd managed to get a mile out of the village and down Maren's long driveway to find the horse.

Sally, listening to the conversation, answered the question casually. "He told me he was there. He's lonely." She said it like it was the most natural statement in the world.

Gillian blushed. "I dinnae ken where she gets these ideas," she said almost apologetically.

"Well, there are stranger things in the world than a special girl knowing where a special horse is. I'm just glad she didn't get lost. I'm out in the hills there, and it's dark. Maybe, if it works for you, Gillian, if she wants to come to visit Laddie again, she can let you know. I can even come to get her for a visit."

"That would be wonderful. That's so nice of ye," Gillian replied. "It's just me here with Sally most of the time. Her dad lives in Edinburgh. I'm a waitress up the road, so I'm gone more than I'd like to be. Sometimes, when I work, Sally gets passed around among my friends. I'm sure she'd love a little time with yer horse. She could even help if ye ever need it. I mean, not for pay," she added quickly.

"That sounds perfect to me. I'm on my own, too, there, so help would be very welcome, and I'd bet you're right," Maren said, turning to Sally. "I bet Laddie *is* lonely. He'd love a visitor now and then. Would you like that?"

Sally nodded her head vigorously, then turned away and walked to the living room and turned on the television.

Maren and Gillian parted ways, both agreeing they'd meet another time to have a glass of wine in the pub together. Maren drove home with a big smile on her face. She had somehow just made a friend and met a little helper. She didn't know Gillian at all, and obviously, the woman had a whole life in Glenmuir. But Maren also felt that, if she were in an accident on her way home that very night, this woman might visit her in the hospital. These were people with generations of roots in this place. People who helped each other out. People who weren't looking for an escape. Maybe she'd actually be able to pull this off. Maybe she'd figure out how people build these lives that look so lovely from the outside.

CHAPTER 6

Maren decided to make a website and design a flyer to put around town to get the word out about her new business idea – horse boarding and riding lessons. She piled the boxes in the upstairs storeroom into a corner so she could make a little office. When she'd moved the final box out of the way, she sat at the little table by the window and saw the pile of photos from the other night. With everything going on, she had forgotten about the mystery woman in the photo. Maybe that's how she became a mystery woman in the first place, Maren thought guiltily. Put aside and forgotten.

She quickly sat down and created a flyer for the boarding business, uploaded photos of the stables from her phone, listed her contact info, and then printed out several copies on the printer she'd picked up on her trip to Inverness. When she'd finished that project, she took the bundle of photos and carefully untied the ribbon again. She looked at the sweet face of the young child, then the school-aged child.

"Who are you?" she asked the girl aloud. She felt a little ripple run through her, like a shiver, causing her to drop the photo. *What the heck was that?*

Imagination, no doubt, she told herself. Imagining ghost stories wasn't hard to do in these mist-covered Scottish mountains. She carefully picked the photo up again and turned it over. Sybil. Sybil McGlashan.

Maren opened her laptop again, went online, and typed "Sybil Mc-Glashan 1936." Nothing. "Sybil McGlashan Scotland 1936." Nothing. On and on, she typed in variations, trying to find any mention of this woman. Did her grandfather really have a sister no one knew of? Is that who Maren was looking at? Uncle Gordon's own father had a sister, and Uncle Gordon never knew about her? He had inherited these boxes of photos when his father died, she recalled, and she doubted he'd ever gone through them all carefully enough to find this mystery.

She must be dead, Maren thought. Easy enough for a child to die in the 1940s. But, something kept nudging her.

"Look, Maren," she almost heard. She felt it, and heard it, but it was inside her head, not out loud. It was another unsettling new feeling. "You must look."

Whatever happened to this girl, it was long before the internet. But there were always birth and death records. She looked out the window. Laddie had been fed. There were plenty of things she could do, including getting the flyers up, but none of it had to happen right that minute.

She went downstairs, put the kettle on and made a cup of strong, sweet, milky tea. To Maren, it felt like a statement that she was about to get serious with her task upstairs.

Back at her desk, she looked out the little window. To the left, the mountains rose abruptly, and in front of her the country rolled out gently, a gray, wet view, but beautiful, nonetheless. There were mysteries in this place. She'd always known that. Mysteries and magic.

She got to work. After a long search, having to spend a precious few pounds to get access to some records, Maren found her grandfather's birth certificate.

Then, with a shock, she found the birth certificate of the woman who *did* turn out to be her Great-Aunt Sybil. Born in Lochend, Scotland, 1936.

But no matter how long she searched death certificates, she couldn't find one for her. She found death certificates for her grandfather, and then her Uncle Gordon, which made her sad to see, her uncle's name added to the centuries of records, one more person gone, a name on a form.

But no Sybil.

Maybe records weren't kept that well in the thirties and forties. Maybe something happened during the war. But she knew this wasn't right. There would be a death certificate if she'd died in this century. On the other hand, maybe she was in America when she died.

Maren spent another hour scouring records in the US. No death certificate. Her grandfather was listed in U.S. death records since he lived there at the time. But no Sybil.

By midday, Maren's back hurt, and she had found no record of Sybil having died. And she had other things to do. Sighing, she closed her laptop, grabbed the pile of papers, and went downstairs.

First, she'd check on Laddie. As she slid the barn door open, his head popped out, and he snickered in greeting.

"Want to go out, sweet boy?" Maren asked. She slid the bolt on his stall door.

He took a few steps out of the stall. He still hadn't shown the slightest sign of aggression. He seemed to be completely sweet-natured, even after having been so mistreated. He walked toward Maren and put his head on her shoulder. Her eyes opened wide, and she stood still, not wanting to spoil the moment. It was what he had done to Sally the night before.

Maren smiled and reached up and scratched his nose. She felt that tingle run through her again, and she knew he was thanking her. They walked side by side, slowly, peacefully, to the back of the barn, and Maren opened the door. Laddie trotted happily out and began to munch on the winter grass. Maren watched him for a few minutes, and then headed inside to grab her bag, the flyers, and her car keys.

She hung flyers at the village shop, the post office, and on the community bulletin board outside the church. Then, she made the drive into Inverness. She'd need to cast a wide net to fill the large stables, so she put the rest of the flyers up in various spots around the city: the feed store, garden center, and anywhere else that seemed like it would be seen by the horse crowd.

As Maren was driving home from Inverness, she saw a sign for Lochend. The town where her grandfather and Sybil had lived as children. Of course! She could go there and ask around. It was a long shot—a very long shot—that anyone would remember Fergus or Sybil, but she didn't have any other idea how she'd figure out what had happened, and for some reason, she just knew she had to keep looking.

As she pulled into the town, she saw the pub on the main road. She parked and went inside. It was a small pub, less charming than the one in Glenmuir. It had a beautiful old wooden bar, but the tables were plastic, and there were three gambling machines in the corner, flashing lights and making annoying noises. There were several old men in flat caps sitting around a table. And two younger men at the bar. Maren walked to the publican and asked for a chardonnay.

Seated with her drink at the bar, she said, "Excuse me, I have a strange question."

"American," the barman said, a statement not a question. "Americans usually do," he said, with an almost smile.

She wasn't sure if he was being friendly or making fun of her, but she went on. "I'm looking for someone."

"Well, we're a small village, as ye see, so maybe I can help ye," he said.

"Great. But, well, the thing is, I'm looking for someone older. She'd be in her late eighties. She was born here, but I don't know much more about her than that. She's my great-aunt. Her name is Sybil McGlashan."

"Any of ye layabouts ken a Sybil McGlashan? Lady about yer age." the publican yelled to the old men at the table.

The two men shook their heads, but one looked into the distance as if scanning his mental files.

"Aye. That sounds familiar. I kent the McGlashans at school. I think there were two of 'em. A boy and a gurrel," he said.

"Oh my God, yes!" Maren blurted out. She grabbed her wine and walked to their table, standing there awkwardly, realizing she couldn't just sit down without an invitation.

"Sit down, lass, if ye like," he said, and she did.

"I was at school with the McGlashans. They lived down the lane from us, och, a lifetime ago, it was. Callum, you knew the McGlashans, don't ye remember?" the man said, turning to his friend.

Callum took off his cap and scratched his head, as if it might help his brain.

"Sybil McGlashan…" he said, looking ahead. Then his expression changed. "Och, aye! I do. Yes, she was a bonnie lass, I remember now."

"Aye, she was," the other man said. Then he turned to Maren and held out his hand. "Andrew Burns." Maren shook it. Andrew then turned to his two friends, pointing. "Malcom." One man nodded with a smile, and "Callum." The man who remembered Sybil nodded at her.

"This is amazing," Maren said. "I just moved to Glenmuir. My Uncle Gordon lived there most of his life, and now I'm living in his cottage. And I found these old photos, and Sybil must be my great-aunt, but I never knew she existed. I think she might still be alive, but there's no record of her anywhere," she explained.

"Well, you'd do best by askin' yer own family, but I'm sure you've started there," Callum said.

Maren looked at the table for a moment, before admitting, "I don't have any family."

"Och, sorry, lass," he said. "Well, my wife'll know more. The women always keep the stories, don't they?" he said. "You jest hang on." To her surprise, the old Highlander got out an iPhone and called his wife.

Ten minutes later, Callum's wife, Maggie, a woman in her eighties, but strong and full of energy, walked briskly into the pub.

"Maggie, this here's Maren. American. Looking for her Auntie Sybil. She knows nowt about her. Do ye remember Sybil McGlashan? We were at school together ages ago," Callum said to his wife.

"Hallo, Maren," Maggie said. Her face was wrinkled but lively. "I kent her, aye. Till they up and moved to America. Anaway, aye, I knew her well. Och, tragic story, my dear. Tragic story." Her eyes filled with tears, which seemed to surprise the old woman. She quickly wiped them away. "Some stories are best left untold, my dear," she said. "Dinnae open a box o' trouble fer yerself."

Maren was riveted. "What do you mean, open a box of trouble? I definitely want to know what happened to her, even if it's sad. Did she die?"

"No. That'd be less tragic, really, though God forgive me fer sayin' it. No, I've no idea if she's still on this side. She may well have died ages ago, fer all I ken. But I'll tell ye the story, if you do want to know."

She did.

Maren got herself a second glass of wine, and one for Maggie, then sat back down.

"She was a bonnie gurrel. And smart as a whip. She lived here in Lochend till she was about, och, I dinnae ken, twelve, thirteen, something like that. She was growing to be a wee bit wild. She painted, gorgeous paintings, even young as she was. Bright colors, I remember that. And she spoke her mind, did Sybil. And she'd get in a wee bind now and then too. Caught smoking once with some of the rougher boys. The school sent her home midday that day. Och, her parents were ragin'. And she had a bit o' temper herself. But that ma of hers was nasty. Mean woman through and through. We all thought we'd ha' a temper, too, living with that woman."

Maren couldn't believe she was hearing these detailed stories about someone who had just been a name on a page a few hours earlier. "But why did I not know about her? My own Uncle Gordon, who lived down the road from here most of his life, never heard of her either, as far as I know. What happened to her?"

"Maybe he didnae ken because it was awful. After the mother died, the father moved her and her brother to America. We heard a few stories, because some of our dads were friends with her dad, and they'd write. Sybil became a painter. She would go to parties and stay out half the night and she ran with a crowd of artists. I think her father regretted movin' her there, America was wilder than Scotland, in that way anaway. And she'd speak her mind to anyone who'd listen. She would talk of the wee folk, the fairy folk, and of talking wi' animals, and of feeling the stones in Scotland calling to her, telling her ta come home. They thought she was mad. One day, a few years after moving there, her father came home, and there she was, in the garden, with a huge pile, burning every one of her paintings."

"Why?" Maren asked.

"No one knew. She said she wanted to start over. New paintings. She had moods, she did. But she was sweet. She was a sweet lass with a nasty mother, and a father whose head was always somewhere else. She got wilder with the talk o' the stones and animals and seeing things that hadn't happened yet. In the Highlands, it's called the sight. She could skree—see the future, looking through a hole in a stone. And, by God, if some o' the things didn't happen!" she said, eyes wide with the memory. "But the father was embarrassed by her. He was tryin' to make a life in American with the rich folks. She was ruining his chances with those kind. That's what my ma told me anaway. We never knew exactly how it happened, or why. But her dad decided she was mad. He brought her back over here, and he had her put away. Locked up. He told the doctors she had lost her mind, and back then, a father only had to say it, and it was done. No investigation, no proof. He told them a few of her stories of seeing the future, talking to animals, burning her paintings, and signed a paper, and the poor, poor lass was locked away in an insane asylum. Old men were always happy to call a woman with the gifts 'hysterical' and 'insane' back then. It didnae take much. We never knew where he put her. Not long after, the father died. And the brother, your grandfather, I suppose, had been sworn to secrecy, to act as if his own sister didn't exist. They abandoned that young woman, only seventeen she was, and no one ever even went to see her after that. The father went back to America, and we never heard about her again. And even if we'd have known where she was, we wouldna have been allowed to see her. She was locked away like a prisoner." Maggie shivered as she finished the tale.

"That is so sad!" Maren said, tears stinging her eyes. She must be misunderstanding the story. This couldn't be possible. She had been locked in an insane asylum for...she quickly did the math...for seventy years! "How could they do that? How could anyone do that?" she almost yelled, ashamed of her own family.

Maggie reached over and patted the back of Maren's hand. "I wasna sure I should tell ye, but seemed right ye should know, as her kin," she said.

"Thank you," Maren said, wiping her eyes. "I'm so glad you did tell me. My gosh, someone needs to know her story. Do you know if she died? Did you ever hear anything else about her?"

"Nae, no' a word. Her father stopped writing to our dads. Probably too hard for him, knowing what he'd done. Then some time later he passed. We none of us ever heard about any of 'em after that. I doubt she'd still be alive, considering the life she must've lived, if ye can call it a life. But I dinnae ken if she's alive or dead, I'm sorry, dear."

"Well, I need to find her. If she's dead, then someone will know where her grave is, and I can honor her by visiting her there, at least. But she could be alive. I mean, she'd be old, but she could definitely be alive!" Maren was getting herself worked up, filled with anger that her family had been capable of creating such unforgivable suffering.

"Whit's fur ye'll no go by ye," Maggie said with a calm smile.

Maren smiled awkwardly. She'd have to learn these Scots sayings. She was too embarrassed to ask for a translation, but Maggie guessed by her expression that she didn't understand.

"It means, what's meant ta happen will happen. It won't pass ye by. And tis true. If yer meant to find her, ye will,

my dear. Maybe it's why yer here," she said, with a knowing look that made Maren think there might be more to that statement than she totally understood.

Maggie winked and rose from the table, giving Callum a little smack on the arm. "I'll burn this old goat's dinner if I dinnae get home, and I'll never hear the end o' that, let me tell ye." She turned to Maren. "Lovely to have met ye, Maren, and if ye need anything ye ken where to find my husband." The men at the table laughed. "But really, we live down the road, Lane House, cottage with a red door. Come by, if ye need anything."

"Thank you so much," Maren said.

After Maggie left, Maren paid for the round of drinks, thanked the men for all their help, and headed to her car and home.

When she got there, she had a message on her voicemail.

"Hallo. My name's Alistair. I saw your paper in town, and I'm looking for a place for my horse. I have him here on our land, but I'm moving to a smaller place with no stables and looking to board him. He's a bonnie boy, no trouble."

He proceeded to give his number and said he'd love to come to see the stables when it suited her. Maren returned the man's call and they arranged to meet the day after next.

Maren couldn't believe it! She'd only put the flyers up that afternoon, and she had a lead already! Then she panicked. thinking the stables weren't totally ship-shape yet. She hadn't expected a response so quickly.

When she got home she changed into her work clothes and headed outside. Maren spent the entire night scrubbing every inch of the barn and organizing all the tack. She lugged in bucket after bucket of hot soapy water from the kitchen. She was on hands and knees, with a stiff scrub brush, music blaring on her phone. It was pitch black outside, but the warm glow of the barn lights and the smell of hay and horse inside made it seem cozy. Laddie seemed to be enjoying the unusual evening visitor and wandered around the stables, keeping her company. He had stayed a sweet and calm horse and was getting less and less shy each day. Maren saw a playful personality emerging. As she was cleaning, Laddie unhooked his empty feed bucket from his stall and gripped it in his teeth, dropping it with a clang on the stone floor right next to Maren. She jumped and then laughed. Was he trying to help, seeing her bent over her bucket? No, he probably just wanted more food.

The sky was just beginning to lighten when she stood and stretched her aching back, looking with satisfaction at the barn. Her uncle would be thrilled to see it solid, intact, and sparkling clean. She finished by scrubbing the flagstone floor with a stiff broom and water, then gathered her cleaning things and walked, half asleep and frozen through, to the cottage.

She knew she should go to bed, but so much had happened in one day, she was buzzing. Her mind kept turning back to Sybil. She would get some rest and then get on her computer. She wouldn't give up until she'd found the poor woman, whether that be locked up somewhere or in a churchyard.

Her phone rang. She wondered who would be calling so early in the morning. She picked it up.

"Morning, lass," Alex said.

Maren's heart did a little flip, she loved that he called her lass, like he'd known her forever. "Good morning," she said back, glad he couldn't see her big smile at the sound of his voice.

"I'll start by sayin', of course ye can say no. I'd almost expect ye to," he added. "But, well, I've a wee favor to ask."

"Hmm, this is a pattern, Mr. Campbell," she said laughing. "Okay, lay it on me."

"I went to see a man about a horse, ye see," Alex said with a laugh of his own. "No, I didn't. It's Charlie, the police called him in the night. They've a farm with several horses in awful shape. I dinnae ken why suddenly it's raining mangy horses. But we wondered if, temporarily again, of course, ye might consider putting them in yer fine stables till we sort them out. There's four. Charlie did say the town'll pay whoever takes them ta cover feed and all that. And a bit more for the trouble. Again, no worries at all if it's too much. I'm sure you've got other plans for yer fine barn than old unwanted horses, but I thought I'd ask." He paused and then added, "There's another pub dinner in it fer ye if ye say yes! This time, I'll take ye to a great whisky pub and give ye a right proper tasting!"

Maren laughed. "Taking on four sick, mistreated horses for an offer of some whisky, let me think about that very Highland-style offer."

Alex's deep laugh made Maren's heart beat faster. "Yer right, not much of a bargain fer ye, is it?"

"Can I call you right back?" Maren asked. "Literally, just give me five minutes to think how, or if, I can do it. Does that work?"

"Of course," Alex said. "Thank you for not tellin' me to away n bile me rheid right off the bat."

Maren laughed out loud. "I have absolutely no idea what you just said to me, but let me call you back in five minutes, okay?"

"Ha, I said I'm glad you didnae tell me to piss off straight away just fer askin'," he translated. "And, aye, take yer time. For the next six minutes," he added. Maren giggled and hung up the phone.

Maren believed in signs and messages. More neglected horses? How was that possible? Was she meant to be taking them all in? Her logical mind told her that a very nice man named Alistair wanted to come by and possibly board his horse here, and that would be steady income and hopefully lead to more boarders. What would four mangy horses be but work? Well, and a stipend, until they found them placement. But she could do both. The stables were huge. It was just one horse looking to be boarded after all, *if* he decided to board. And the new ones could easily be kept separate, in the far end stalls, until they had been checked out and cleared to be together. If they were here long enough for that to even happen.

She tried being logical and measured, but she already knew what her heart was telling her loud and clear. She called Alex back and said, "Bring them over, I'll have stalls ready."

"I'll book a table at that pub!" he said, then thanked her before hanging up.

Maren took her tea and wandered back to the stables, still in the filthy, wet clothes from the night of cleaning. She leaned her head in and yelled, "Laddie, you're getting friends!"

A few hours later, Charlie drove up in his truck. This time, he pulled a large horse trailer behind.

"Maren, yer a saint. I told Alex not to even call ye, it's askin' so much. I dinnae ken what's happening with all these horses. Maybe it's the cold and the farmers running out of food midwinter, but two rescues in so short a time, that's no' normal up here. We're no' all horrible to our beasts, I promise ye."

"I don't think you are, and I'm happy to help," Maren said.

The sun had broken through the clouds, and as Charlie unloaded four emaciated horses, heads hanging low, sunlight fell in a beam like the heavens shining on them. Maren smiled.

"Hello, sweet things," she said softly, as each one was led by and into the stall she'd pointed out for Charlie to put them in. "You're safe now, don't worry." She felt a tingle of exhilaration, and something else, pride maybe, that she could say those words and offer that to a being who had been through what she had been through as a child. To be able to say the words to these helpless creatures that had never been said to her, at least at home. "You're safe with me."

Maren kept looking to see if Alex was coming but was disappointed, he never showed up. She tried to sound casual as she asked Charlie, "So, is Alex coming today?" She was pretty sure she failed the casual test.

But Charlie was busy with the horses, and he was a guy, she reminded herself with a little laugh. He probably hadn't noticed the tightness in her voice as she asked it.

"Aye, he'll be here. Stoppin' by, he said, but on his way to Inverness to his brother's restaurant to see what they need, so just poppin' in."

"Oh, okay, whatever. He doesn't need to, if he's busy," she said, then told herself to shut up before she started babbling.

Charlie was in the stall of the second horse, examining it. Fortunately, the first one did not have mites. He seemed to just need some good care and food.

At the sound of a car, Maren poked her head out of the barn to see the little red sports car pulling up. Out of the passenger side, Alex stood up.

He didn't even walk all the way over. He just yelled, "Everything okay, Charlie?"

"Aye!" Charlie yelled back.

"Maren, thank ye so much, yer truly a kind lass. I wish I could stay, but we're running late fer a meeting," Alex said, turning back toward the car.

The beautiful blonde sat in the driver's seat again. She smiled and waved from the car, and Alex jumped back in, and they drove off.

Well, that is that Maren thought. No more nonsense. You've had enough broken hearts. Don't be an idiot and pine after a man who is taken. A kind man. And funny. And sexy. And smart. *Maren!* she shouted in her mind. *Enough.* And with that, she hardened herself a little and flipped the switch in her heart to the "keep it light" setting.

Charlie finished examining all four horses. No mites or mange. That was a huge amount of work saved. They all got vitamin injections and vaccinations, and Charlie unloaded hay, timothy grass, and three fifty-pound bags of feed pellets into the feed room of the stables.

"I didn't have time to sort it today, but there'll be a check for ye tomorrow from the animal welfare society, for caring fer the wee beasties while we find them a home. Thank ye, Maren," he said with a warm smile.

Charlie had a kind face, very round, with freckles. She wished she could feel an attraction for him, purely as a distraction from her disappointment over Alex. But she couldn't. And right away, she was glad. She liked Charlie, in a simple but genuine way. It was nice to have a friend.

"Cup of tea?" she offered, starting to feel the effects of having been up all night, now that the adrenaline of the day was wearing off.

"I could murder a cup o' tea," he said, and she smiled at the expression.

In the kitchen, his mouth fell open as he looked up at the sky through the hole in the roof. The fox, a frequent visitor to the kitchen now, jumped up on the table, cabinet, and out the hole, and Charlie let out a yell.

Maren smiled. Her visitor had become like a friend and she had given him a name. "That's Clive."

"He's yer pet?" Charlie asked, looking shocked.

"No, he's a fox that lives in the garden. But he visits me in the kitchen most days. He's not dangerous. I've got someone coming tomorrow to start fixing the roof. Alex gave me the name of someone who does roofs and said he's very good. Though I'm sort of sad about it, to be honest. But it is ridiculous. I know, I need a roof."

Charlie looked at her with a mixture of shock and amusement, as if he was having to recalibrate his opinion of her to someone who was half-mad, or half-wild, living with foxes in her house, rain and snow falling right into her kitchen.

"It is dangerous, ye ken. Foxes are wild animals. They bite if scared," he said. The vet in him clearly made him want to be sure she understood what she was dealing with.

"I know. But Clive and I have an understanding, don't worry. And after tomorrow, I'll have to visit him in the garden. No more kitchen tea parties," she said with an exaggeratedly sad expression. "I'm going to be sensible. Boring as that is." She laughed.

Charlie shook his head, chuckling. "Americans," he said.

Though she responded with another laugh, Maren felt sure this wild piece of her nature was far more likely to have come from her Highland blood than from Boston.

After tea, Charlie fed and watered the horses, so they were settled till evening, and suddenly Maren couldn't keep her eyes open. She had been up for over twenty-four hours.

She went upstairs and headed to her little bedroom, now aired out and fresh, and warm with the furnace running, but as she passed the little office, her mind went back to Sybil. When she thought of Sybil, feeling a bit tired seemed a feeble excuse not to at least have a quick poke around on the internet, though she didn't expect to find much.

She opened her laptop, and as it started up, she looked out at the garden. The sun was out. The grass in front of the house was just stubble, but she knew it would be green in a few months, and the pink rose bushes in front of the cottage would bloom and smell wonderful. She knew this from what her uncle told her and again wished she'd be able to see it in color. But she'd feel the change, and smell the flowers at least. She looked further ahead, to the ben, rising in the distance, and felt called to it, like something physically pulling her. "Tomorrow," she said to the mountain. "I'll wander tomorrow, I promise."

And the mountain seemed satisfied with that and let her go.

Maren paused, staring at the cursor blinking on the computer screen. She didn't know where to start. A simple Google search by name hadn't done much. If her aunt had been in a medical facility all this time, maybe she could find her via the national health system. After an hour of searching, again unsuccessfully, to find her aunt in a care home, she decided it must be a privacy issue. You couldn't expect to find a list of names of people in the hospital.

Her final attempt before she was headed for a nap was to call a number for national health and see if she could at least get a nibble on her line. After being given four other numbers to call, Maren got a woman on the phone, who told her that, if her aunt was in a nursing home in Scotland, Maren would have to prove she was a family member, and then they would be able to give her some information. Maren's heart raced as the woman said it. She could do that! She could prove that!

But they wouldn't even say if her aunt was alive until Maren could do that. The kind, but businesslike, woman gave Maren the address for the office of the NHS in Inverness and told her she should call and book an appointment.

Maren called the number and, surprisingly, was able to make an appointment to meet with someone in just three days' time. She'd need to print out birth certificates and other things to show her relation to Sybil, but for now, she felt she'd done enough for one day. Her eyes were starting to close by themselves, whether she liked it or not, so she stumbled to her bed, climbed under the duvet, and was asleep before her head hit the pillow.

CHAPTER 7

The next morning, Maren dressed in her work clothes and went to the barn. Four new, skinny heads leaned over their stalls as she entered. Three of the horses were light colored, she could tell that at least. And one was very dark, he looked black to Maren. The black horse's name, she'd been told by Charlie, was Sultan, and he was understandably mean. She was surprised they weren't *all* mean after the mistreatment they'd endured. But having learned how to handle horses, she knew how to behave, not just with the easy ones, but with the hard ones too.

She dumped big scoops of grain into each of their feed buckets and used the hose to fill their water buckets, all from outside their stalls. She would take a day to get to know them a bit before squeezing in an enclosed space with them. She may have tea parties with a wild fox, but she wasn't going to get in a tiny box with an angry two-thousand-pound beast.

She scratched the heads of the three light horses. One had a white star on its forehead, so she decided to call her Star. One bobbed his head up and down with such force every time she walked by that it reminded her of an eighties headbanger band, so she named him Bang. Maren had to stare at the third light horse for a while to come up with a name, then she noticed he had a large white patch on his side that looked just like the continent of Australia so she named him Ozzie. To those friendlier horses, she held out her hand and offered carrots. She wanted to slowly let them know that, when she walked into the barn, good things would happen.

When she got to Sultan's stall, he kicked at the wall. He looked like a biter. And a biter could take your finger off. A kicker could break your leg, or kill you, if it landed in just the right spot. There was horse whispering, but then there was foolishness. She would have to take her time with him.

She dropped the carrot into his bucket, and he snatched it out and ate it. Finally, she went to Laddie's stall. He was such a sweet horse. He held his head out for his morning nose scratch and gently took the carrot from Maren's hand.

Then it was time for business. Maren went back inside, showered, and changed into jeans and a black turtleneck, put on a touch of makeup, and waited for Alistair to arrive. A potential client. Potential income. There were two men coming to start work on the kitchen roof that day. There had been lots of expenses already at the cottage. She was quickly running out of money so she really needed this man to board his horse. She knew, in small communities, word of mouth was the best way to build a business.

When she saw his car pull up, Maren smoothed her hair and stepped outside with a smile.

"Hello," she said holding out her hand. "I'm Maren Phillips."

She didn't know why she'd been expecting an old man. This guy was her age, and handsome. Black hair combed neatly to the side, dark eyes, a strong jaw. They grew the men handsome in the Highlands, Maren thought, with a hidden smile.

"Alistair McCain," he said, shaking Maren's hand. "People call me Ali."

"Hi, Ali. I'm so glad you called. You're looking for somewhere to board your horse?"

"Aye, I am. I've been living on a property with a barn, but it's too much work. I'm too busy to be mucking stalls. I'm in banking and don't have time for all that," he said with a slight wave of his hand toward the stables.

Maren wasn't sure why, but she felt slightly insulted.

"I've just taken a gorgeous flat in Inverness, and obviously, haven't a spot for a horse," he said. He flashed a big, broad smile. Maren's heart skipped a beat.

"Well, then you're in the right place. Room for horses is what I have in spades. Do you want to see the stables?"

"Aye, I do. Thank you," he said, following her across the yard.

Maren slid open the barn door and they stepped inside. She had cleaned it so well it practically gleamed.

"Impressive!" he said. "This is a bonnie stable you've got here."

"Thank you. It was my late uncle's favorite part of the farm," Maren said.

"I can see wh—" Alistair stopped midsentence as five scrawny horse heads appeared over the tops of the far stalls.

"Oh, I see you have some boarders already," he said, walking toward the animals. The corners of his nose curled up very slightly, clearly in distaste at seeing the skinny, dirty horses.

"Ahh, yes, I can explain. These are rescue horses. They just arrived last night, well, except for Laddie," she said, pointing at him. "He's been here a few days. They're just stopping here till they can be found permanent homes, but they're not ill or contagious with anything. They're in great health except for being malnourished, and we've had them checked out by a vet," she said, with a feeling of pride that she was helping these animals in need.

Alistair didn't seem to see it that way. "That's nice of you to do," he said with a cold tone in his voice, "but my horse is an expensive thoroughbred. I certainly don't want him being around horses who might be carry-ing disease, or who are ill-tempered."

"I do completely understand," she said, and she meant it. "I can get you a vet's certificate that they aren't sick, if that would help."

"You know, I think I'm going to think about it," he said. He flashed her his big smile again, but this time it didn't have the same effect. "Your stables are bonnie, no doubt. I just have to be sure it's the right fit. I'm sure you understand. I'll be calling you, and thank you," he said, heading back toward his car.

Maren's instinct was to go after him and try and talk him into it. Like she had with every man, in every situation in her life, she suddenly real-ized. But, when she looked back, and saw the goofy, pathetic horse heads looking at her with curiosity, she unexpectedly laughed. Luckily, Alistair had his back to her and didn't notice. She wouldn't try and talk anyone into anything. That's not how she was going to live anymore. With men, with work, with herself, even.

"Okay, that makes sense. Thanks so much for coming by," she said, and she found she truly meant it, and felt friendly again toward him now that she had changed her perspective. It was fine if he didn't board here. She'd find someone else.

When he got to his car and turned around, he seemed slightly offend-ed that she hadn't pursued him and tried to talk him into it. That was the feeling she thought she was getting from him, anyway. He certainly looked like the kind of guy who was used to being pursued.

Maren went back to the stables and said out loud to herself, "I will find horses to have here!" Laddie kicked his stall and Maren laughed. "Oh my gosh, you're right. Laddie. I do have horses here already!" She had five horses in her stalls, horses that, at least in the short term, she would get a stipend to keep, and she hadn't had to do a thing to bring them in. They had dropped out of the sky into her care. Wasn't that how things sometimes happened if they were meant to be? No banging your head against a wall. Just allowing things to happen naturally. She cocked her head and looked at the horses in a different light.

A horn honked and Maren jumped, startled out of her daydreaming. Four men were getting out of a van and Maren realized they were the roof repairmen. They were polite but not talkative. Maren spent half the afternoon trying to spark conversation and show them that she was a friendly American. They didn't seem to care, so finally she left them to their work in peace.

***

The next morning, pile of papers in hand, Maren jumped in her scrappy little car and bounced down the road to the city. The office for the Scottish National Health Service was a large modern building on the edge of the city. It looked out of place among the ancient stone buildings of Inverness. Maren was directed upstairs to a waiting area, and she sat next to a fake ficus plant and read old magazines. It was just like every waiting room in the world.

After about half an hour, a voice called, "Maren Phillips."

"Yes!" Maren said, her heart in her throat. She followed the man into a small office.

"How can I help ye?" he asked. The man was gray-haired and had kind eyes. But he looked tired. She was glad it wasn't later in the day. Would he be less likely to help the more tired he got? she wondered.

"My name is Maren, and I'm trying to find my great-aunt. It's a bit of a long story, but my family sort of…lost touch with her, years ago, and I've just realized she may still be alive, and I'm trying to find her."

86

The man chewed on the tip of his pen while considering what she'd said. "So, yer American, but yer great auntie is Scottish?"

"Yes. My great-grandfather moved to America from near here and brought his two children with him." Maren felt strange saying that, like she was lying, but it seemed to be true, there *had* been two children. "One became my grandfather, the other, her name was Sybil. I can't say for sure if this part is correct, but I was told she was brought back many, many years ago and placed in a mental hospital. I'm desperate to find her. She'd have been there on her own all this time."

Clearly this wasn't the usual story people came to him about. This was no normal pencil-pushing situation, where someone wanted to query a charge or sign someone up for healthcare.

He slowly shook his head. "I'm sorry to hear that. That did happen generations ago."

"Yes, and I know she might not even still be living. She'd be in her late eighties, but I just have to find out, even if it's just to know where she's buried. But, in case she's alive, I mean, if by any wild miracle she's alive, I have to find her!" she said with urgency. It wasn't how she'd planned on handling it. She had thought detached and businesslike would be the way to go. She didn't want to freak the administrator out, or make it seem like this might turn into a lot of work. All he had to say was no, and she'd have no recourse. She'd have lost any chance of ever finding her.

But, instead, the man—Dennis, apparently, by the name on the plastic name placard on the desk—looked sympathetic. "Let's see what we can do."

Maren knew she was in.

"I'll need to see some proof yer related, of course. Privacy and that," he said.

Maren was prepared. It was amazingly simple to get documents for dead people, she'd found.

She handed the pile of documents to Dennis and laid out the photos of Sybil and her grandfather as children, explaining who everyone was. She was aware that the people in the photos could be anyone, and it wasn't proof of anything, but she thought it might help to see the innocent face of the woman she was now trying to find, a woman whose life had been stolen from her.

Dennis looked carefully at all the documents, and touched them gently, one at a time, as if making some sense of it all in a file in his mind.

"Well, I can see yer kin. Ye did a braw job with the documents," he said.

Maren smiled, nervous but hopeful.

"Let me see what I can find. We have a database of everyone in our care. If she's alive and in a hospital or care home, she'll be in our system. And if she's deceased, she'll be in there too. I'll search by family and birthdate, too, as there may be more than one Sybil McGlashan. Give me a wee moment, dear. Can ye go get a cuppa tea and come back in a bit?"

A bit? Maren had anticipated this would take weeks.

She tried to hide her excitement, and casually said, "Of course. I will do that. Would two p.m. be a good time to come back?"

"Aye, that should do it. I will see ye then. I cannae promise anathing, but I'll do my best," he said with a warm smile, and Maren felt so lucky to have ended up with this man across the desk and not some short-tempered person who couldn't be bothered.

Maren left in search of a tea shop where she could go and bite off all her fingernails for two hours.

***

When she returned to the office at two on the dot, Dennis was beaming.

"Yer no' going to believe it, but I found her," he said. He was clearly enjoying being involved in the adventure of finding the mysterious woman.

"No way!" Maren yelled. A woman across the hall shot her an irritated look. "Sorry," she said, grinning. "No way!" she said more softly. "I never in a million years thought you'd find her that quickly. Thank you! So..." She paused, knowing the answer to this question would determine a lot. "Is she alive?"

Dennis smiled, "Aye. She is. She's alive and in a nursing home no' far from here. About an hour's drive, in a town called Mullach. If ye like, I can contact them and tell them yer kin and will be visiting. If, of course, ye want to do that. I dinnae ken the state she'll be in at her age and after... well, after where she's been," he said with a sympathetic look.

"Where has she been?" Maren asked.

"Yer story was right," he said. "She was in a hospital for what we now call mentally ill. Back then, it was the St. Joseph's Hospital for the Insane. No' a pretty place back then. Much changed now, with so many different laws protecting patients. But I wouldna have wanted to be there in the fifties. She was there for almost seventy years. The mind reels. After that, she was transferred to this lovely nursing home, and has, thankfully, been there since."

Maren got chills over her whole body. She felt like she had just been plugged into a live circuit.

Maren drove home on a high. And at the same time, she felt completely overwhelmed. It had all happened so quickly. Who was this woman? Why had they locked her away? And would Maren's vision of a sad, lost, old woman be accurate? Or would she go there and find a crazy, screaming, nasty person? Maren had no doubt, *she'd* be a nasty, bitter person herself, if her life had been robbed from her.

Did she really want to go and see this woman? She'd barely gotten settled in her life here, and she needed to start focusing on making money. She needed to think. She wanted to create a life on purpose there. A life with intention, not stumble into things that felt heavy or messy that she then had to run from in six months, or weeks, like she usually did.

Maren decided she needed some help lifting her mood, so on her way home, she parked her car in front of the village green and walked along the road to the pub. It was dark and cold. But the days were slowly edging longer, she could see that.

As she walked, she looked at the glow of the windows from the row of pretty, attached stone cottages that lined the street. One had their curtains drawn, and she could only see light along the edges of the window. In the next window, a family sat in their living room, watching television. A child was coloring in a coloring book, and the woman had a glass of wine and laughed at something the man next to her said, presumably her husband.

The next window revealed an old couple. Maren could see through the sitting room to the kitchen, where the woman was cooking, the man was on the sofa reading a newspaper. She could hear the faint sound of classical music.

As she walked past the last cottage, she suddenly started crying. It had just been a long day, she told herself. And she was hungry. But she knew what it really was. She wanted that. She wanted that life. *A* life. Her whole life, Maren had walked past the warm glow of lights in people's houses and wanted to be inside. Wanted to be invited into those lives, where people cooked dinner and read newspapers and had children making a mess and laughing. She resented never being invited inside. It hurt that, for thirty-five years (barring her summers with her uncle), she had walked the globe, looking in on other people's lives. But never the one inside the home. Never the one with the life and the partner and the dinner simmering on the stove.

In an instant, like a bright light switching on, Maren realized she had spent her whole adult life trying to be invited into a life. But she'd been looking for the wrong thing. She didn't need to feel lonely because the whole world seemed to have these full lives, with people who loved them, where she was on the outside looking in.

It wasn't about getting *invited* in. It was about *building* a life of her own.

Even after moving to Glenmuir, she'd been hoping to be invited into someone's life. Maybe Alex's, Charlie's. Even Gillian's.

For the first time, Maren wanted to be inside the glowing evening home, but not in someone else's life. *She* had to build that life herself. The way into the bright living room on a dark evening, with people and meaning and dinner on the stove wasn't through someone else's door; it was through her own.

Her heart felt tight with both loneliness and joy at the realization that everything she'd ever wanted was possible and that it didn't depend on anyone else. It could be hers, but she'd have to make it herself. She could have it tomorrow if she wanted it. But it wasn't just standing in a home that made it, it was the energy of it. It was truly feeling in her heart that she was home. Then the rest would follow. That's how she would end up on the inside of the evening window.

She wiped her eyes and smiled as she walked into the pub. And saw Alistair.

He was leaning with one elbow on the dark wood of the bar, one foot up on the brass rod that ran along the bottom. He saw her and smiled, and with a jerk of his head, motioned for her to come over.

"Hi there. On yer own?" he asked.

"Yes, just need a hot meal and can't be bothered to cook," she said.

Alistair motioned to the barman. "A…?" He looked at Maren with raised eyebrows.

"Oh, red wine, please. Thanks," she said to Alistair.

"Red wine, Ewan, thanks."

"Right ye are," the barman said and turned to pour her drink.

There was, to Maren, an uncomfortable silence, as the only thing she knew about this handsome man was that he was looking to board his horse. But she didn't want to ask about that and seem pushy. She smiled awkwardly.

"How's that lot o' ragtag horses you've got there? Very nice of you to take them on. Hopefully, they'll get them off your hands soon," he said, and she was glad it was he who had broached the subject.

But she felt slightly insulted at the way he did it. Suddenly defensive of the "ragtag" group of horses, who'd ended up looking ragtag through no fault of their own.

"They're great, actually. One of them is a bit high-spirited, but he'll come around. The rest are sweethearts. They just need a little love, and they'll be gorgeous in no time," she told him.

"I did actually find a place for my horse," he said. "No insult to yer beautiful stables at all. Just found a place closer to my new apartment and it's—" He paused looking for a phrase, "—better suited."

Well, you can shove your fancy horse where the sun doesn't shine, Maren thought. But, of course, she didn't say it. And as soon as she'd had the thought, she was mad at herself for being childish. This man had simply found a better-suited place for his horse. It had nothing to do with her. She'd have been stressed out with his horse there, and she was glad he had chosen another spot.

"I'm glad you found somewhere that works so well," she said, and she meant it.

"So, tell me about yerself," he said, giving her a generous look up and down, looking like he appreciated what he saw.

Maren's stomach fluttered. An image of Alex's face came to mind, but she swatted it away. He had a beautiful girlfriend. And Maren was allowed to have some fun. Maybe more than fun.

Maren told Alistair her story, the version that left out the horrible childhood, that was too dark for a flirtatious conversation. She finished with how she had ended up in Glenmuir.

"And now your turn," she said with a smile.

"Let's see. I'm from here, I grew up in the large house on the far edge of the village."

Maren knew of the house, a huge stately home, made of light-colored stone and set amid beautiful lawns and gardens.

"Of course, I was sent to boarding school in England," he said, which explained his accent, Maren thought, a mix of English and Highland Scot. "Most people from…well, from my kind of family, send their children to boarding school in England. I lived in London for about a decade. Then, once my father got sick, I moved home to take over. And as I can work from almost anywhere now, with the internet and teleconferencing, I fly down to London once or twice a month, but other than that, I work from the Inverness office or home."

"Why did you get an apartment, if your family owns that beautiful big house?" Maren asked.

"Oh, I'd never live in it. I'll help run it, and I suppose, one day, maybe I'll be forced to live there, but it's drafty and old and I like modern. My apartment is floor-to-ceiling glass, clean lines, brand new. Suits me much better. My father is in fits about it, but as long as he's alive, I can put it off. Wool cardigans to keep the constant cold out is not my cup of tea, I'm afraid."

Maren thought this was sad and couldn't understand choosing glass and modernity over tradition and history and a beautiful family home, even if it was cold. But then she smiled and almost laughed out loud. She'd been living in a cottage with a hole in the roof, having tea with a wild fox and enjoying it. So. clearly, they had different ideas of what a happy home looked like.

"What are you smiling at?" Alistair asked, and he couldn't help but smile in return.

"Just thinking how far my cottage is from your sleek apartment," she said. "But I guess I'm half wild, so maybe that explains it."

Alistair laughed. "I like that."

At that moment Maren watched Alex walk in and see Alistair and her laughing together, very close together, at the bar. Alex sat in a booth near the fire to have a quick pint and bite to eat. He didn't come over to say hello. And the few times she caught him looking over at them he looked almost angry. She was confused but thought it was rude, so she ignored Alex and laughed louder at Alistair's jokes.

***

A few days later, Maren woke before dawn. She put on a thick sweater, jeans, wool socks, and her rubber boots made a cup of hot tea, grabbed her down jacket, and went outside. First, she opened the stable door and fed and watered the still-sleepy horses, and then she went to the garden. She had been testing out the herbs and the withered vegetables. Every time she touched them, color rose up the food in a wave of pure magic and her hands buzzed. And when she ate the food, she was sure that magic got inside her. She couldn't put a finger on it, but it felt healing and uplifting every time. There was never color anywhere except the food, as if there were a message to be had. As if she were meant to be cooking and experimenting. She longed to see color elsewhere, but even without that she was still thrilled, and confused, by the mystical garden. After the garden, Maren walked up into the hills.

The land had been calling to her since she'd arrived, but things had been happening so fast she hadn't had time to answer the call. As she headed to the path leading up into the hills behind the farm, the sun crested over the highest peak, and a brilliant shaft of warm light pierced the darkness.

Maren headed down the hill, into the thick copse of woods. As she walked, she felt a hum like thousands of bees. Or like an electrical current. It was both inside and outside her body at the same time. By the time she was in the center of the woods, it was almost scaring her. Her whole body was buzzing.

Then, as she made her way out of the woods, it slowly stopped, and the moment she stepped out into the morning sunshine, it was gone. Her body felt cleansed. Pure. *What was that?* More magic, she thought. It was a strange combination of disconcerting and comforting.

She inhaled deeply and walked on. The path wound in a gentle arch between two high hills. Off to the right was a thick patch of brambles, she left the path and walked on the uneven hard ground until she reached it. There were large thorns, and by their size, she thought they must be blackberry bushes…an enormous mound of blackberry bushes. *I'll have to make jam and pies and all sorts of things to keep up with these.*

A stiff wind blew suddenly, out of nowhere, and one of the bushes seemed to open like a door. For a brief moment, Maren could see a large stone. Then the wind instantly died, and the bush folded back over, and she could see only bramble again. There was certainly something unusual about the land. She'd felt it as a child, but then she'd had no fear. *I guess children are so magical, it seems normal.*

She walked on for a long time, up to the high ridge, where a Highland view came into sight that took her breath away. From the top of this peak, land rolled on as far as she could see, hills, and in the distance, a dark loch, and beyond that, mountains, white-peaked with snow. Maren stood with her face to the sun, her head back, soaking up the view and the feeling and the freedom and the joy of this new life that was hers. It was hers. Whatever else she didn't have—husband, children, job, all of it—she had this, this land, this view, this feeling. And she smiled.

In the distance, a movement caught Maren's eye. A huge buck strode regally toward her. His antlers were enormous, his eyes intense, and he walked until he was only a few yards away and then stood facing her, stock still. He stared at her, his warm breath puffing into the cold air in white clouds.

Maren held her breath. A mixture of fear and excitement coursed through her.

Then he snorted and turned his back on her and strode into the distance.

Maren had no idea what this animal messenger meant, but she felt the thrill, and the honor, of having been in its presence. She thanked him, turned, and headed back on the long walk to the cottage.

***

At nine a.m., Maren dressed in her most sensible clothes. She wore black trousers and a white sweater with small hoop earrings. With a little make-up, and a touch of rose water, she headed to the car for the drive to Mullach. She hoped that the NHS worker, Dennis, had kept his promise to alert the care home that she was coming, otherwise Sybil would be in for the shock of her life. Well, she probably was anyway.

Maren was scared. Scared of what she would find, what state her aunt would be in, if she would be raging mad, or just raging. Scared of what stories she might hear about what she'd been through, or about her family. But none of that mattered. All she knew was she had to meet her.

***

In the nursing home, the mornings had a very precise schedule. After those needing help with washing and dressing had been tended to, everyone sat in the cafeteria and ate breakfast, while kind nurses came around with tiny paper cups filled with each person's morning medications. Miraculously, Sybil was on nothing. She was blind, but other than that, she was healthy.

She had her egg and toast and tea and waited. The evening before, the head nurse, Abby, had come into Sybil's room while she was listening to the radio. She'd sat on the end of her bed, taken Sybil's hand, and told her that someone was coming to see her the next day.

"Yes," Sybil had said.

"I'm sorry, dear. Maybe you didn't understand. It seems you have a great-niece, and she is coming to see you tomorrow!" Abby said, this time with more enthusiasm.

But Sybil had known someone was coming. She'd first felt it, then seen it in her mind. She didn't know who it was. But she knew. Sybil hadn't expected it to be family, and it made her both excited and nervous. She was old and blind and had been treated harshly by family all her life. Family made her nervous. But the stronger feeling was of peace. Sybil knew most of all that when things were meant to be, there was simplicity and ease. And that's what she felt from this visitor. There would be simplicity and ease. And dare she even hope it, maybe even happiness.

"Yes, thank you, Abigail," she said. "That is very exciting."

That satisfied the nurse, though she likely had expected more surprise from her patient. The next morning, Abby made sure Sybil was in her best outfit and ready to be met.

Maren pulled into the parking lot of Mullach Residence. It was a big, old, stone house now turned into a nursing home. It was lovely, which was surprising. Many nursing homes weren't as charming. When she walked in, a combination of food, and something else, maybe muscle rub cream, or something medicinal, filled the air. It was slightly depressing. But a cheerful woman greeted her at the door.

"Hello, dear," the woman said.

"Hello, I'm Maren Phillips. I'm sure this is a bit of a surprise. Hopefully, Dennis from the NHS told you I was coming, I'm—"

"Oh, you're Maren!" the woman said with a huge smile. "I'm Penny. Oh, my goodness, we've talked of nothing else since last night. We cannot believe someone has come to see Sybil. Our hearts have broken for the poor dear, all alone all these years, and not even a card at Christmas. Oh, my dear, yes, we ken who ye are. Come in, she's expecting ye."

The woman led her into a sitting room full of recliner chairs, each with a silver-haired person in it. Some playing cards, some knitting, some watching TV, some napping. One woman stared off, unseeing, into the distance.

Penny approached her and gently touched her hand so as not to startle her.

"Sybil, dear, you've got a visitor. Do ye remember your wee talk with Abby last night? This is Maren, she's yer great-niece, Sybil. She's American. She's come to see ye!"

Sybil moved her head around as if she were trying to see.

The nurse motioned for Maren to sit and take Sybil's hand, which she did. It felt far too familiar to be holding her hand before she'd spoken a word, but Maren could feel her aunt relax. Her hand was bony, and her veins were large and dark. Her skin felt thin, like delicate paper. She looked so vulnerable.

Maren started right away. "Hello. I am so very, very happy to meet you. My name is Maren Phillips. I'm so incredibly sorry I never came to see you before, but until last week, I didn't know you were here. No one ever told me. I'm your brother Fergus's granddaughter. I've just moved here, and I'm so sorry you've been here on your own!" To her surprise, Maren found she was crying, and she sniffled loudly.

"Och, dinnae cry, my dear," Sybil said, and she reached her free hand up and brushed away Maren's tears. "I wish you weren't seein' me like this. I'm blind, ye see."

"I'm sorry, Sybil. I'm sorry that has happened to you. But I'm just thrilled to meet you."

"And I you." Sybil smiled, and Maren grew uncomfortable at the realization that this woman, who had been locked away like a prisoner for seventy years, was the one comforting her.

"People tell me I look like your brother," Maren said, making conversation.

"Och then, yer tall are ye?" Sybil asked.

What a memory. She certainly didn't seem insane. "Yes, I am, actually, and I've dark coloring like him too."

"He was a handsome man," Sybil said, looking wistful.

Maren paused, wondering how much to ask. How much would Sybil want to share, or even remember?

As if reading her mind, Sybil patted her hand. "Shall we walk round the gardens, dear?"

"I'd love that," Maren said. She nodded at the care worker standing nearby watching them. "Is it all right if…" She paused, and instead of saying "Sybil," she said, "Is it all right if my great-aunt and I walk in the garden?"

Sybil smiled. The aide said it was just fine, and that it was a lovely day out. It had turned into an unusually warm day. She went and fetched Sybil's coat, a long black woolen coat that must have belonged to someone else, as it was far too big for her. Maren supposed all Sybil's clothes must be from some charity or another. No one else would have bought her any.

Again, Maren's heart hurt looking at the old woman, drowning in someone else's huge coat. But Sybil smiled and linked her arm through Maren's, and the two walked out the big French doors and into the sunshine.

Sybil was tall and willowy, with gray hair pulled up into a bun, from which a few long wisps had fallen loose. They blew around her in the wind. Her skin was like porcelain, a combination of the British climate and not having spent much time outdoors, Maren imagined. She looked much younger than she was. Her unseeing eyes were striking, and her cheeks were flushed and healthy. She was beautiful, and something about her felt very powerful.

"I want to hear all about you, dear. I never imagined I had family," Sybil said.

Maren desperately wanted to know about Sybil, not talk about herself. But she said, "Well, to start with, your brother had two children in America. One was my Uncle Gordon, who moved to Glenmuir as a teenager, and whose cottage I inherited when he died. The other was my mother. I grew up outside Boston with my family and spent my summers here with my uncle. I just moved here recently."

Sybil got a wistful look. "All this time, to think of all the life that was going on out there that I dinnae ken." Then she straightened up. "I cannae tell you how happy I am you've found me, dear. And I suppose you're probably wondering how I got here, aren't ye, lass? And why ye didn't know about me?"

"Yes!" Maren said, relieved she didn't have to bring the subject up. It surprised her that Sybil seemed to know exactly what she was thinking. "I will tell you all about me, but, yes, I want to know what happened, if you're willing to tell me. I mean, I know we just met...you don't have to tell me, obviously," Maren stammered.

"It's all right, dear. I'm old now. And things that made me angry for years don't cause a fire in me now. I won't bore ye. I'll tell ye straight. We can start with that and get it out o' the way. There's much nicer things to talk about." Sybil stopped and turned to face Maren. "I didnae ken why I was put away. And the doctors had their own ways about them. But eventually I understood why it all happened. I was a wee bit wild, ye see. I painted. I painted what I saw, and what I saw was beautiful. Things from this world, but things from the other world too." She paused as if remembering... "Aye, yer wondering if I was really mad. But no, I'm no' mad. I have the sight...second sight. There are many of us have it. It's strong in Highland folk. I dinnae ken what it's like now, but forever it was known that some here had the gifts. Second sight, skreeing, reading stones, even workin' a bit o' magic. Och, it was known forever. But I think after the war, the world wanted safety. Wanted to feel they could control everything and hating what they couldnae. That's what I came up with, thinking about it anaway. But we were always there. Still are, I know. I feel them, the ones with the gifts. They're still all over the Highlands."

Maren spoke up. "Yes, they are. It's more accepted again now. Not by everyone. I'm sure many people still think they're crazy, or making things up. But there's a new respect for it, at least in America, I know there is."

"Aye, you do ken it. Because ye have it. That's for certain."

Maren's eyes grew wide. She didn't know what to say.

"Well, ye know yerself ye have it. But anaway," she continued, even as Maren stared at her in shock. "I was a painter and had a temper and had the sight, and I was always embarrassing my father. He wanted to rise up the social ladder in America, and I was in his way. One day, I'd had a time of it, and I lost my temper and burned all my paintings in a big drum in our garden, just as he was having people over for a fancy garden party. And that was it. He packed me away. Tricked me, really. Took us over on the ship back here to Scotland. I thought I was on a lovely holiday. And then one day—" Sybil stopped suddenly.

Maren could see by her expression, the haunted look in her unseeing eye, that she never thought about that day. She'd probably forced it out of her mind for decades. It had to have felt like the day her life ended. Maren couldn't even imagine what that sense of betrayal had been like. The day her entire future had been stolen from her.

"I think I'll just sit down, dear, if ye dinnae mind," Sybil finally said.

"Of course. I'm sorry, I'm tiring you out. Let's sit." Maren led her to a bench, and they sat down.

"I'll get it out now, and then the story will be done, and we'll no' have to fret over it again. Not now that I know I have family. New family," Sybil said. She smiled broadly and felt for Maren's hand. "And I wouldna tell it to anyone here. I can only tell it to those who ken, who are safe, as I ken you are, my dear. Anyway, my father brought me over to Scotland, and one day took me to a hospital. An asylum. I was handed over to men in white smocks and pulled into a long corridor. I looked back down the hall, and there was my father, signing a paper. And that was it. I never saw my father again. I never even had a letter from him. Not once. My brother did write to me a few times. Very few. He'd send the hospital a few pounds at Christmas, and they'd buy me chocolates or socks or the like. But he never visited. I never knew what happened. I was told I was insane. And the longer they locked me up, the more I felt it and acted it. I was like a wild animal. I'd been caged, and I was powerless to get out. Then, finally, I gave up. I retreated back inside, and my life became only about the spirit since my body was in such an awful place. And the more I went inside, the more freedom I found. My gifts got me locked away, but then they set me free. I'd travel the Highlands. I'd sit in the ancient stone circles. I'd talk with the dead and with the animals. And I'd paint it all…that saved me. They love a craft in a hospital," she said with a laugh that brightened her face. "So, they got me paints, thank the Lord. Och, aye, I had a wonderful time when I closed my eyes and went away."

Tears streamed down Maren's face as she listened to the heartbreaking story and looked with wonder at the resilient old woman.

"Dinnae cry, my dear," Sybil said, patting Maren's hand.

Maren's eyes widened. How did she know she was crying? Sybil was blind, and Maren had been careful not to make a sound, not wanting her to stop. But when she thought for a moment, she knew. It was the same feelings she had had her whole life and often didn't know what to do with. She felt she had suddenly met someone she was always meant to have known.

Sybil pulled her coat around her tighter as the wind blew, and Maren realized she must be cold. She was so thin, and the wind had changed. It wasn't warm anymore.

"Shall we go inside?" Maren asked.

"Aye, let's do that."

Maren held her arm and led her to the warmth of the sitting room, where tea appeared before them.

"Now, tell me more about yerself, dear," Sybil said, taking a nibble of a tea biscuit.

Maren decided to tell a little more of her story. "I had a bit of a rough start. My parents died when I was eighteen, in a car accident. They hadn't been the best parents…they drank. A lot. Growing up, I spent all my summers in Glenmuir, at my Uncle Gordon's cottage. My summers here in Scotland were the best part of my life as a child. Gordon died two years ago. He'd never married, and so he left me his cottage. After my parents died, I guess I felt a bit lost, and I've bounced around since then. I've been very lucky. I've seen a lot of the world and had incredible experiences."

"How lucky ye are, dear. How wonderful. You were independent. That's what I always longed for. But now yer home, lass. That's why ye came back," Sybil said. It wasn't a question. It was a statement. And she was right.

Maren left after their tea. She could see Sybil was very tired. Her visit must have been quite a shock. Though she also laughed when she thought that maybe it wasn't quite as much of a shock as Maren thought it would be. Clearly, Sybil had a mysterious way of knowing things. But it had been enough for one day.

The whole drive home, Maren had just one thought, *how do I get her out of there?*

CHAPTER 8

Maren pulled up to the cottage and sat in her car for a moment. She'd have to contact Dennis at the NHS on Monday and find out if there was any way to get Sybil out. Jumping in without thinking again, she laughed. Sybil could have major health issues and need nursing care, for all Maren knew. And where would she live? And how would that affect Maren's new life? It was, for sure, without question, a terrible idea. But it didn't matter, if there was any way on earth she could make it happen, she was going to. It was the right thing to do.

She could give Sybil a late chapter to her life that would, at least in one tiny way, heal the wound of the injustice of the rest of it.

A car pulled in behind Maren. She turned to see it was the women from the other day. The Sisters of the Stones. Maren had missed a call from them two days ago but had been so busy with other things she'd completely forgotten. They were surprised as Maren got out of her car at the same time they did.

"Hallo!" they all said as they walked toward her.

"Och, dear, we didnae mean to disturb you. We hope it's all right we just showed up. We didnae ken how else to reach you" Isobel said.

"You're not disturbing me. But it's freezing. Let's go inside to talk."

The women said that would be lovely and all bustled into the living room.

Once everyone had a cup of tea in hand, Maren asked, "What can I do for you?"

"Well, dear, we wondered if you'd made any progress in finding the stone circle on yer land. We ken it's here, but we cannae figure out where from the old map we have. We're hoping we're not wrong and that it's somewhere else entirely," Isobel said.

"I'm afraid I really haven't had a moment to even think about it. I'm so sorry," she said. The women must have wondered what a single woman in the Highlands was doing that she hadn't had a moment to herself. Abandoned horses, secret relatives, and a crumbling house were the answers to that question. "But you're free to have a wander around the property if you like."

"Now that's just what we were hoping you'd say! Thank ye so much!" Phillipa said. "Would it be alright if we had a wee wander now, as we're here?"

"Why not?" Maren said, though, really, she just wanted to be alone to soak in a hot bath and relax and think about everything that had happened that day. She supposed she could do that, even with them there.

"Well, it won't be light fer long, so if yer sure, we'll go have a wee wander now then. Yer verra kind, thank ye, Maren," Clara said.

They all put down their teacups and hurried out the door. They stood in the front garden for a bit, looking around, clearly discussing which direction to walk. If there were standing stones that were thousands of years old, it's not like they'd have a path leading right to them. They could be anywhere.

Even so, the women headed up the footpath into the hills, toward the little woods in the valley. Maren smiled and put the tea things away, poured a glass of red wine, and went and soaked in a long hot bath.

When she got out, her phone was ringing. It was Alex.

"Hello, neighbor," he said.

Maren smiled. "Hello, neighbor."

"It's verra last minute, but my dad and I just wondered if you'd like to come for dinner. We had some lovely local steak dropped off today, and we're cooking, so thought you might like a break from cooking and come have a wee bit o' dinner and company."

A break from cooking? Maren laughed to herself. She kept *meaning* to cook something nice, but so far she hadn't. Her stomach did little flips at the thought of dinner in Alex's house, meeting his father. But she told herself to calm down, remembering his girlfriend. Still, friends were nice, too, even if not as nice as lovers.

"I'd love to," she said.

"Wonderful! How's six o'clock?"

"Perfect," she said. "I'll see you then."

After hanging up, she looked out the front window of her bedroom. The minivan was still in the drive. It was getting dark. The women must still be looking. Otherwise, if they'd found something, she was sure she'd have heard about it.

Now what am I going to wear? She turned to review her wardrobe. Alex might have a girlfriend, but she wasn't going over there looking like a frump.

Maren still hadn't seen Isobel and her friends return, and their car was still there as she left. She drove the short distance down the road, then bumped her car into the cobblestone yard at Alex's farm. The house was large, made of gray stone, with a chimney rising on either end of the solid square home. It had a shiny black front door, with two windows to the right of the door and two to the left, and five upstairs, evenly spaced, giving the home an orderly appearance. It was simple but beautiful, a house meant for the ultimate practical job—farming—but the farm of a prosperous farmer when it was built, no doubt. Not a sod-covered croft or even a little cottage like her own. The stability and practicality of it made her feel safe. She loved things built of stone. Scotland was all stone, she thought as she parked. Not many trees, like in America. But it was also a statement, a commitment. That this building, the stone walls on the fields, the churches, were to stay. They wouldn't need changing, wouldn't be torn down for something new every ten years. You could rely on it, even centuries later.

When Maren got to the front door, she looked in the window and saw Alex's father talking and Alex laughing. He had a drink in his hand, his back to a roaring fire in the kitchen woodstove. He was broad and strong, and his hair reached to his shirt collar with a slight wave in it. His jaw was square, and his eyes twinkled when he laughed, like someone who truly knew how to enjoy life, which made Maren smile herself.

Alex looked over and saw her. She was mortified that he had seen her smiling at him through the window like a fool, but he just grinned even wider and came to open the door. "Great, yer here. Come in, lass!"

Maren's smile returned.

Alex led her into the kitchen and turned to his father, a bald man with a ring of white hair round the sides of his head, twinkling eyes, and a kind face. He was still handsome, and Maren saw where Alex got his looks from.

He rose and offered his hand. "Hugh Campbell. It's a pleasure to meet you."

Maren shook his hand. "Thank you so much for inviting me. It's a pleasure to meet you too."

Within a minute, she had a short glass with a dram of whisky in it, "to get the chill out," they said. With a silent chuckle, she wondered what excuse they used in summer.

"Alex is just finishing dinner. He's no' a bad cook, so why don't we sit by the fire while he does all the work," Hugh said with a smile.

"That sounds wonderful to me." They sat in the armchairs by the fire, watching Alex in the kitchen.

"I hope ye don't mind our old chairs. We're just two bachelors here. We don't fuss with fine furniture," he said, but she could tell he didn't really care what she thought. He was just being polite. She liked that.

"Not at all!" Maren said. "Your home is beautiful, and I love old things. They're such a comfort, I think."

"Well, then, you'll love me, lass. I'm ancient!" Hugh said, and they all laughed. Hugh was both elegant and down to earth at the same time. "I kent yer uncle well. He was a good man."

"I like knowing that you were friends. It sounds cliché, but it's like he lives on when I meet someone who knew him."

"Aye, that's true. He had a great sense of humor, yer uncle. We had a laugh many a night at the pub or at his place. We'd walk, too, up the hills, and even bagged a few munros together. Tough old codgers we were together," he said, looking off into the distance, as if remembering adventures past and bodies younger.

"Bagged a munro?" Maren asked.

Hugh laughed. "Och, I ferget yer no' Scottish…yet," he added with a wink. "Munros are mountains in Scotland. Ben Nevis is the tallest munro in Scotland. We didnae top that one, but we bagged a few o' the others together. Wonderful walks, food in packs on our backs, great time to talk. They were good days, those," he said.

She loved that. Climbing a huge peak…and they refer to it as "going for a walk" in Scotland. In America, it would be a hike. She'd always felt so much pressure the few times she'd been asked to go for a hike. Like she somehow had to be intense and tough. Walking sounded much nicer.

"That sounds quite a challenge, climbing a…munro," Maren said.

"Well, yer a lang time deid," Hugh replied.

Maren looked at Alex with an expression that she was sure would quickly become familiar to him...she needed a translation again. Alex noticed from the other side of the kitchen.

"It means, literally, you're a long time dead. It's like—" he thought for a moment, "—seize the day. Live life to the fullest!" He and his father raised their glasses to the statement, while Maren looked on, grinning.

Maren liked Hugh instantly. He would be the kind of man to do the right thing, to stand up for someone, to make someone feel comfortable, and to speak his mind without offending, all signs of true class, in her opinion. He also had a great sense of humor, and they talked and laughed for half an hour, while Alex finished the meal and put it on the table.

"If you two layabouts are done blathering, dinner's ready," he said, as he deposited the last of the dishes.

The large kitchen table had been laid with a tablecloth, the first time in ages, according to Hugh. Alex pulled out a chair for Maren, and when she and Hugh were seated, he placed a perfectly cooked steak, beans, and potatoes onto her plate. There were homemade warm rolls in a basket in the middle of the table.

"This looks amazing!" Maren said.

"Let's hope it tastes amazing," Hugh said with a smile and a look of skepticism.

Alex rolled his eyes.

Maren took her first bite and closed her eyes and said, "Mmmmmm," without even meaning to. It was hearty, comforting and nourishing. Combined with the dram of whisky now warming her stomach, she felt her whole body melt in pleasure. The company, the kitchen with fire blazing, the meal...she felt herself get emotional and was afraid she might start to cry.

Stop it. These stoic Scotsmen wouldn't have her over again if she started crying at dinner for no reason. Though it wasn't for no reason. She knew that. It was because this felt like a life. A real life. These were real people. And, for some reason, they seemed to like her. Her soul was being nourished just as much as her belly.

Alex poured red wine liberally, and the meal was wonderful. They all talked and laughed easily together. After dinner, Alex made coffee and produced an apple tart with heavy cream. Maren was afraid she was going to fall asleep right there at the table. It had been such a long day, and the food, company, and warmth made her eyes want to close, no matter how much she fought it.

"Cook doesnae clean," Hugh said as they all rose after dinner.

"I will definitely do the dishes," Maren said, embarrassed that a man in his seventies or eighties, she wasn't sure which, was going to do the dishes while she sat by the fire.

"Absolutely not!" Hugh said. "Yer our guest. You sit. But you can invite us next, and I'll let ye do all the work." He winked.

Maren wasn't used to receiving. She only felt comfortable giving. Always giving, never being willing to accept. Giving was safe. Everyone liked to take. But receiving, that made her heart seize up. That was vulnerable. That was saying you wanted something or, worse still, needed something from someone else. Even allowing Hugh to do the dishes made her uncomfortable.

But she was wise enough to sit with it. To not be rude and insist on washing up. To receive. And, as soon as it didn't seem desperate, she'd have them over so she could repay the kindness.

"How do ye like it there, lass? In the cottage?" Alex asked as he poured more wine into her glass.

Maren's head was beginning to spin, but she didn't want to break the spell. Clearly, two whiskeys and two glasses of wine didn't have the same effect on a brawny tall man as it did on her.

"I love it," she said. And she meant it. "The workmen have almost finished fixing the hole in the kitchen roof, and the big window in the living room has been replaced. I've got heat and electricity, so I'm living like a queen now. But, really, I do love it. I feel like I'm home. Oh, and the horses!" she added.

"Och, aye, how are they?" Alex asked. "It's one o' the reasons I wanted to have ye over. Yer so kind, and I'll tell ye, you've got a reputation in the village already as being a bit of a hero, landing one day and takin' on Glenmuir's mistreated beasts the next!"

Maren smiled. She had a reputation in the village? That felt good.

"They're wonderful," she said. "I do need to make some time to get the new arrivals out and make sure they're really okay. One of them will need a bit of handling...he's a wild one, but they're all great horses and gaining weight every day. Laddie is a sweetheart. I'm going to see if he'll let me ride him soon."

"That's wonderful," he said. "We havenae forgotten about them. Charlie's still working on finding a rescue fer them. Somewhere that can keep them, so they can have a good end to their lives, since they've no' had a good start."

Maren suddenly had a thought. A rescue. A horse rescue. Wasn't she already an unofficial horse rescue? Didn't *she* want to give these horses a better second half to their lives after their awful first halves? Wasn't she trying to do that for her own self? Must be the whisky. How would she start a horse rescue?

But then she heard a voice. It said simply, "You already have."

And she knew it was right. When something was meant to be, it might involve huge amounts of hard work, like a horse rescue would, but it also came with ease. Things just showed up. Like the horses had. Maybe she didn't need to make money renting stables to people for their fancy horses. Maybe she could run a horse rescue for neglected, mangy, magnificent creatures no one wanted. No one but her. There must be stipends for that. And with some riding lessons...

Maren was excited as she suddenly knew exactly what she was going to do. At the same moment, she felt her head swirl as all the booze of the night hit her. It was time to go home. Though she wasn't sure how she was going to get there.

As she stood to say her goodbyes, she swayed. Alex stood up.

"Thank you so much for the most wonderful evening. Everything was delicious, and it was so nice to meet you, Hugh, and to have such great company," she said with a big smile.

"Yer welcome, bonnie lass," Hugh said, hand still in soapy water in the sink. "Come again soon. Any time ye just feel like a wee bit o' company, drop by for a cup o' tea or a dram. Sad to say, I'm here most o' the time now, old codger that I am," he said with a charming smile.

"I will, thank you!" Maren said.

"I'll walk ye out," Alex said.

A thousand butterflies started frantically flying around inside her belly and her chest. She was buzzed and happy and excited about her future, and she felt like throwing caution to the wind. But she wouldn't throw herself at him, much as she wanted to. She really liked this man. And he had a girlfriend.

She wouldn't start to burn down the life she had just barely begun to build.

Maren and Alex stepped outside into the dark night. The shock of the cold air on Maren's flushed face felt delicious and cleared her head a bit. She could see her breath in the light of the window. Beyond that little puddle of light was pitch darkness, except for the small lights in the village far off to the right. It felt almost holy in its stillness and darkness.

"Lass, ye cannae drive, ye know," Alex said.

"I know," Maren said, feeling embarrassed. She hadn't realized how the drinks were catching up to her. At least this time she wouldn't get on the back of a motorcycle, let alone drive a car, like this.

"I feel terrable. I should drive ye, but I'm afraid I'm no' really fit myself. I did have a whisky or two before ye arrived. I was a bit nervous cooking for a lass," he said, with a smile that came with a twinkle in his eye, which made it a little bit hard for Maren to breathe.

"But it's no problem, I'll walk ye home! It's a braw night out, a great time fer a Highland walk. Get some good fresh air in us," Alex said.

He whistled, and Finn appeared suddenly at his feet, tail wagging wildly, wondering what unusual adventure he was about to go on at nine o'clock at night and in the dark.

"I love it. Perfect solution!" Maren agreed.

"I'll run and grab a torch." Alex disappeared into the barn.

Maren had spent enough time in Scotland to know that a torch was a flashlight. But some part of her wouldn't have been surprised if he had appeared with a huge flaming stick. In a kilt, ready for walks, or maybe even sword-slashing battles.

Her mind was running away with her, and she laughed.

He came to her side and pointed the beam of light onto the path. "Stick close," he said to her.

"I will." She brushed against him as they walked side by side into the night.

On the way up the hill that divided their farms, Alex told Maren the story of how he'd tried to shear a sheep when he first started farming. The beast had thrown him, and he'd fallen, and instead, cut a huge line of his own hair off down to the scalp. Maren laughed so hard she couldn't breathe, and she had to stop walking.

She returned with a travel story about how she and her friend had run out of money in Spain and snuck onto a farmer's field to camp, only to wake up and find themselves surrounded by massive bulls. At which point, they ran screaming from the field, losing half their belongings and never going back for them. This got loud bursts of laughter from Alex.

When they reached the top of the hill, it was pitch black except for the front light of the cottage down below. Maren was sad they were almost there.

"So do ye like it?" Alex asked.

Maren wasn't sure what he meant. In her whisky-sodden brain, she thought he meant walking close together in the dark, laughing and talking and feeling his solid body next to hers.

Luckily, her logical brain stepped in before she reacted to that thought. "Oh, do I like it here in Glenmuir?" she asked.

"Aye," he said.

"I love it." She smiled in the dark. In the back light of the little flashlight, she saw him smile too. "I wanted to find a place that felt like home, and I have."

"And ye dinnae miss whatever, or whoever, you left?" he asked.

Maren wondered about the second part of the question, what he was really asking.

"I don't. I didn't really have much to leave," she said, feeling embarrassed at the statement. She thought about padding the stories and spinning them to make her former life sound amazing. But she didn't want to. "I was lonely. And a bit lost, really, if I'm honest," she said. "From the outside, it looked great, I had wild stories and life of adventure. And I actually really did love it, for quite a long time. But by the time I decided to come here, I was just lonely. I didn't really have much of a home life growing up. That's a story for a different bottle of whisky," she added with a laugh, and Alex laughed, too, but looked at her with sympathy. "I got really good at not relying on people. Most of my life, I have found people to be completely unreliable."

"Not all of them," Alex said with a kind smile.

"Well, that hasn't been my experience. But I'm sure you're right. So, I'm new at this building a home and putting down roots thing. But, so far, it's amazing. Just simple. And fun and…it feels like home." Tears welled in her eyes as she said it, just as they reached the front of the cottage.

Alex noticed and laid a hand gently on her shoulder. "Well, I'm glad yer home too," he said.

Maren felt warm all over and turned to face him. His kind eyes smiled down at her, his hair moving in the wind.

Suddenly, his smile faded, and he looked at her with an intensity that made her take a tiny gasp as a tingle ran through her body. She looked back at him and felt a tension pulsing in the air between them.

Alex looked down at Maren. Her hair flew around her face in the wind, and she felt her lips part. Maren felt desire run through her body and the look of seriousness on Alex's face made her think he was feeling the same. Maren saw him ever-so-slightly lean toward her and she was unable to breathe for a moment.

Just then Maren swayed very slightly, and Alex took hold of her arm to steady her. The spell was broken, he leaned back and looked at her now with a small smile.

"I'm afraid I've gotten ye drunk, lass. Not very gentlemanly of me," he said. And with that he helped her to her door, said goodnight and headed back up the hill, a small pool of light in front of him, Finn at his heels. She knew he was being a gentleman by going home, but she was so disappointed and frustrated she could have cried. Then she felt disappointed and frustrated in herself, wanting a man who was taken. She went upstairs and flopped on her bed fully clothed and fell asleep.

CHAPTER 9

In the morning, Maren's head was pounding. She took two Tylenol, went to the kitchen and a few minutes later, took her steaming mug of tea and walked to the stables. She thought back to the night before, embarrassed that she'd gotten drunk at a dinner with Alex's father. But then she thought Alex was a little drunk himself so maybe it hadn't been too obvious. She hoped not. She also remembered the moment by the cottage door at the end of the night and felt irritated again. She slid the barn door open, batting the annoying thoughts away like gnats. Inside, she was greeted by the usual sniggers and blowing of nostrils. This was the magic of animals. No matter what else was going on, they made Maren feel calm and loved.

Sultan was weaving, putting his head in and then out of his stall over and over and over. Maren knew it was a sign of anxiety. It was time she did some work with these horses.

Charlie had texted to say he was coming over later that day to check on them, and Maren was going to ask about keeping them. At some point she'd go to the village hall to ask about permits to start a nonprofit and start applying for some kind of funding. She didn't want these gorgeous animals going anywhere.

After feeding them all, she walked to Sultan's stall.

"Shhh. It's all right, sweetheart," she whispered.

He still weaved, bobbing his head in and out.

"You want to come outside with me?" she asked.

She very slowly reached up with a halter. Sultan looked at her and stomped his foot. Maren was nervous. She would be stupid not to be. Horses could be dangerous, and this one was angry. By moving just inches at a time, she was able to reach up and place her hand, holding the halter, next to his neck without him flinching. He stopped weaving as if calmed by the touch. She gently placed the halter over his head.

Amazingly, he stood still as she tied the little leather buckle at his cheek. She gently clipped on a lead rope, slowly slid the bolt back and opened his stall door. She was careful to be out of the way in case he bolted.

He did the opposite. Like most animals, including humans, who acted aggressive and tough and mean, he was, in fact, really just scared. Unsure of himself.

Slowly, he stepped out and into the corridor. He saw the pasture out the open back door of the stables and headed toward it, hooves echoing on the stones. The other horses watched him. When he got to the field, he stepped onto the grass and stopped.

Maren slowly took off the lead rope and stayed next to him. If she got very quiet and still, she could connect to his energy. She could feel the pulse of the beast. She knew they could feel her energy all the time. For humans, it took a bit more effort to get to that place.

After a moment, she felt the connection. Sultan dropped his head, as if exhaling and relaxing for the first time. Maren walked ahead slowly, and she heard Sultan follow. She walked in large circles in the field. Sultan was free to run off in the huge pasture. But he didn't. He was tethered to Maren by energy, by a budding trust, by a feeling of safety.

And, so, the two danced together in the field. Eventually, Maren laughed and ran a little bit, and Sultan trotted behind her. When she stopped, Sultan wandered over slowly, lowered his head, and placed his nose against her forehead. They stood like that for a long moment, Maren crying, feeling this mistreated animal being vulnerable and trusting.

She reached up and scratched his nose. Sultan looked at her, his huge wet eyes soft now. Then he turned and ran. He ran and bucked, delighted in the freedom and the feeling of grass and a full belly and kindness.

When Maren turned around, she jumped. There, standing silently, was Sally.

"My gosh, you surprised me!" Maren said. "Hi, Sally. I didn't expect to see you here."

"It's Saturday," she said, laconic as ever.

"Yes, it is, you're right," Maren replied. Gillian didn't appear to be with her daughter. "How did you get here?"

"I walked," Sally said.

Maren was worried about this new pattern. The road from the village to the farm was busy and winding and there certainly wasn't a sidewalk. She would have to come up with a plan with Sally's mother, if this was going to be a regular thing.

"I wanted to see the horses," she said.

"Well, you are in the right place," Maren said. "I'm just about to turn them all out. After that, you can help me muck out if you like. It's not the most fun part, but it's an important job."

"Okay!" Sally said with an eager smile, as if she hadn't just been asked to shovel horse manure out of a barn.

Maren had Sally wait in the tack room as she let all her charges out to graze and run and feel the sun on their backs. Once the horses were in the pasture, Maren closed the door back into the barn, gave Sally a mucking fork, put a wheelbarrow in the corridor outside a stall, and told her she was running inside for a minute.

Once inside, Maren grabbed her phone to call Gillian.

"Hi. Gillian?" she said when her call was answered.

"Hi, Maren," Gillian said, Maren's name popping up on Gillian's phone since they had exchanged numbers.

"She's here," Maren said.

"Oh my gosh, Maren. I'm so sorry. I'll come get her. I told her she may not walk over to yer place uninvited. I'll come straight away."

Maren almost said, *Don't worry about it, she can come any time she wants!* And part of her would have meant it. But this practicing adulthood thing popped back into her head. She didn't actually want a child showing up any time unannounced. She was thrilled to have her…sometimes. But it also wasn't safe for Sally to keep doing this. "Okay, we can talk when you get here. We'll figure it out."

When Gillian arrived, Maren made them both a cup of tea, and they went and stood in the doorway of the stables as Sally happily lifted pitchforks full of straw and manure, shook off the loose straw, and dumped the manure in the wheelbarrow.

"She loves the beasts, this one. I swear she's Dr. Doolittle. It's almost as if she can talk to 'em," Gillian said. "She would rather spend time with animals than people. I try and get her to have girls over from school, and sometimes she does, but mostly, she wanders the village visiting people's dogs and cats and chickens. She walks to the beat of a different drummer, this one."

Maren thought back to school herself. She wasn't different in that same way, but she had always felt different, knowing she had this secret life at home, never able to invite someone over to play, always scared someone would find out how she actually lived. School could be hard.

"She seems a very sweet girl," Maren said. "She's very welcome here. Why don't we come up with a schedule, so she knows she's coming back, and doesn't have to walk on that busy road."

"Are you sure?" Gillian asked. "I dinnae want to impose. I know yer just settling in."

"It's no imposition, I mean, she's cleaning poop out of stalls while I have a cup of tea. This could work well!" Maren said, and Gillian laughed.

"How about twice a week, if that isn't too much for her? Or once, whatever you like."

"That would be grand. I could pay you for watching her. How about I pay you in bottles of wine now and then," she said with a smile, probably not wanting to offend her by offering cash.

"I feel the beginning of a beautiful friendship," Maren said.

They shared a laugh.

"Sally, come here, wee one," Gillian called.

Sally put down the rake and walked over.

"How would you like to come here two times a week and help wi' the horses?" Gillian asked.

"Really?" Sally jumped up and down with obvious glee.

"Yes, but only if we agree, no more walking here on yer own. It's no' safe, and Ms. Phillips doesnae want ye here all the time," her mother added.

Sally looked serious for a moment, considering whether she would agree to the terms.

Maren added, "First of all, you can call me Maren. And I think this is a good idea, Sally. I'd love to have your help. There's so much to do with horses!"

Standing tall, like she felt needed and proud Sally nodded and said with great seriousness, "Okay. I'll do it."

Maren and Gillian smiled at each other.

***

Later that afternoon, Maren walked over the hill to Alex's farm to collect her car. She was disappointed no one was there. She came back and found a bottle of Cabernet sitting on the big stone front step of the cottage with a little tag with a heart and "Gillian" written on it. Maren smiled.

She poured a glass and lit the fire. The cottage looked beautiful. In the kitchen, a large window in front of the deep stone sink overlooked the front garden. The wooden farm table was scrubbed and clean in the middle of the room, the cabinet stood against the far wall, full of her uncle's dishes and pots and pans, and on the other wall was the large Aga stove, softly, continuously, producing a gentle heat. A wood stove stood in the corner of the kitchen, next to a door that led directly outside.

Maren had oil, electricity, and hot water, and had, by then, washed every linen in the house in the washing machine kept under the kitchen counter. She had laid a beautiful tablecloth, white with a tartan edging, on the kitchen table. It looked white with various shades of gray in the checkered tartan pattern. She wished, as she so often did, that she could see what the colors were. In the middle of the table was the basket full of colorful vegetables she'd picked and that eased the longing.

With the fire lit and wine in hand, horses fed and bedded down for the night, Maren felt something deep inside. Something unfamiliar. Maybe it was more an absence of something than a presence. An absence of the feeling of panic, of anxiety, of wanting to get up and run. It was the feeling of peace. Of belonging. Not clinging to the edges of someone else's life. It was a tiny feeling of being in her own life. Like a new flame. She felt protective of this feeling. Like she needed to cup her hands around the delicate flicker and let it truly catch. She felt at peace.

Then she thought of Sybil. Of wanting her to feel that peace too. To feel she had a home. A life. She would call Dennis at the NHS, to see if there was some way she could get her out of that nursing home. At least for a weekend.

In the midst of these thoughts, Maren's phone wrang.

"Maren?" a man's voice said.

"Yes?" she replied.

"This is Ali. Alistair McCain."

"Oh, hi," Maren said, surprised. Had he changed his mind about boarding his horse?

"I don't know what yer doing this coming Saturday, but there's a party at the pub fer Glenmuir's birthday, and I wondered if ye'd like to go."

Maren sank into a nearby chair. Why would rich, handsome Alistair McCain be asking her to a party? He must have a hundred girls he could ask. She was flattered, but without meaning to, she thought of Alex. Did she want him to ask her instead of Alistair? She pushed the thought away. He'd be there with his girlfriend.

"That sounds great, thank you," Maren said, and she felt fairly sure she meant it. "But what do you mean Glenmuir's birthday?" she asked with a little laugh.

"Smashing," he said. "It's the three hundredth anniversary of our village. There's a bit of a do every year, but this year, being three hundred, should be grander. Just a party and a load of drunk Scotsmen at the pub, but everyone goes, and it's good craic. I'll swing by yer place about two on Saturday. Parade starts at three."

"Wonderful, thank you. I'm really looking forward to it," Maren said.

She hung up and sat by the fire. She had the TV on, the news, talking about the weather. It then switched to reporting on a donation that had been made to a local village school, little children standing in their neat uniforms, looking bored, while a woman spoke about early learning and fundraising. Then it went to a bit about a local farmer who'd gone viral on YouTube. Maren almost couldn't believe this feeling she had. Happiness.

She remembered the vegetables in the kitchen and decided it was high time she tried her hand at cooking. She loved to eat, and, in her mind, she had collected flavors and spices and meals on her world travels, the way others collected stickers or little silver spoons. From fried scorpions on a stick to green curries with lemongrass to buffalo tacos. She loved it all. She just didn't know how to cook much besides frozen dinners and spaghetti.

That was going to change. She went to the kitchen and smiled as she saw the vegetables. Carrots, kale, rosemary, sage, onion…that might make a good soup. A perfect small meal on a cold night. She googled a recipe. She'd need chicken stock and ginger, she had both of those, having filled the pantry after her big food shop, though the ginger was powdered, she'd have to buy fresh next time.

As Maren chopped the onion and carrot, she felt an energy pulsing through her. It felt healing. Not physically, so much as emotionally. Like someone was laying a gentle hand on her heart, which had hurt for so long. But it wasn't a sad feeling. It felt peaceful and joyful at the same time. It took her breath away.

She stepped back, startled. But things were surprising her less and less, these days, so she simply closed her eyes, let out a big sigh, and leaned into the feeling.

She tossed the vegetables in a big pot with butter and salt, and instantly the kitchen began to smell wonderful. She heard a scratching at the kitchen door and went to investigate. She opened the door off the back of the kitchen very slightly and there was Clive. The gorgeous fox who had been her friend and companion during her first, wild days there.

"Clive!" she said with a smile. She didn't open the door any further; he was a wild fox after all. If he got inside now, he wouldn't have a way to easily get out, and that could go bad fast.

A sort of chirping sound came from outside…or a tiny, high-pitched bark. She closed the door and went to get a big flashlight she'd bought on her trip to town. She opened the door again and shone it into the side garden. Under the bushes, at the edge of the lawn, she saw three tiny fox kits. Little, yelping puffballs.

"Oh my goodness, Clive, you're not a Clive!" Maren burst out laughing. "I guess you're a…Clover. How's that?"

The fox tilted her head to one side.

I'm sure she knows how to feed her kits, Maren thought. She'd probably just come to show them off. Maren went to the fridge and got out some bacon. She walked over and gently laid it just inside the doorway. Clover walked in, comfortable as ever near the room she had safely lived in for who knew how long before Maren fixed the roof.

The fox picked up the bacon, looking at Maren, before she returned to the garden.

"You're welcome," Maren called after her.

She watched Clover take the bacon to the hungry kits, and everyone yelped and dug in. Baby foxes, how wonderful! Spring was coming.

CHAPTER 10

At nine a.m. the next morning, Maren made a phone call.

"Hello, Dennis? This is Maren Phillips. You helped me find my great-aunt, Sybil McGlashan," Maren said.

"Och, aye, of course I remember ye. Did ye go see her?" he asked enthusiastically.

"I did. It was lovely. And I have a question. I wonder if I could get permission to bring her here for a weekend. Is there a way to get permission to do that?"

"Aye, it shouldn't be too hard. Ye could arrange that right with the nursing home," he explained. "As her next of kin, which ye officially are in her file online now, ye could definitely do that. You'd have to start by asking her if she wants to, obviously. And it would depend on her medical needs. I dinnae ken her state. If she's verra ill, they won't let you. But, otherwise, if Ms. McGlashan wants to go, they can sort that out with ye at the home."

"Wonderful!" Maren said.

She hung up and drove to the nursing home right away.

Once there, seated with a cup of tea, holding Sybil's hand, Maren asked, "Would you like to come to my house for a few days?" Maren remembered she had a party to go to Saturday. "Maybe this Sunday, for two days, for a visit?"

There was a long pause as Sybil thought. Maybe she wouldn't want to, maybe she was scared to. Almost her whole life had been spent in institutions.

"I'll have to check my diary and see if I'm free," she finally said, very seriously.

They both burst into laughter.

"I'd love that, dear," Sybil added. "Aren't ye kind? Goodness." She paused as the reality of leaving the nursing home for a few days seemed to sink in. "I've no' been out on my own, able to do what I like, in almost my whole life. I…" She looked like she might cry.

"I'm sorry!" Maren cried. "Have I upset you?" She clasped Sybil's hand between her own.

"No, no," Sybil protested. "Just the thought of it is so *exciting*. There's nae anything wrong. But the thought of leaving does make me think of a lifetime lost, really. I cannae get it back. I'm old. Every year, I'd hope someone would come fer me. And no one did." Sybil paused and stared ahead. Then she smiled. "Until now." She squeezed Maren's hand. "But it's water under the bridge, so no sense in crying over it. Maren, I'd love to visit ye for a few days. Thank ye, my dear."

Leaving her great-aunt, smiling in her chair, Maren went to talk to the head administrator and sort out the details.

***

The next day, Charlie called and told Maren that she had been approved for a grant for the horses. He had applied on her behalf after dropping the four horses off, and now he said he'd drop off a check for her later that day. Maren felt proud and official, receiving money for helping the sad horses, who were less sad every day. While she had him on the phone she asked,

"Who actually owns these horses? I mean, if I worked with them and knew they were reliable and steady, would I be able to give lessons with them?"

Charlie was quiet for a moment. "That's a good question," he said. "I dinnae ken who owns them actually. Maybe the village, as the village animal welfare took control of them. I'll find out fer ye. That would be great if you could make use of them. Does this mean yer thinking of keeping them?"

Maren hadn't thought it all the way through, but she said emphatically, "Yes." And she knew she meant it.

"Wonderful! Okay, let me find out about the wee beasts, and I'll also ask how ye apply to be an official rescue, that way ye can ask fer donations, and the town may have more stipends. I dinnae ken, but I'll find out," he said. "Yer an interesting lass, Maren Phillips, that's for sure. And a good one."

They both hung up the phone and Maren walked out to the stables and slid open the huge door.

"Hello, everyone," she said.

The horses all snuffled and stuck their heads out for their scratches. It was a day for grooming, and one by one, Maren went into their stalls and put on a harness, walked each horse to the front of the stables and attached the harness ropes that hung on either side of the stable door so that the horse stood looking out, its harness gently held on both sides by the rope.

Maren started with brushing. It was amazing how quickly the animals were recovering, like they'd been just waiting for the chance to spring back to life. There were still some bare patches on Star, but mostly, she brushed away dust and dirt and saw thick coats and a shine beginning to appear on all of them. They'd all also put on weight and the pathetic ribs sticking out were quickly being covered by healthy muscle.

As each horse had its coat brushed, Maren looked into the eyes of each one. Sultan still looked a bit wary, or maybe it was just that he'd always be a bit wild. Each horse had its unique energy, and when Maren approached them gently, softly, they yielded to her willingly. When she had come out to groom them several days before, she'd been stressed, with workers in the house, worrying about money, wondering what the heck she was doing in the Scottish Highlands. It had been a hard day, and she'd tried to lift Laddie's back legs to pick the mud out of his hoof, but he wouldn't budge. The simple movement he knew so well, when she ran her hand down the back of his leg and gently lifted his hoof, was met with stubborn resistance. And no one could make any horse on earth do anything unless they were willing. They were two thousand pounds of solid muscle.

She had tugged and pulled in frustration, and finally that day, having had enough of struggling, she realized it was her energy that was the problem. But she was too tired to do anything about it and had returned him to his stall. She'd pick his hooves the next day.

But today, calm, excited about claiming these animals as her own, peaceful in her own energy, she slid her hand down Laddie's leg and effortlessly lifted his foot, rested it on her bent knee and used the pick to get the packed mud out of his hoof. Like it or not, horses were a pure reflection of one's energy, one's emotional state. You could say what you want, or act like you were relaxed, but a horse's reaction to you told the truth. Told you what you were, in fact, feeling.

Feeling connected with the horses right then, Maren had another idea. Maybe it wasn't just *lessons* she was going to give. Maybe this was what she was meant to do. There were lots of places one could take riding lessons. But Maren had the gift. Her uncle had told her so since she was a small girl. She could communicate with the horses in a special way. She had studied horse whispering on one of her stints out West in America.

Maybe what Maren could offer was *healing* with horses. She felt the tingle, the sparkle, and instantly knew that was exactly right.

"What do you say, Laddie? How about a ride today?" she asked the gentle horse.

He turned to her, ears forward in the horse language of being relaxed and happy. She patted his neck and went to get a blanket and saddle. Maren hadn't ridden in a few years, but the motions were deeply ingrained, so she threw first the blanket, then the leather saddle, over his back, reached under and tightened the buckle, and switched the harness from the simple grooming one to a leather halter, slid the bit of the bridle into his mouth, and led him to the pasture. The other horses all looked on with curiosity.

In the field, she put one foot in the stirrup and threw her other leg over Laddie's back. To her complete surprise, she almost burst into tears. The feeling of riding, of being atop a horse, of that union with the powerful animal, was so beautiful. She had forgotten how much she loved it. Laddie was a perfect gentleman, allowing her to walk him and direct him easily. Again, she had to be very aware of her own energy. She was connected to the horse like they were plugged into one another, so it was almost as if the horse did what she wanted just by her thinking about it. The gentle pressure with a calf to move in one direction or another was just an extra hint.

After ten minutes or so, Maren gave a squeeze with both of her calves. "Hup."

Laddie broke into a canter. Maren let her body glide with the huge movement as he loped in a big circle around the field. After a few rounds, feeling that mix of excitement and fear that always went with the next move, she squeezed again, and Laddie broke into a full gallop.

Maren's hair streamed behind her, and she smiled to the point of almost laughing. It felt like freedom. It felt like flying. It was dangerous, always, and that was part of the thrill. But Laddie galloped with joy like he was loving it, too. As his hooves thundered beneath her, Maren moved in total unison with the huge animal.

After a big loop around the field, Maren gently pulled on the reins. "Whoa." She forced her bum into the saddle as a message to slow. Laddie responded right away, slowing to a walk. He was still recovering his strength and hadn't been ridden in…she didn't know *how* long. She didn't want to exhaust him.

Maren let go of the reins and let them fall on Laddie's back. She leaned forward and patted his neck, whispering in his ear, "What a good boy, Laddie."

Then she lay back still seated in the saddle, but with her back along Laddie's back, resting her head near the horse's tail. Laddie dropped his head and began grazing on the spring stubble of grass. Lying with her eyes closed, face up to the sky, horse beneath her, Maren felt almost sensual. As if she were melting. She let her arms fall to either side of her and she smiled.

After a few moments, Maren sat up, scratched Laddie's head, threw her leg over, and jumped down. She removed the saddle and bridle and let him stay out in the field as she walked back toward the stable, saddle over her arm.

Alex was waiting by the barn.

"Oh. Hi," she said, quickly wondering how long he had been there. Feeling embarrassed that he had seen such an unguarded moment. Alex looked embarrassed too, like he had witnessed an intimate moment he hadn't been invited to see. "I didn't know you were here."

"I know, I'm sorry. I wasn't spying," Alex said. "Well, maybe I was a little. You looked beautiful out there."

Maren's face heated and her heart started racing. *Did he just call me beautiful?* Or, no, he said her *riding* was beautiful.

Alex cleared his throat. "I've that check for ye. Charlie got called away and wanted you to have it right away." He held out an envelope.

"That's so exciting, thank you!" Maren said as she took it.

"He also said to tell ye you can apply through village hall for horse rescue status, or online, and then yer free to keep these lucky beasts. They belong to the village since they were seized, and they'll go to whoever will take them, so they're yours if ye want them," he said with a big smile.

"Horse rescue?" He lifted one eyebrow and gave her a crooked smile.

"Yes! I love having them, and I want to work with them and then give lessons, and do healing work. It's a long story," she said with a smile. They both looked out at the horses now all in the field. "I wish I knew what colors they were."

Alex's brow furrowed. "What do you mean?"

Maren turned to him. "Oh, never mind," she said, embarrassed. She hadn't meant to say it out loud.

"Tell me, lass."

Maren paused. Then said, "I'm colorblind," and shrugged her shoulders. "Everything is just gray to me. Well, black and white and gray."

Alex cocked his head slightly and said softly, "I'm sorry, lass." Then he turned back to the horses and leaned on the fence with his arms folded and said, "Sultan is black, I think ye kent that."

Maren folded her arms and leaned on the fence next to him, looking at the horses and smiling.

"The one you call Ozzie is…he's a light yellow. Like the color of honey. Bang over there is a beautiful deep brown. Chestnut really. The one with the star on her head is a light yellow too, another honey-colored one. And then there's Laddie. Laddie is a verra light gray. Like a mist," he said and he turned to face Maren. She turned toward him and their faces were so close she could feel his breath on her. He looked at her with a softness and kindness that made Maren smile softly, and he smiled back.

They turned back to the field and leaned on the fence in comfortable silence for several minutes, watching the horses. Then Alex said. "Did ye hear about the Glenmuir party this weekend?"

Maren wondered for a moment where he was going with the question. Was he leading up to asking her? Of course, he wasn't, he'd be there with the gorgeous blonde.

So she said, "Yes. Alistair told me about it."

Alex looked taken aback. "Alistair McCain?"

"Yes, he had come to look at the stables for his horse a while back. We met then."

"Oh," Alex said.

He almost looked disappointed, which left Maren feeling confused. Why would he care who she went with?

"Okay, well, ye'll have a great time, I'm sure. I may see you there. I mean the whole village goes so…" He trailed off. After a few more moments leaning on the fence, Alex stood up and said, "I'd better be off."

As he turned and left, Maren felt frustrated. The lovely moment with Alex had ended with talk of Alistair and thoughts of the blonde. She was going to a fun party with a handsome man, so why did she always have to complicate her life?

Shoving the man drama aside, Maren went in and heated up a bowl of the delicious soup she'd made from the garden. As she sat at the table to eat, the sense of centered calm she had felt just moments before on Laddie was gone. She didn't know why, but she felt lonely and upset.

She lifted a spoonful of the creamy, fragrant soup, and as she ate it, a warm glow spread through her. It was delicious. It tasted of colors and of life. But it wasn't just the taste. She had felt it the first time she'd had some the other night. A soothing energy flowed down her throat as she swallowed, which then spread through her whole body. Like a gentle glow. Like a strange nonphysical hug. She almost laughed at the thought. What was a nonphysical hug? She felt calmed. Healed.

Feeling grounded again, Maren poured a glass of wine and went upstairs to see what she had that she could wear to the party.

***

Saturday was beautiful, thankfully. Not as cold as it had been. The weather flip-flopped between frigid and hints of warmth. This day there was a touch of spring in the wind.

At two p.m. on the dot, Alistair pulled into the driveway at the cottage. Maren had let her hair curl, and it fell in waves down her back. She had put on makeup and wore black jeans, a form-fitting black turtleneck, and black boots. On top, she wore the new fitted oilskin jacket she had bought in Inverness. Her outfit struck the exact right balance of sexy, and not trying too hard.

When she opened the door, Alistair's eyes grew wide. Maren felt she looked both pretty and natural, his expression made her think he thought so too. It was a combination that undid many men, and she knew it. Alistair looked handsome in jeans and a collared shirt with a dark wool sweater. Preppy and neat. It was only the look in his eye that made Maren wonder if he was as safe as he looked. It intrigued her. Her gut told her to just observe. To take her time.

"You look stunning," Alistair said.

"Thank you," Maren replied. "You look very handsome."

"Why, thank you," he said with exaggerated formality. "Shall we go? The parade starts in an hour. I hope you like bagpipes!"

The main street of the village was lined with people. Maren thought every person for miles around must be there to create such a big crowd in such a small village. There were strings of Scottish flag bunting hung across the main road, and children ran around waving tiny Scottish flags on sticks.

Alistair and Maren found a spot near the edge of the road. She looked across and saw Gillian, who smiled broadly and waved. Maren waved back, noticing how nice it felt to know someone. She scanned the crowd, but she didn't see Alex.

A high-pitched sound rang out, clear and loud, and then a huge sound, that felt almost three-dimensional, as others joined in. Bagpipes. Rows of men and women in kilts stepped in time together as they came toward them around the bend of the main street. The sound of bagpipes filled the air, and Maren felt it fill every cell of her body. To any Scot, or half Scot, as Maren considered herself, the sound made the hairs on your neck stand up, made your heart race with pride, and often brought a tear to your eye. As the group marched toward them, and the sound got louder, Maren felt all three things. She understood how this sound rallied men to run screaming into battle in the past, and how they were outlawed by the English centuries ago in an attempt to thwart that burst of Scottish pride and bravery. It was a powerful feeling, and everyone standing there felt it, she was sure.

Men beat huge drums, which resonated through the street, along with the crisper sound of the snare drums punctuating the music. Thrilled, Maren looked around at the cheering crowd with a new sense of joy. After the bagpipers faded into the distance, various children's clubs, girl guides and scouts, and the Women's Institute marched by, followed by a farmer on a tractor. The mayor of the village brought up the rear in a vintage convertible MG, waving and smiling.

The crowd cheered as he went by, signifying the end of the parade.

The families with young kids headed home or to the green to kick a ball, and most of the adults headed to the pub. Half the village had beaten them there, and by the time Maren and Alistair arrived, people were already spilling outside, standing in front of the thatched building, drinking in the cold.

"Aren't they freezing?" Maren asked, laughing.

"Och, no, they're Scottish. This is braw weather!" Alistair said with a laugh and a look of pride.

They stepped inside to blissful warmth. The pub was packed. They inched their way toward the bar and finally managed to get a glass of wine for Maren and a beer for Alistair. Alistair he saw a group he knew, and they waved the couple over.

"Ali!" One man drunkenly stood up and slapped him on the back.

"Bruce!" Alistair returned the slap to his back.

"Who's this bonnie lass?" Bruce asked.

Alistair put his arm around Maren's waist. "This lovely lass is Maren Phillips. Just moved to the village from America."

Maren wasn't sure how she felt about his arm around her waist. It seemed presumptuous. She didn't even know him yet. But his arm stayed there, as if to make a statement.

She looked through the crowd and spotted Alex across the room. He was taller than almost everyone else. As the crowd parted for a second, their eyes met. Then his gaze dropped slightly. She realized he'd seen Alistair's arm around her.

When his gaze rose again, he and Maren locked eyes. Suddenly, it felt as if there was no one in the pub but the two of them. Maren's breath quickened and she felt herself flush.

He stared unsmiling, intense…and something else. Was he hurt? Or worse, disapproving? Maren wanted to peel Alistair's arm off and go to

Alex, but when Maren's gaze shifted, she noticed the beautiful blond woman next to him.

So instead, she nuzzled closer to Alistair and laughed at some stupid joke he told. When she lifted her glass of wine to her lips and glanced back seconds later, Alex was gone.

After an hour, Alistair and all his chums, who turned out to be golf club friends, were so drunk, she could barely understand them. She sat at the table while they continued to tell golf stories, not making any effort to include her in conversation, laughing loudly at every little thing each other said. Maren was bored to tears. The pub had started to thin out, and Maren was thinking of leaving when she saw Gillian and Sally walk in.

She turned to Alistair. "I'm going to go say hello to Gillian."

He turned to her as if he'd forgotten she was there and just shrugged.

Maren felt like she might cry, but it quickly turned to anger. Why should she care if he was ignoring her? She barely knew him.

"Gillian!" Maren called out across a few heads.

Gillian's face lit up. So did Sally's. Maren's heart recovered instantly from her hour with the idiots at Ali's table. Gillian waved her over, and the three of them ended up at a small table someone had just left.

"How are you?" Gillian asked when they were all seated with their drinks—seltzer for Maren, who had had two glasses of wine already, gin and tonic for Gillian, and lemonade for Sally.

"I'm good, thanks. Were you at the parade?" Maren asked Sally, to include her in the conversation.

"No," she said, looking a little shy.

"Sally isn't a big fan of crowds and loud noises," Gillian explained with a sympathetic smile.

"Oh, I understand that, Sally," Maren said. "I like a crowd now and then, but I'd much rather be on the farm with the horses."

"Me too. I want to see the horses. When is it my day to go to the farm, Mum?" Sally asked.

"Soon," her mother answered.

"Good." The answer was enough to satisfy her.

A group of girls came in with their mothers, who were clearly all friends. The moms went to the bar, laughing loudly and talking. The girls looked aimlessly around the pub until they spotted Sally. They sat at the table just behind Maren, Gillian, and Sally, and started whispering and sniggering, looking over at Sally. Sally saw them, as did Gillian and Maren. They said nothing. But they had their eye on them.

One girl said, "I'm Sally. Yes. No. That's all I know how to say. I have no friends and I'm weird."

Another girl joined in. "Hi, Sally. You are weird. No one likes you."

The girls burst into laughter. Gillian and Maren both stood up without thinking and turned to the girls. Sally's head hung low, as she stared at her hands in her lap, where she was picking at her nails.

Maren knew she should let Gillian take the lead, but having been that girl, the strange outsider, something deep inside her stung so badly, the words just came out. "That is no way to talk to someone. That's bullying and it's not okay."

She looked at Gillian, in case she'd made her mad by jumping in. Gillian raised her eyebrows, but she was smiling. Maren looked over to the bar, where the group of mothers was now all looking over.

"Your children are bullying Sally," she said to them.

One woman stubbed out her cigarette. "No they ain't. They're having a laugh. Kids are kids. Don't get your knickers in a twist." As the moms all laughed, it was crystal clear where the pack bullying behavior was learned.

"No, they are not just being kids. They're having a laugh, but at someone else's expense. That's bullying. You should teach them better," Maren said.

The woman stood up unsteadily from her bar stool.

Gillian intervened. "Carol, sit down. We are leaving anyway. But Wendy is bullying Sally. We've talked about this before. I'd appreciate it if you would talk to her about it. It has to stop."

Maren shot a glance at Sally, shoulders back, smiling and looking proud at being stood up for.

Gillian, Maren, and Sally got up and left.

They walked toward Gillian's house, along the row of attached village cottages. Once seated at Gillian's kitchen table, Maren realized she'd walked out without even telling Alistair. Thinking over the incident with the bullying girls, the awful mothers, and the terrible hour she'd spent at the pub with Alistair, Maren burst into laughter.

"What's up?" Gillian asked, smiling just because Maren was laughing.

"Just not how I thought today would go. I walked out on Alistair. I'm supposed to be spending the evening with him." She got out her cell phone and texted him that she'd left.

Alistair texted back, "Oh did, you? Okay." Which made Maren realize he hadn't even noticed. "Might have been nice of you to tell me before walking out," he added a minute later. She texted back saying, "I wasn't having a very good time, you seemed more interested in your golf buddies than including me so I didn't think you'd mind. I hope you have a good rest of your night."

"Well that's ducking rude," he texted back. Maren was glad of the autocorrect error, it made it slightly less jarring than reading the word he clearly meant to write. "You're pretty full of yourself. One little chat with my friends and you get all offended. I won't waste my time again, don't worry."

Maren sat in silence. It seemed an awfully nasty response to the situation. He hadn't even noticed she'd left. It was clearly more about his ego than her leaving. But the text struck a nerve. After a moment she realized why. It was just like what Trey had said to her in the hospital. Telling her that expecting basic kindness was overreacting and demanding. But then Maren smiled. She was changing. She didn't for one moment believe it and instead she turned her phone off and put it face down and shrugged.

"Did you want to spend the evening with him?" Gillian asked.

"Not at this point. I mean, he's pissed drunk, and oh my God, is he a boring drunk." She laughed.

"Good choice," Gillian said, and Maren felt there was something more in that statement. That maybe she meant something beyond having walked out of the pub.

Later, having had a wonderful time talking and laughing with Gillian, Maren thanked her very much and got up to leave, then realized she'd come to the party with Alistair and didn't have a ride home.

"I feel absolutely awful bothering you, but I don't have a ride home."

"Och, that's no' a problem at all. Come on Sally," Gillian called into the living room, "We're going to give Auntie Maren a ride to her farm."

Maren's eyes stung at the endearing name. Gillian was becoming a real friend. The kind who would come visit you in the hospital if you were in a motorcycle accident. Maybe even the kind who would bring you food and plump your pillows.

***

The next morning, Maren got the cottage ready for Sybil's visit. She was going to pick whatever vegetables were left, ready to cook a wonderful dinner, tidy the house, and get her uncle's bedroom ready for her visitor. Excitement and nerves followed her around the cottage. Maren's morning routine had become one that was soothing and fulfilling. She would make a strong cup of sweet, milky tea, don her work coat and wellies, and feed, water, and visit the horses.

In the stables, she filled their buckets with grain and water, then opened all the stall doors to let them out. She wandered into the pasture with the horses following her like she was the Pied Piper. It made her laugh every time. The sun had a new warmth to it, it was almost March.

The horses all ran joyfully to the far edge of the field, clearly feeling energized by the warmth.

Back in the cottage, Maren took the clean linens that had been drying on the line and went up to her uncle's bedroom. Earlier in the week she'd had a new mattress delivered and now she made the bed and placed a small bowl with a handful of dried lavender blooms. Maren had found a large patch of lavender in the herb garden, dead now in late winter. Knowing Sybil couldn't see a vase of flowers, this seemed a nice addition to the room. She pinched a few tiny leaves to release the scent, and the room filled with their soothing smell. She laid a fresh towel and washcloth folded at the foot of the bed, then stood in the doorway feeling satisfied. She looked at her phone and realized it was time to get dressed and go pick up her great-aunt. Her great-aunt. Family. She smiled.

***

Her car crunched up the gravel driveway of the nursing home. She parked and went in, nervous and excited. The things that could go wrong with a plan never seemed to really dawn on her until it was too late. Would Sybil turn out to actually be insane and now she'd be in a cottage alone with her? Or would her needs be more than Maren could handle? She started to panic, but in the end, she told herself to stop imagining things and to trust her gut, which told her that everything would be fine.

The nurse gave Maren a small bag of Sybil's things, and the two walked to the living room, television droning on in the corner. Sybil stood by a tall window, the warm sun falling on her upturned face. Maren smiled.

"Sybil?" she said.

Sybil turned, a smile spreading across her face. "You've come. How lovely!"

The nurse took her hand and led her to Maren. She took Sybil's hand from where it rested on her forearm and placed it in Maren's. A handing over of a life, of responsibility. Maren wanted to cry.

"Ready?" Maren asked. "Do you have a handbag or anything you need?"

"Och, dear, I've been locked away since I was a young girl. I've never had a handbag. Though I always wanted one. I loved to see the Queen with her little bag on her arm everywhere she went. I always wondered what was in it," she said with a laugh.

Maren felt like she'd been punched. What a stupid thing to have asked Sybil, who had basically been a prisoner her whole life. Of course, she didn't have a handbag. The lack of freedom even in such a small detail of the woman's life was heartbreaking.

Maren slowly led her to the door, across the small patch of gravel, to the car. Maren waved at the nurses standing in the doorway, who waved back, looking thrilled to see their ward have someone come for her after so many years.

As they drove, Sybil said, "My goodness, I haven't been in a car in seventy years! Well, except when they moved me from the loony bin to this nursing home. I guess, at some point, they decided I was so old I could clock out the rest of my days safely there. But this feels nothing like the cars of my youth. I feel like we are gliding on air!"

"Technology has come a long way, Aunt Sybil," Maren said, and the words filled her heart.

Sybil clearly had the same reaction. "Aunt Sybil," she said wistfully. "My dear, you have made a verra old woman verra happy."

Maren reached over and held Sybil's hand, giving it a squeeze. "And you've made a young…well, almost young, woman very happy too," Maren said, and they both laughed.

At the cottage, Maren got out and walked around to assist Sybil.

As she rose from the car, Sybil turned in a slow, full circle. "Oh, my dear. What a place! Do you feel it? The magic is strong here. Thank you, thank you for this." Tears filled her eyes, then overflowed.

Maren wrapped her arms around the thin, bony shoulders. "Thank *you*, Aunt Sybil. I'm all alone in the world. I have been for so long. It's you who should be thanked. I am so happy to have you here." Her own tears joined in.

"Och, look at us, two wild crying women. I ken we're related, that's for sure." Sybil grinned and Maren took her arm and slowly led her into the house.

Maren described each of the downstairs rooms to her as they went, and Sybil held out her free hand and slowly felt around her, for furniture, for doorways, telling Maren she was creating a map in her mind of where she was. It was a straight shot from the living room to the kitchen, through the little entrance to the other side of the cottage, and Sybil felt around the kitchen for the stove, the table, the fridge.

"Maybe, one day, I'll cook something!" she exclaimed. "I never have, of course."

Again, Maren was struck by the tragedy of her aunt's life. Of course, she'd never cooked. Patients in a mental ward weren't typically given knives and hot stoves to use.

"I'd love that," Maren said. "I am a terrible cook, so I can't teach you much, but I've been experimenting here, and I'm starting to love it. We can cook together."

Sybil agreed that sounded wonderful. "I think I'll just sit down, dear." She put a hand out, as if looking for a seat.

"I'm so sorry I'm tiring you out," Maren said. "This must all be a lot for you. Let's sit down, and I'll make us a pot of tea."

"That sounds lovely."

Maren led her aunt to the living room, sat her on the big, soft sofa, and lit the fire to take the chill out of the room.

"A fire! Och, I remember this smell. Well, my goodness it takes me right back to being a child!"

Several minutes later, Maren came back in with the tea tray. Sybil's head was tipped forward. She was sound asleep. The comfort of the home, the fire, the company, and the exertion of the day had worn her out.

Maren quietly put the tray down, poured herself a cup of tea, and sat in an armchair by the fire. As she smiled at her aunt's sleeping figure, she wasn't sure she had ever felt so happy.

After her tea, Sybil was still asleep, so Maren snuck out to check on the horses. They were all out in the field on the beautiful warm spring day, soaking in the sun and eating the first green shoots of grass. Maren filled their feed and water buckets earlier than usual for their dinners so she wouldn't have to come back out later.

Laddie came in from the field as he always did now when he saw her. She scratched his head and gave him a carrot from the bag she kept in the feed room. He chomped contentedly and watched her go about her chores.

Maren heard a small sound. A squeak. Or more like high-pitched noise that was a cross between a bark and a cry. A baby fox? Had Clover brought her kits to the barn?

She followed the weak sound into the back of one of the empty stalls. There, huddled in the corner, was a tiny kitten. He was the size of a small teacup.

"Oh my gosh!" Maren said.

Laddie clomped slowly over to see what was going on. The little creature looked up and let out a pathetic meow. Maren didn't see or hear any other kittens in the barn.

"Where is your mom, sweet thing?" she asked.

She checked every stall, and the feed and tack rooms, but didn't find anything. She didn't want to take him from his litter, but there didn't seem to be any other cats around. "How did you get here, little thing?" she asked.

He replied with another wide-mouthed squeak.

Maren didn't want to take him into the cottage if his cat family was still around, so she decided to put out a little bowl of milk for now and check later to see if he was still alone.

She went inside, glanced in at Sybil to make sure she was still asleep and got a small saucer and a bottle of milk. She went back to the barn and placed them in the stall.

The kitten got up instantly and wobbled over to the saucer, hungrily lapping up the milk. Maren refilled it, and he emptied it again. Maren grabbed a big handful of clean straw and spread it in the corner, and the kitten walked back to the corner and plopped down, and instantly fell asleep.

Maren headed back to the cottage, threw a log on the fire, took a book off the big bookshelf, and settled in while Sybil slept.

Not long after, her aunt slowly raised her head and opened her eyes. "My goodness I guess I needed a rest," she said with a smile.

"Yes, it's been quite a day," Maren said. "I'm glad you rested."

"My dear, I should love to wander on the land here, if I may. There's something calling to us here, talking to us. I think ye hear it, too, but maybe ye don't ken it yet. Aye, it's calling to us. I will take ye there if you like."

Maren was intrigued. "Yes, I'd love that," she said, wondering what exactly Sybil meant. For now, Maren was hungry and assumed Sybil must be too. She wanted her aunt to decide what they did every step of this visit, not having had any control over anything in almost her whole life. So, she asked, "Aunt Sybil, what would you like to do for dinner? Are you hungry?"

"Och, I could eat a horse," she said with a laugh. She thought for a long moment and then said, "Maybe I'm asking too much. And do just tell me, dear, if I am. But I wondered, it's been so long. Might we go to a pub for dinner? I went a few times as a bairn, and whenever I'd see a pub on television, I remembered exactly how it felt to be there. Och, I'd love that, if it isn't too much to ask."

Typical British, Maren thought. Americans asked for the moon. Here was Sybil, imprisoned her whole life, wondering if a pub dinner was outlandish.

"Of course, we can. I'd love that!" Maren said. "There's a lovely pub right in the village. It's just five minutes in the car."

"Och, what a treat, my dear. I can't tell you what a gift you are giving an old woman."

Maren went over and hugged her aunt. "You are the one giving the gift," she said.

She helped Sybil up, walked her to the bathroom, waiting outside. She then led her to the car.

They parked in front of The Red Stag. Maren helped Sybil out of the car and into the pub. When they opened the door, the now familiar rush of heat and light and smells of beer and food greeted them.

"Wonderful," Sybil said the moment they entered.

A few people said hello to Maren, and everyone stopped and watched as the American led a clearly blind old woman to a table by the fire. A few raised their eyebrows at one another, probably wondering what this newcomer was doing with the old woman.

Maren went to the bar and ordered a glass of merlot for herself and a whisky for Sybil, which Sybil had requested with a mix of childish delight and a hint of rebellion. While she was at the bar, Alistair, who had been watching the two women, approached Sybil at the table. He was drunk.

"You look like a nice woman," he said, sounding not at all nice himself. "Be careful with that one," he said, jerking his head toward Maren at the bar. "Thinks she's better than everyone else. Typical American," he sneered. "Don't trust her."

Sybil, surprised by this interloper, felt the negative, almost violent, energy of the man. She was not intimidated and simply said, "You can go sit down now. My lovely niece will be right back and we don't require yer company."

Alistair looked surprised at her reply and said, "Huh. I see where she gets it." And he stormed back to his table.

Maren returned, sat down, and raised her glass, then realized Sybil couldn't see that. She clinked her aunt's tumbler, and her aunt said, "Sláinte."

Maren replied, "Sláinte," and they took a sip of their drinks.

Sybil closed her eyes as the smooth single malt Oban slid down her throat, as if the earthy, musky slightly burning sensation Maren knew it gave, was the best thing she'd ever tasted.

"Och, aye. I remember it now. Oh wonderful!" she exclaimed, and several old men with bellies to the bar smiled.

The door opened, and Maren looked up to see Alex and his father. Her heart leapt.

"What am I feeling, my dear?" Sybil asked. "Something is stirring."

Maren's eyes widened, shocked by her aunt's perceptiveness, but also a bit disturbed by it. Could she have noticed that Maren's heart skipped when she saw the brawny Highlander?

Just then, a third person walked in behind Alex and his father...the beautiful blonde. Alex's girlfriend. Maren's heart sank.

"It's nothing, Aunt Sybil," she said, irritated with herself for feeling deflated. Again.

"Aye, I think it is, in fact, nothing, my dear," said her aunt, pointedly looking in her direction.

Maren frowned. What in the world did she mean by that?

Alex saw them and his face lit up. He waved and the three walked over to their table.

"Hallo there, Maren," Alex said, then he paused and looked at Sybil, waiting for an introduction.

"Hi, Alex," Maren said. "Hello, Hugh. This is my great-Aunt, Sybil."

Everyone greeted her. "Hello, nice to meet ye."

"Maren, I didnae ken ye had family here," Alex said.

"Neither did I until very recently!"

"There sounds like a story there," Hugh chimed in.

"Aye, there certainly is," Sybil replied, with a smile, looking in the general direction of the group.

"Och," Alex suddenly said, straightening, "I dinnae think ye've actually met Kate, have ye? Kate, this is Maren, the American I've been telling ye about. Maren, this is Kate. My sister."

CHAPTER 11

Sister? Maren stood, speechless, for several long seconds. She wasn't sure, but her mouth may have actually fallen open. The gorgeous blonde woman was his sister?

Her heart was now flopping around in her chest so hard she felt sure the whole pub could see it.

She quickly scanned her memories of seeing the woman, and there hadn't been any reason for her to jump to the conclusion that the woman was his girlfriend. Other than the fact that they were together often and around the same age.

Sybil seemed to pick up on the uncomfortable silence. "How lovely to meet you, Kate."

This snapped Maren out of her trance, and she pulled herself together. "Yes, so nice to meet you."

"Alex has told me all about you," Kate said.

He has? More heart pounding.

"Oh, that's nice. He is so nice. It's really nice having him as a neighbor." *Oh my God, shut up, you idiot.* How many times could she say "nice" in one sentence?

"Will ye join us fer dinner?" Alex asked.

Maren wanted desperately to yell, *Yes!*, but she knew the day had been an enormous one for her aunt. They were still just getting to know one another, and she was in a crowded pub for the first time in seventy years. The right thing to do would be for the two of them to have dinner on their own.

"I would love that, but my aunt and I have a lot of catching up to do," she said, and her body relaxed. She knew this was right. "But we'd love to another time," Maren added.

"We'll hold ye to it," Hugh said with a smile, looking at Sybil when he said it, rather than Maren.

Sybil smiled at him. Maren wondered if she knew Hugh was smiling at her. It was becoming clear that her vision was related to much more than just her eyes.

Maren read the menu to Sybil, who commented that she was happy to find that many of the items were the same all these years later. Though vegan shepherd's pie and Thai chicken pizza were certainly new. The women laughed at that and both ordered bangers and mash and red wine.

When Sybil bit into her fist mouthful of the steaming hot dinner, her eyes closed. She let out a quiet sigh of pleasure.

"Oh, my dear, you have no idea how good this tastes. Och, they try their best at the home, but this is heavenly."

The barman overheard the comment and called over, "Good scran, is it?"

Maren frowned in confusion. "Sorry?"

"Good scran, that?" he repeated louder, and Sybil nodded.

Alex had overheard the exchange from their nearby table. "Scran," he translated for Maren. "It's Scot's fer good, greasy, delicious food."

Maren laughed and called back to the barman, "Aye, great scran, this!" Everyone laughed.

During the meal, Sybil and Maren talked about life, about adventures had and adventures not had. Of memories of family, and of the present, their meeting. The whole time, Maren kept glancing up at Alex, who was talking and laughing with his family, but who was staring at her every time she looked over. He watched her with a mix of amusement, interest, and something else. She wasn't sure, but she thought it was the look of desire. She was fairly sure she was looking back at him the exact same way.

Back at the cottage, both Maren and her aunt were exhausted.

"I think I'll go straight to bed, my dear. It has been such a wonderful day. I'll never be able to thank ye," Sybil said.

"Of course. Let me go up with you."

She gently led Sybil upstairs and showed her where the bathroom was, directly next to the bedroom where she would be staying. Then, she led her to the bedroom, and Sybil walked around, feeling the doorway and furniture, making another mental map. Sybil got out the toiletries in plastic containers the home had packed for her, along with her flannel nightgown, and carried them to the bathroom, feeling her way there.

A few minutes later, she returned, and Maren, waiting there, asked, "Are you going to be all right on your own tonight? I mean, I don't really know what I should be doing for you. Can you get to the bathroom in the night and get back to bed, that sort of thing? I don't mean to insult you, I just don't know what I should be doing." Her great-aunt looked so fragile and vulnerable in her floral nightgown.

"Yer a kind soul, dear. But, aye, I'm fine getting to and from the bathroom. I'll wait fer ye in the morning going downstairs, but I'm fine tonight." She sat on the edge of the bed. "Ooh, lavender. What a lovely thing to have brought in." Her cloudy eyes filled with tears.

Maren reached down and hugged her aunt tightly. Her shoulders were thin and bony, but there was that steel strength to her that Maren felt again. Strength, and a wildness, somehow. Like a storm. Or maybe more like the sea. She kissed her aunt on the cheek and wished her a good night.

Maren went back and sat by the fire and let the blissful warmth ease her body and mind. It had been quite a day. Just as she was thinking how lucky she was to be beside a crackling fire on the chilly night, she remembered the kitten.

She threw on her coat, stepped into her wellies, grabbed a flashlight, and went to the stables. The horses seemed surprised to see her after dark. She found it so comforting that they were there, sleeping or quietly munching on hay all night. She made her way to the back stall and shone the light in the corner, and there he was. Alone, curled up in the straw, shaking. He looked up at the light, and let out his tiny, weak meow.

Okay, that's it. No mama cat has come back for him. He's coming inside.

"Hey, sweetheart. Want to come inside with me?" She gently scooped him up. He didn't resist.

Inside, Maren got him another saucer of milk and put a cushion on the floor. After he drank the milk, she placed him on the soft cushion by the fire, where he instantly fell asleep. She'd need supplies, but for tonight, she'd need a makeshift litter box. She hoped he knew how to use one. Kittens usually instinctively did. She got out the plastic dishwashing basin from under the sink and filled it with torn up newspaper. It wasn't a great setup, but hopefully, it would do the trick till the morning.

***

When Maren came downstairs the next morning, Sybil was already sitting in the living room. The little kitten was curled up, asleep on her lap.

"Good morning!" Maren said, surprised to see her there.

"Good morning, dear," Sybil replied with a smile. "I found a little friend this morning." The little puff ball purred loudly as she stroked its head.

"I'm sorry I wasn't up to help you downstairs," Maren said, hoping her aunt hadn't struggled in the new setting. "And yes, this is a kitten who seems to be alone. I found him in the stables last night.

"Och, no, I was fine. I decided to give it a try on my own, and it was no trouble. I'm used to seeing inside, so I did that to find my way." she said.

"Seeing inside?" Maren asked.

"Aye, I can't see things outside, but I see just fine inside. Of course, to the sweet nurses, I call it being blind. But, oh, the things I can see that they can't!" Her face lit up. "But you ken all about that, I think…"

Maren thought for a moment. "I think I do, yes." She thought of the land calling to her, of talking with horses, of being able to connect to places or people in her mind's eye.

"Let's start with some breakfast," Maren said. "Then I'll just zip into the village shop for some cat food and litter. Then we can do whatever you like for the day. How is that?"

"My dear, that is the most heavenly thing I have heard in seventy years," Sybil replied.

An hour later, Maren returned with cat food, bowls, litter, and a litter box. She got the kitten set up in the broom closet, then returned to the living room. Sybil was not there, and Maren panicked for a moment.

She found her standing in front of the cottage, face held up to the sun, smiling. Maren grabbed both their coats and headed outside.

"Here you go, Aunt Sybil," Maren said, offering her the oversized coat.

But it was surprisingly warm outside, and Sybil declined. "Och, I dinnae need it, my dear. Let's soak up this gorgeous sun today."

Maren agreed, the warmth felt blissful seeping into her skin after the long winter.

"Would you like to meet the horses?" Maren asked.

"Aye, I'd love that dear. But first…" Sybil said, trailing off. There was a long pause. Then she continued, "Something's been calling to ye here, dear, and you've no' been listening."

A shiver ran through Maren. Sybil was right. Maren *had* heard the land call to her, over and over, beckoning her to explore, as if it had something specific to tell her. But she rarely made time to follow the message and walk the paths.

"You're right!" Maren said. "How on earth did you know that? I mean, I think you're right. It's subtle. But it is like something out there on the land is calling to me. I've just been busy and…well, maybe lazy more than busy. I just thought I was imagining it or that I'd get to it another day."

Sybil turned to face Maren, looking very serious. She reached out and felt for Maren's hands, then clasped them in hers.

"No. You must never get to those messages another day, Maren. You must make the time, and you must listen. Those are the most important messages in life. They aren't to be trifled with. Everyone can hear them, but some hear them much louder than others, like me. And like you. That's the mists talking to ye, lass. Dinnae ignore it." Sybil looked so serious as she said this that it scared Maren a bit.

"Okay," she replied.

"It's callin' from that valley, isn't it, dear?" Sybil pointed in the direction of the little dip between the hills that held the copse of trees.

"How did you know there's a valley there?" Maren said, feeling a bit alarmed at the actual physical example of this old woman's ability to see without her eyes.

Sybil just smiled.

"Yes," Maren finally admitted. "That path calls to me. It's so weird."

"Not weird, my dear, just a different voice. A different way of hearing things," Sybil told her.

"Yes, that's exactly right! It's like I hear it inside, or actually, like I *see* it and hear it. But, at the same time, it feels like I'm imagining it or making it up."

"That's just because yer new to it, dear. The more you listen, the more you'll ken it's real. Verra real. And you'll trust it. So…shall we walk and see what's been trying to get your attention, then?"

"Yes!" Maren said. "But are you up for it? I mean, it's a decent walk to get over the hill here behind the cottage, and I don't really know where it is we're walking to."

Sybil smiled a knowing smile. "It's fine, my dear. I ken where we're going."

Maren suspected her aunt was talking about more than just the walk they were about to take.

At the top of the rise on the hill behind the cottage, they stopped to rest. Sybil sat on a large stone and caught her breath. Below them was the small valley with the tiny woods at the bottom and, though Maren couldn't see it over the trees, she knew the large bramble was just beyond that. From where they sat atop the stone, you could see rolling hills, one after another. Maren looked over at Sybil and noticed a tear rolling down her cheek.

"Are you all right, Aunt Sybil? What's wrong?"

"I'm free, my dear. I'm free. It's a tear of joy."

Maren hugged her.

"It's just down there," Sybil said, after a moment. She pointed toward the huge blackberry bramble next to the trees.

"Yes, I felt that too!" Maren said, stunned. She helped her aunt stand and held her arm as they descended the path into the little valley.

"I need a staff," Sybil said at one point. "I'll find the right stick while we're walking. It'll help."

Maren kept her eye out for one. At the bottom of the hill, they entered the copse of trees.

"There." Sybil pointed to the side of the path.

Sure enough, there was a long, straight tree branch that must have fallen a long time ago, as it was smooth and dry. Maren was about to ask how Sybil knew it was there, but she knew the answer. She picked it up and handed it to her.

"Och, that's lovely, thank you," she said. "Ye ken, staffs like this, and magic wands, are just branches that fit a person. That call to them. Then we ask the energies of the universe, the sun, the earth, to collect in them. And we put our own energies into them, and that's what creates the magic. It's the concentration of energy that makes magic, my dear. Remember that. It's the focus. The intention, the picture in our mind. That's all it is," she said.

A little thrill went through Maren at getting ancient wisdom from a true Highlander with the sight. She had meant to get her aunt out of the home as a gift to her *aunt*, but it was turning out that the gift was Maren's.

When the two reached the huge bramble, Sybil stopped and sat on a fallen tree and gestured with her hand toward the bushes. Maren knew it was a sign that she was meant to continue on alone. Whatever was in there was what had been calling to her since she'd first arrived on the farm.

She walked over, wishing she'd brought gloves or pruning shears or something. Instead, she picked up a long stick and began pushing the long thorny tendrils aside to make a tiny path through the bushes. The sharp thorns scratched at her skin, and at one point, her sweater got stuck on a thorn and tore. But she kept going. The feeling of being pulled forward got stronger and stronger with each step she took, until she was trembling.

She took her stick, shoved a huge branch aside, and stepped forward.

Her mouth fell open. In front of her was a large clearing, and in it was a perfect, ancient stone circle! Large, gray, monolith stones stood, jutting out of the ground like pillars, sacred, powerful, and silent. This must be what the Sisters of the Stones had been looking for.

Maren felt a jolt of electricity through her whole body, and she stumbled, nearly falling. With her mouth agape, she slowly walked to the stones. It was as if she was in a cathedral, and she felt an intense reverence for the stones. The ground beneath her buzzed as she neared.

She silently asked the stones if she had permission to touch them. "May I?"

She felt a sense that she could.

As she stepped inside the circle, the light changed. Once inside, everything around her was bathed in a soothing light. She slowly approached a stone, lifted her hand, and placed the palm flat against it. A surge of energy ran through her hand, arm, and then her whole body, freezing her in place. But rather than being scared, she felt the most profound sense of peace she had ever felt.

She closed her eyes and let the energy flow through her like water, like powerful, charged waves. Eventually, she was smiling and crying at the same time. Yes, that was it. These ancient stones were telling her that she was home.

Suddenly, an image appeared before her. Wind whipped around the enormous standing stones, silent and powerful. A woman stood, her long robe flowing around her, holding her hands up, not quite touching the stones. Her robe looked like something out of a medieval book. Slowly, the figure turned and walked to the edge of the stone circle and held out her arms. Into them, a young woman, scared and shaking with cold, placed an infant. The baby didn't cry. It hadn't the strength. "Heal my child," the woman said desperately through tears and the robed figure turned back to the circle. She held him up to the sky, turned him to the directions of the earth, then placed him on a sheepskin, now wet and cold, on the ground. After a moment she picked the baby up and whispered gently into its ear, "Slainte mhor agus a h-uile beannachd duibh". Then she returned the child, now wailing heartily, to his mother's arms where he was instantly put to her breast and covered under her woolen shawl. He suckled hungrily. The mother beamed. The child was cured. Then the figure turned toward Maren and Maren gasped. The face of the figure looked just like Sybil. Then the image faded, like smoke clearing, and Maren was again alone in the stones.

Maren emerged from the blackberry bramble scratched, bleeding in a few spots from the thorns. Her eyes were wide and her heart was racing.

Sybil could clearly feel Maren's emotions and beamed back. "Ye found it then, did ye?"

"I did. Oh my gosh, it's incredible. It's standing stones, a stone circle. Like a mini Stonehenge. It's the most beautiful thing, I can't believe it. It's just powerful and calm and intense and beautiful!"

"Och, that it is, my dear," Sybil said calmly. "Ye'll have to lead me there one day. After ye've cut some brambles back," she added with a laugh.

"Aunt Sybil, I saw something. I…," Maren trailed off, not sure how to describe what had just happened.

Sybil smiled peacefully. "Tell me, dear."

"It was a woman, two women, dressed in ancient robes. And a baby, he was sick, and the old woman cured him. I mean it was like I was really seeing it, not imagining it. I am freaked out, to be honest. I mean what was that?!"

"Ahh, a vision. Oh my dear, what a gift. That's the circle talking to you. Nothing to fear. You're home now, lass. You're where you're meant to be. Magic will be finding ye more and more. If ye let it."

Maren sat in stunned silence. She was either losing her mind or finding her path. Or both. She smiled and went to take Sybil's hand and help her up.

They took their time walking back to the cottage, Maren still trying to make sense of what she'd seen. Sybil grew tired as they walked, leaning more heavily on her staff. They rested often, and when they got home Sybil went upstairs for a nap.

While she slept, Maren went to the garden to see what was left to pick for dinner. Sage, rosemary, a few leaves of kale and onions. Once again, as she reached into the dirt to pull the onion, or snipped the leaves of the herbs and kale, color filled the vegetables.

But, today, as she placed the food in the little basket and stood up, the basket fell out of her hands. She gasped.

She spun around, staring wildly at the trees, the hills, the garden. Her hand flew to her mouth, and Maren burst into tears. There was color everywhere!

She was seeing the whole world in color for the first time. The new grass starting to push through the spring earth was a brilliant…green. She'd never seen it, but she knew that's what it was. She turned her face to the sky…blue. Deep and rich, dotted with fluffy white clouds. The door to the garden shed was dark. She didn't know what she was looking at. It was a color. But what color? Hadn't her uncle once said it was red? Is that what red looked like?

Maren could hardly breathe. To suddenly see the world with this incredible new vision after thirty-five years of grayness was almost more than her brain could process. To see what the rest of the world had always seen, the beauty of it, almost broke her heart.

She picked up the basket and rushed into the house, racing from room to room. The Persian rug was deep red, like the shed door but darker, the bowls and pitcher in the kitchen had blue stripes on them. She had bought oranges, and seen carrots, so that must be what orange looked like. She ate it all in hungrily, scared it would disappear as inexplicably as it had appeared like it did the first time in the garden. But it didn't.

By the time Sybil came downstairs an hour later, Maren was still as excited as a child on Christmas morning. But she had at least stopped crying. She would tell Sybil about the miracle over dinner. Maren had prepared baked chicken thighs with thyme and onion, mashed potatoes with a hint of rosemary, and sliced carrots, from a recipe in a cooking magazine she had bought at the shop – and immediately subscribed to.

Sybil was using the staff she'd found in the woods to touch on doorways and the feet of furniture, like an earthy, magical version of the white stick the visually impaired often used. Maren loved that Sybil was making herself at home and finding ways to move around on her own.

"I smelled something delicious and had to come look," she said with a smile.

Maren led Sybil to the dining table, then poured them each a glass of wine and placed a plate of the delicious fragrant dinner in front of them. Sybil took a bite and closed her eyes.

"My goodness, that is delicious!" she said, savoring the bite. "In fact, it's not just delicious. I dare say this food is healing, my dear. Some food is food, some is medicine. The earth here holds magic, and I feel it in the food. And it comes from you too. This is something special," she said and she took another large bite.

"Thank you, Aunt Sybil," Maren said. "I have to tell you something crazy. Or at least it seems crazy. But…well, anyway, I have always been color-blind. But when I picked the vegetables in the garden here a few weeks ago, I saw color for the first time in my life. Just on the vegetables.

It was like they were magic. Well, today when I picked them, the color moved to everything. To the whole world. I can see color now!

Everywhere. I mean I can't understand what happened, but I can see color. It's so beautiful, I still can't believe it's real. And I don't know why, suddenly, today, the color moved everywhere. And *stayed*."

Sybil was silent for a long moment. Then she simply said, "I do."

Maren could come up with no logical explanation. Then, that inner voice, or rather inner *image*, showed her the stone circle. "Was it the stones?" It had seemed magical at the time, but enough to bring color to her world?

Sybil smiled. "Och, dear, you're a fast learner. Yes, it was the circle. It's a healing circle. There are different kinds of stone circles. And this one here is a healing circle. It healed you."

"The circle?" Maren said, wanting to keep an open mind.

"There are more ways than one to understand the world. For most of time mysterious forces were understood as vera real and powerful parts o' life, ye ken. Only recently have they been cast out of culture…well, cultures like yours and mine. Many a place still know them. And what is a fact, lass? It's something that's true. We cannae prove everything that's true. Not yet anaway. Trust yer heart. I know ye do, and I ken ye hear its call louder than most. Dinnae be afraid of it."

Maren knew she was right, and she did believe in things that many would call unbelievable. She had seen things on her travels that no Western scientist could explain. And she felt in her bones it was true. Still, she was shocked.

"I hope ye'll let me come for a wee visit again," Sybil said, softly, "if it's not too forward to ask. And maybe then I can go to the circle with you."

"I would love that, and yes, of course you can come again," Maren said, suddenly feeling like she might cry. Her aunt was expected back at the nursing home the next day. "I'll clear the brambles for your next visit." Then she had a thought. "Maybe the circle will cure your sight, too, Aunt Sybil!"

Sybil smiled a sweet, knowing smile. "Maybe, lass. But I dinnae think so. The circle only cures things that are meant to be cured. My sight is long gone, but my second sight is strong. For me, this is how it is meant to be. But sure we'll see what happens if I make it there one day."

"Of course, you'll make it there. I'll make sure of it!"

"Well, then, I'll look forward to that, my dear. I will indeed," Sybil said.

***

The next day, Maren drove her aunt back to the nursing home, where she was greeted with excitement and lots of questions about what she'd done and where she'd gone. Maren was glad it was such a nice place, but still, it was a nursing home. Sybil would go back to sitting in front of a television all day and being alone.

As her aunt walked away in her oversized wool coat, into the sitting area, after they'd said goodbye, Maren knew she couldn't leave her there. She'd ask Dennis if it was possible, then she'd ask her aunt if she wanted it, but Maren decided then and there that she was going to get her aunt out of there for good. She was going to bring her home to live with her, to let the last years of her life be good ones. She'd call Dennis in the morning.

When Maren arrived back at the cottage it felt lonely. It hadn't before. Maren knew the cure for that. She started by going inside to visit with Mac, the name Maren and Sybil had come up with for the little orange kitten. When she walked into the living room, Mac came tumbling toward her, his purr loud as an engine. He was sweet, friendly and into everything. He had followed Maren everywhere for the two days since she'd brought him in from the barn. Having lost his family once, he was clearly determined not to lose Maren.

"Hey, Mac. How's my boy?" Maren said, reaching down and scooping him up in the palm of her hand and giving him a scratch behind the ears. The purring turned up a level. "Want to come feed the horses?"

She carefully put him down and changed from shoes to wellies. On her walk to the stables, Mac stayed at her heels. Her mood instantly lifted at the sight of the horses. They were all in the field just at the entrance to the stable, waiting for dinner.

As Maren scooped the grain pellets into a big bucket, the sound drew them inside. Each one slowly, calmly, clomped into their stall, and one by one, Maren filled their buckets and then took the hose and filled the water buckets.

She then sat on a chair in the middle of the stalls. "You'll never believe the day I had yesterday! I found a stone circle! I mean an ancient, sacred standing stones circle, right here! It had been hidden all these years—" As she said it, her mouth fell open. "Oh my gosh, Hidden Stone Farm! That's the name of our farm, guys. That must be why. It was amazing. I'll take you there some time," she said, not sure which she'd take first. Laddie probably. Then she said out loud, "I have to tell the Sisters of the Stones!"

Mac kept himself busy, pouncing on bits of hay and chasing invisible things around the corridor of the stables. Maren laughed and watched him for a long time. And by then she wasn't sad and lonely. She was happy. And she was excited.

***

Each day was warmer, and it was really beginning to feel like spring. Maren decided to take stock in the garden. It was time to start sowing spring seeds, so she sketched out the long beds on some paper and decided where she'd plant lettuce, kale, peas, and later beans, then tomatoes, peppers— hot ones and sweet ones—cabbage, zucchini, pumpkins, and more. She was excited and planned a trip to the garden center later that day.

Mac was great company and frolicked in the garden until he was worn out, at which point he found a spot of warm sun, curled up, and instantly fell asleep.

Maren spent two hours at the garden center and came home with not just seeds, but compost, a few seedlings, and a hose. She also came home with six tiny chicks. Impulsive as always, Maren had seen the little yellow puff balls at the garden center, peeping and chirping, and decided on the spot that the farm needed chickens. Her uncle had had some, and she knew the old shed he'd used as a coop was still standing. She'd added a feeder, water can, food, heating lamp, and wood shavings to her purchases.

She laughed at herself as she arrived home and started unpacking. Would she ever learn to look before she leaped?

Mac came out to see what was going on, and he cautiously approached the box that was moving and making funny sounds. He bravely put his nose against it, and then leapt back in fear when a chick cheeped. Maren laughed at his antics.

She started by raking out the debris on the ground of the old chicken shed. It had one window with glass still intact, and inside, there were three long roosting bars at increasing heights that ran from one side of the shed to the other. Otherwise, it was empty. After cleaning it out, Maren dumped the bale of wood chips on the floor of the shed and spread them around. She then filled the three wooden nesting boxes she'd bought with straw from the stables. She set up the food and water, and the circular pen the man at the store had told her to keep them in at first. She then attached the heat lamp the little chickens would need for those first few weeks until they grew large enough and had adult feathers to keep themselves warm. The days were getting warmer quickly, so she knew they'd be okay soon even without all that.

The final step was carefully taking each little chicken out of the cardboard box and placing it in the pen. They cheeped and scurried around and found the food and water. All had something to eat and drink, then, exhausted from the afternoon's excitement, they curled up under the heat lamp and fell asleep.

"Have a good nap, girls" Maren said.

She latched the coop door closed and walked back along the garden beds to the cottage. Her plan was to call Dennis at the NHS and see if there was any way to get her aunt to move into the cottage with her.

But the plan got sidetracked when she found a big sheep standing in front of her cottage.

"I know where you belong," she said to Houdini, with a laugh. She didn't see Alex anywhere, so she figured she'd do him a favor, and if she was honest, use it as an excuse to see him, and walk the sheep over the hill to his farm.

She hadn't seen Alex since the night at the pub. She found she'd spent quite a lot of her time thinking about him. Now that she knew Kate was his sister, her thoughts had a very different feel to them.

Maren, with no border collie to assist, got out a horse lead and put it around the sheep's neck. She gave it a tug. "Let's go."

The sheep didn't move. It didn't look that big, but she realized it must weigh a couple of hundred pounds.

"Come on. Hup. Walk on," she said, thinking horse language might get a result.

Nothing.

She went to the barn and grabbed a bucket of grain and held out a handful of it. The sheep moved toward her and used its velvety lips to suck up the grain. "Good, girl. Or boy," she said.

Over the next fifteen minutes or so, Maren used a combination of pulling and enticing to get the sheep to the top of the hill. She could see Alex's farm down below, but she had run out of grain, and Houdini seemed to know this. So Maren started tugging. Then she went behind and tried pushing. But the sheep was having none of it.

Finally, Maren gave a big tug on the lead. It slipped out of her hands, and she fell backward into a big muddy puddle.

"Damn!" She stood up and wiped mud off her face, which, in fact, just spread it around. She shoved her hair out of her eyes. "Git, come on, please, can you please just walk?" She wasn't sure what to do. Would she have to just let him go after all that effort?

She turned her head when she heard a sharp, loud whistle, and she saw Alex standing at the foot of the hill. Finn was bounding toward her.

Maren quickly undid the lead, and Finn swept around behind the sheep and expertly and effortlessly moved it down the hill. Alex was waiting and opened the pen door so Finn could chase it in. He closed the door and latched it.

"Come on down!" Alex called up to Maren.

She slowly descended the hill, wet, and covered in mud. This was not the entrance she had intended to make. Alex was fully laughing by the time Maren reached the bottom.

"How dare you laugh at me. I was doing you a favor!" Maren reprimanded him, then burst into laughter herself.

"Come inside and get cleaned up. I'll pour ye a dram to warm ye," he said with that smile that made her feel fifteen.

In the kitchen, Hugh sat by the fire reading the newspaper. He looked up, raised his eyebrows and grinned.

"Maren's had a wee bit o' trouble with Houdini," Alex said, smiling back at his father.

"Aye, I can see that," Hugh said.

"Toilet's through there if ye want a wash," Alex said, pointing at a door by the stairs.

"Thanks," Maren said.

She went and washed her hands and face in the sink. When she came out, Alex handed her a tumbler with an inch of amber liquid in it.

"I was jokin' earlier. Thank ye fer bringin' him home. I'm sorry he's troublin' you still. I've got te find where he's getting out. And I will," Alex said.

"It's no bother. I thought it would be fun to walk him home. I guess it's not like walking a dog." She laughed and sipped at the whisky, which burned her throat, then warmed her.

"How are you, Hugh?" Maren asked.

"Braw!" he said. "Never better."

"Glad to hear it!"

"Well, I'm off," Hugh said, folding the newspaper and getting his coat.

"Dad volunteers in the village. Home Keepers. He drives old folks who don't have a car or who can't drive. To do their shopping, to the doctor, those kinds of things. Helps them be able to stay living at home longer than they would. Of course, he's an old codger himself, but he doesnae seem to ken it," Alex said laughing.

"Haud yer wheest," Hugh said, with a chuckle. "I'm no' ready to pop me clogs yet! Maren, ye look lovely, even covered in mud. I'll see you two later." He headed out the door to his car.

In the silence, Maren realized they were alone for the first time. She sensed Alex was thinking the same thing.

"Well, yer here. I can whisk up some scran, if ye like," Alex said.

"Aye, that'd be grand," Maren replied in her best Scottish accent. "But you've cooked for me already. Why don't I cook something this time?"

"Well, it's been a long day. I won't say no if yer sure. I planted seeds for the summer gardens or started to. My back's killing me, to be honest."

"That settles it, you have a seat, and if it's okay, I'll look through what you have and make something," she said.

Alex refilled their whiskies and sat at the kitchen table while Maren found a beautiful piece of salmon, some dill, potatoes, and salad.

"What did you plant?" she asked, partly because she was going to plant her own garden the next day and wondered if she'd planned the right things.

"Och, lots of things. From lettuce to peas to onions and garlic. Then I started hundreds of seedlings in the greenhouse for tomatoes and squash and things to do in the ground a bit later," Alex said.

"Hundreds?" Maren asked.

"Aye. Remember, I'm no' just a sheep farmer, lass." He laughed. "I grow and sell veg to a lot of the farm-to-table restaurants in the area, including my brother's place in Inverness. It's a lot of work, but I love the freedom of working on the farm, and the satisfaction of seeing fine reviews for restaurants serving food I grew from a seed."

"That's amazing," Maren said. "I've never gardened much, but I'm replanting my uncle's garden this week. Maybe I can pick your brain if I need to."

"Pick away!" Alex replied.

While Maren was mashing the potatoes, adding a small crumble of bleu cheese she'd found for some extra creaminess and flavor – a trick she'd learned from her new obsession with online cooking sites. Alex put a log in the woodstove. She noticed the muscles in his back as he leaned over and tossed the wood into the fire.

When he stood up he flicked the hair out of his eyes and turned around and caught her looking at him. He stood still for a moment, their eyes locked together. Maren found it hard to breathe. And she was embarrassed that he'd noticed her staring at him, but now that he was looking back, she found it impossible to look away.

Alex smiled his teasing smile, but there was a seriousness to his look too. She knew the look. Desire.

Maren suddenly felt a wave of heat rush up her body. Alex walked over to the table. He looked down at the bowl of mashed potatoes, then with a smile he dipped his finger in and scooped some up and slowly ate it. His lips were full, and he had stubble on his face. Maren wondered what it would feel like to kiss him.

"Delicious," Alex said, looking straight at her.

After a long silence, Maren finally said, "Um. We should eat." She wished she'd thought of something wittier, or that she'd had the nerve to dip her own finger in the mashed potatoes sensually. But, instead, she felt like a teenager, unsure and nervous.

She wasn't normally like that around men. She was usually fun and flirty and bold. But when she thought about it, that was with men she didn't care about. Where it all felt like a game, like all of her relationships had for years. This felt different. It scared her. And thrilled her.

Maren served the meal, and Alex said it was the best dinner he'd had in ages. Maren felt proud of her burgeoning cooking skills. She wasn't the poor girl making canned spaghetti from the shop anymore. They talked about themselves, their pasts, their farms. Maren told Alex about Sybil, and he was fascinated, and horrified, to hear Sybil's story.

"Will ye have her to yer house again?" he asked.

"Yes. In fact, I'm hoping to be allowed to have her move in with me. I mean, I haven't asked her yet," Maren said, "but if she wants to, and I can, I will. I want her to have some sort of life after all these years. And I love having family. Plus, she's fascinating. I can learn a lot from her."

"Well, that's a big undertaking, and a grand one. You're a good woman for even thinking to do it," he said.

For the first time, Maren realized there could be a downside to having a blind eighty-eight-year-old in her care. It might make dating and spontaneous adventures more of a challenge. But she shook off the thought. She knew it was the right thing to do. And she wanted to do it.

After dinner, Maren had to get back to feed the horses and check the baby chicks. Alex drove her home to the cottage.

As Maren reached for the door handle to get out, Alex stopped her.

"Maren."

She liked the sound of her name on his lips. "Yes?"

Alex looked at Maren, still with small patches of dirt on her forehead. He smiled. Maren looked at Alex. She realized today was the first time she had ever seen him with color. His hair was light brown, his eyes were a bright blue and his blue shirt made them seem even brighter.

"There's a wedding coming up. A friend o' mine. In a big country house in Lochend. Two weeks from Saturday. Would you want to come with me?" he asked.

Maren had to force herself not to yell "Yes!" before he'd even finished the question. She made herself take a breath and pause before she said, "That sounds great. I'd love to," with far more composure than she felt.

"Grand!" Alex said with a smile. "If ye've no' been to a cèilidh yet, yer in fer a treat!" he said.

"A cèilidh?"

"Aye, I dinnae think you'd even consider yerself married in the Highlands if there isna a bit of a cèilidh. It's a sort of wild party, lots of drinking, whooping and dancing. Stripping the willow, tossing each other aboot. That sort of thing," Alex said enthusiastically.

"Stripping...?" Maren asked, slightly alarmed.

"Stripping the willow," Alex said with a laugh. "No' stripping. I'm sure ye've seen it. Highland dance where laddies and lassies swing each other round and move down a line. Lots of flingin' each other aboot and yellin'. I'll teach ye. It's no' hard once ye ken the few steps."

"That sounds very romantic," Maren said with a laugh.

Alex laughed. "It's beats doing the YMCA like at an American wedding!"

Maren laughed out loud at that. "Okay, you've got me there." Then she added seriously, "It sounds wonderful, I can't wait." She sat there, looking into his eyes, wondering how long she could stay before it started to look pathetic. Like she was hoping for a kiss.

Which she desperately was.

After a moment, she pulled on the handle and opened the car door at the same moment it seemed like Alex had leaned toward her. *Damn!*

But it was too late. She'd started getting out, so she kept going, cursing herself for not waiting another moment.

She turned and leaned her head back into the car. Alex's gaze dropped unconsciously to the top of her button-down shirt, which now showed just the very top of the swell of her breasts as she leaned in.

"Good night," she said somewhat breathlessly.

Alex looked up, into her eyes, where she was sure he could see her desire clearly now. "Good night."

Maren closed the door and walked into the cottage, and as she heard him drive away she did a dance like a teenager with a crush, which was exactly how she felt.

CHAPTER 12

The next two weeks were busy. Maren planted her garden, mostly seeds, some seedlings. The chicks were growing quickly and were almost ready to start roaming free of their coop. Mac was growing, too, and was wonderful company in the evenings, curling up on her lap and purring as she watched TV or read. He followed her around all day, too, and the horses had gotten used to him. She had spent one night in a panic, unable to find him, but eventually had followed the sound his meows to the old cottage out behind the grove of oak trees that sat several hundred yards behind the main cottage. Maren hadn't explored the old cottage, hadn't had a reason to.

But she opened the door that night and found Mac sitting inside looking nervous. Maren eventually found how he'd gotten in. One window was very slightly ajar. He must have forgotten how he'd gotten in and become trapped. She picked him up and he started purring wildly. Maren smiled and carried him as she had a look around the cottage. It was in good shape. Dirty. Unused for many years. But solid and cozy. Maren closed the open window and walked back to the garden, Mac now asleep in her arms.

The horses were all coming into their own. Maren now rode Laddie and Star regularly, and both Maren and the horses clearly loved the feeling of freedom walking into the hills or galloping through the fields.

Every day for those two weeks Maren had ridden out to the stone circle and worked at cutting back the mass of thorny bushes that blocked it. At the end of each day, she was scratched up, bleeding, and sore. But happy. She would end by quietly entering the circle and sitting, reverently, respectfully, silently. Sybil had suggested she bring little offerings, which she did. A handful of birdseed. A daffodil. Sometimes she saw images… some that seemed ancient. Images of people or of things, often stones, or fires. Sometimes she heard things in that unspoken way she was getting used to, where information would just arrive in her mind, in her body, without her actually hearing it. Several times, she saw food and the horses and crowds of people. She wasn't sure what to make of those visions, but she knew the answers would come.

But most important of all, Maren had gone to see Sybil at the home and asked her if she'd like to move to the cottage.

It had taken Sybil by such surprise. She had been speechless.

Then, she had quite calmly said, "Oh my dear Maren. I'd love that, dear. I cannae believe yer asking. But I'd love that. If I wouldna be too much trouble."

Maren was thrilled and assured her she wouldn't be. Maren went straight from there to Inverness to see Dennis at the NHS to start the paperwork. Sybil would be moving to the cottage the following week.

And all the while, Maren was getting more and more excited about the wedding. She bought a new dress for the occasion, a deep red, fitted dress and black high heels. She had even bought some new makeup and felt like Cinderella getting ready for the ball as she fed chickens and mucked out the stables that morning, filthy and smelly, eager to get her chores done so she could transform into a princess.

At three p.m., Alex's car pulled up outside the cottage. Maren's stomach was so full of butterflies she felt almost sick. She was scared. She was scared at how fully her heart, her stomach, and her mind fluttered and flipped when she even thought about Alex. She didn't like vulnerability and she felt very vulnerable starting to care so much for someone. Especially when she didn't even know if he felt the same. She started feeling irritable, she wasn't even sure why.

Maren realized she was starting to ruin the evening before it had even begun, so she shut off her mind and went to the mirror to check her makeup and regroup. When she heard Alex's knock, she grabbed her little black clutch and opened the door.

There, framed by the doorway, was Alex. He was dressed in a kilt made of Campbell tartan and she loved that she could finally see the blue and green in the pattern. He had on the traditional short black jacket, socks, a sporran, and even a dirk tucked in his sock.

Maren was unable to breathe for a moment. He was stunning. Tall, broad, and dressed in his Highland best, he was a thing to behold. Alex seemed to be having the same reaction when he saw Maren. His mouth fell open slightly and just stared at her. Maren smiled. It was the reaction she'd been hoping for when she bought the red velvet dress, cut low enough to show her voluptuous breasts, but not low enough to be vulgar. The dress hugged her hips and showed her fit, slim legs. She had bought black high heels to complete the outfit and she wore her hair down. It fell in soft curls down her back and she had on more makeup than he had seen her in before.

They stood in silence for several seconds, drinking each other in, before they simultaneously realized they were staring hungrily at one another and started talking at the same time.

"Wow, you look absolutely stunning," Alex said and at the exact same time Maren said, "You look so handsome in your kilt!"

They both laughed, and Alex held out his bent arm, like the chivalrous romantic that he looked. Maren slid her arm through his and he walked her to the car.

On the drive to the wedding, Maren said, "You look very good in that kilt." She's wanted to say sexy but held back.

"I know." He laughed. "I'm kidding. But we do love our kilts here. Do ye ever wear the McGlashan tartan?"

"No," Maren said. "I never really thought to get anything tartan."

"Well, it's your clan. You can wear it if ye ever decide to," he said.

Maren made a mental note to look up the McGlashan tartan. She loved how it had been a way of communicating your clan and your loyalties for hundreds of years. It was another thread in this tapestry of belonging to truly think of herself as a McGlashen, which she was.

The wedding was held in a small stone church in Lochend. The groom was a school friend of Alex's, and the bride a friend of his sister's. It was a moving ceremony, with love and tenderness palpable between the couple. Maren thought she would love someone to one day look at her the way the bride and groom looked at one another. Like they were the luckiest people on earth. Maren had never been looked at with real love. Not as a child, and not in any of the frivolous relationships she'd had as an adult. It made her sad as she sat in the ancient church. But it also gave her hope to think she was changing her life. Maybe one day, that kind of love would be hers.

After the ceremony, everyone met at a big country estate a few miles away for the party. When Alex and Maren pulled up to the venue, Maren's eyes grew wide. It wasn't just a large house. It was a castle. Built of gray stone with a slate roof, huge windows on the ground floor, and windows above those with pointed dormers topping them off. On both ends of the house were round turrets with pointed roofs. Now she really *did* feel like Cinderella.

They parked on the gravel lot to the side and Alex, again, gave Maren his arm. It was both romantic and practical, as the gravel path to the front door was treacherous in her heels. Alex's arm was solid muscle, and her fingers itched to move and feel more of it as they walked. But she kept her hand casually draped over it instead.

Inside was magical. The huge entrance hall had been decorated with candles and little lights. An enormous, dark wooden, carved staircase led upstairs, with large portraits of people who must have been very important in their day, men and women dressed in the clothing of their various times.

Immediately as they entered, a young man in white shirt and black trousers appeared and held out a tray of champagne flutes, bubbles cheerfully rising in the golden liquid. They each took one, and Maren blissfully sipped the drink. They were directed to an enormous room to the side of the entryway, paneled in dark wood floor to ceiling. It had a fireplace so big Maren could have stood up in it, with a fire blazing away. Tables stood along the walls, a buffet of delicious food—cold ham, roast beef, potatoes, salad, rolls, cheese, and fruit. On a table in the corner was a beautiful three-tiered wedding cake. The center of the room was completely empty, and Maren knew that was probably to make room for dancing. She'd watched some YouTube videos of cèilidh wedding dances. She was no expert, but she hoped not to totally embarrass herself.

As the party progressed, there were speeches, food, and lots more champagne. All the while Maren and Alex talked, laughed, and chatted with the people sitting near them, never taking their eyes off each other for long. Both clearly recognizing the look of desire in the other.

Then the whisky came out, and before long, the music started. Fiddles and traditional round drums started a quick, lively song, and couples young and old drifted toward the center of the room. Alex raised an eyebrow at Maren, who laughed and nodded. He rose and held out his hand

and led her to the floor. Everyone lined up along either side of the dance floor, and then it began—pairs coming to the middle of the row and linking elbows, swinging around, then heading back to the side to do the same with a different person, who twirled to them. Down the line this went, with people whooping and laughing. At one point, they ended up in huge circles, spinning around, all holding hands.

Finally, the dance ended. Everyone cheered or whooped, and they all laughed, out of breath and ready for more. Maren messed up the steps occasionally, but she was quick to laugh easily at herself before jumping right back in. She was happy. Full of champagne bubbles, romance, and music. Her face shined, and she smiled with her eyes, as well as her lips. Alex couldn't help but smile himself as he looked at her, and several times Maren looked over and caught him doing so. She would smile extra brightly at him, then go back to twirling and dancing.

By midnight, people were exhausted, happy, and many of them seriously drunk. Maren recognized a few people she knew during the evening. Charlie was there. And Alistair. He'd brought a woman, whom he proceeded to ignore the whole evening, like he had done to Maren a few weeks before. Alex and Maren chatted with Charlie and with some other friends of Alex's. Alistair was in a corner, talking more and more loudly, till it became clear that a problem was developing. Alex and Charlie turned to see if they needed to intervene. Alistair was yelling at a man, who looked completely confused to find himself on the receiving end of the tirade.

"She's with me, you ass!" Alistair shouted, suddenly protective of the woman he'd been ignoring all evening.

"Och, no offense intended, my friend. I was just having a chat. No worry." The man turned to walk away.

"Keep yer filthy hands to yerself! It's not my fault ye cannae get a lass to come with ye. Ye bastard!" Alistair yelled.

The man on the receiving end looked much less friendly now. "Shet yer pus, or I'll shet it for ye!"

Alex and Charlie walked toward the two, as did several other large men, one of whom said, "All right lads, head yer ways and leave it be."

Alistair gave the man a look that could kill. The man looked dumbfounded but shrugged as he walked away and let out a little laugh. Alistair glared at Alex and Charlie like they'd spoiled some sort of fun for him in preventing a fight. Then he looked over at Maren and curled his lip, as if the very sight of her were distasteful.

Alex came back to Maren. "Seems like the party's no' headed anywhere good. Shall we go?"

"That sounds like a good idea," Maren agreed.

They said their goodbyes and headed out into the warm spring evening. It was dark out, and many guests had already left. Alex told Maren to wait by the front, and he'd bring the car around so she didn't have to wobble through the gravel. He disappeared into the darkness.

As she waited, Maren felt an arm on her shoulder. She turned quickly to see Alistair standing behind her. Close. There was no sign of his date, who was no doubt still inside wondering where he'd gone.

Irritated, Maren shrugged to get his hand off, which seemed to anger him.

Alistair stepped in front of her, frowning at her gesture. He put his hands on both her hips.

Maren shoved them off. "What are you doing? Get off me."

Alistair reached for her again, this time putting a hand behind her head and pulling her toward him. He was so drunk, though, he stumbled.

Maren cried out in protest and slapped him across the face.

Infuriated, Alistair lifted his hand, about to slap her back.

Out of the darkness, Alex appeared. Without a word, he punched Alistair, sending him stumbling backward. Alistair rebounded, lunging forward and punching Alex in the stomach.

Alex groaned, but struck again, harder, and Alistair crumbled to the ground. Luckily, no one else was outside to see this, as Maren immediately felt incredibly embarrassed to be in a brawl at a wedding.

"Are you all right?" Alex said, rushing to Maren's side.

"I'm fine. My God, what the hell was that about?"

"I dinnae ken. He's drunk, that's fer sure. And he's always been an ass with women. He's known for it," Alex said. "But this is a new low. As far as I ken, anyway."

"Well, thanks for warning me before I went out with him," Maren said, only half joking.

"I dinnae ken you'd go out with him. And I didnae like it at all when I saw it."

Maren realized he was right. He couldn't have known she would go out with him.

"Let's get out of here." Alex led her to the car just as Alistair staggered to his feet and spit blood on the ground from his busted lip.

"I wouldna want you anyway!" he yelled at Maren as they drove off.

Maren wrung her hands in her lap and tried to breathe slowly to calm her racing heart.

They drove in silence and Alex seemed to feel her upset.

After a few minutes, Alex said, "I'm so sorry lass. I've no idea what is wrong with that man."

"It's not your fault. But I agree, there is something seriously wrong with him!" She turned to face Alex. "Are you okay? That was quite a punch you took." As she said it, she felt a mix of concern and pride having watched a man slug someone who had been mistreating her.

"Aye, I'm fine lass. Thank ye. Takes more than that ta hurt me," he said. He reached over and placed his large hand on top of hers and left it there.

They drove the rest of the way in silence. As the Highland roads twisted and turned, they both relaxed from the ordeal, and Maren eventually turned her hand over and interlaced her fingers with Alex's. He glanced over and smiled, sending new flutters through her stomach, along with a heat that pulsed through her whole body.

When they pulled up outside Maren's cottage, her heart was pounding. She hesitated before reaching for the car door. Alex looked like he might reach over and pull Maren toward him, but then seemed to think better of it.

"Thank ye for a braw evening, Maren," he said instead. "I will see you again soon for sure."

Maren thought she might burst into tears. She had been longing to be alone with Alex all evening, to at least kiss him and know whether he wanted things to go that way too. And now he was basically telling her to get out of his car.

It was never worth it, trusting people, hoping.

"Okay. Thanks," she frostily replied.

She got out of the car, went inside, and closed the door.

Inside, Maren peeled off the red dress, trying not to cry. She yanked on sweatpants and a big sweater, along with her rubber boots, and went out to the barn, Mac tumbling along behind her.

In the barn, the horses were half asleep. It was quiet and calm. Maren sank to the floor outside Laddie's stall.

"I should never get my hopes up," she said, as Laddie bent his head over the stall door and snuffled her hair. She was unsure if she was hurt or angry. Or both.

Laddie simply grabbed a mouthful of hay from the straw bag hanging on his stall wall and munched, unconcerned. His presence eventually calmed Maren. As she relaxed, the evening caught up to her, leaving her exhausted. She went inside and went to bed.

***

A few days later, Maren woke up early, cleaned the house, drove to the village shop, stocked up on food, and headed to the nursing home to collect her aunt. She'd spoken to Alex only once, briefly, when he had called to see how she was after the Alistair incident. She told him she was fine. She pretended she had to go and got off the phone quickly. It didn't seem he was interested in her the way she was in him, so she hid her hurt with busyness, working long hours with the horses, riding them, coaxing them to walk with her without a lead, or at the stone circle battling thorn bushes.

But when the day came to collect Sybil, Maren wasn't pretending to be anything. She was excited, and honored, to be bringing her aunt home. She had never felt *she* had a home, but now she had met someone who had one even less than she. And she was determined to give her aunt, and herself, everything they hadn't gotten in their lives—stability, comfort, love, and happiness. It was a tall order, but Maren felt she could do it.

When she arrived at the nursing home, Sybil was ready. Of course, she was. In some ways, Sybil had been waiting for this moment for seventy years. She had a pathetically small bag sitting on the floor next to her, and she was dressed in a skirt and blouse with the oversized winter coat on. But, still, she had a power about her that made these things, which might have diminished someone else, seem trivial.

Maren announced herself and her aunt's face lit up.

Had she doubted Maren would come? Maybe getting hopes up was something Sybil had also learned not to do.

"Ready, Aunt Sybil?" Maren asked.

"Aye, dear. I couldna be more ready."

They both thanked the kind nurses at the home, who filed out with them so they could wave. Maren glanced at Sybil as they drove away, wondering if she would have a big reaction to being free for the first time in most of her life. Instead, Sybil had a quiet, peaceful smile as she faced the window and let the sun hit her face.

Before Maren could ask how she felt, Sybil said, "I was always free, my dear. Now my body is just matching my soul."

And once again Maren was surprised. Then she, too, smiled, understanding perfectly.

At the cottage, Maren and Sybil unpacked her few things in her room, a flannel nightgown, a bag with toothbrush and comb and a change of clothes, a sensible skirt and polyester blouse they'd given her to take home.

"Aunt Sybil, would you like to buy some new clothes? I haven't been shopping since I moved here, and it might be fun."

Sybil thought for a moment before answering. "Well, I wouldn't put you out, my dear. But, my, I haven't bought clothes since I was a young lass. Wouldn't that be fun! Maybe just one or two things."

"It's a date!" Maren declared.

***

That evening, Maren cooked steak and potatoes, sliced thinly and sautéed to a crisp with sea salt and rosemary. On the side, was a small plate of sautéed kale from the garden. Sybil commented again that there was something special about the food Maren prepared.

"Maybe because you cook with love, dear," she said.

That must be it! She felt almost giddy. She was so happy when she cooked now, in her own kitchen, sometimes with things from her own garden, soon with much more from there. And now for someone she loved. It was a kind of joy Maren hadn't felt before.

After dinner, they sat by the fire, and Maren gently asked, "Sybil, what did you love to do before they put you in that awful place? What made you happy?"

Sybil didn't have to consider her answer for long. "Paint. Och, I loved to paint. And they let me even in the hospital. Oh, the colors I can still see when I think back. Aye, painting was always my passion, dear." Then after a long pause, she added, "And what makes you happy, Maren?"

Maren hadn't expected the question. Flustered, she realized she didn't know the answer right off. There had been travel and adventure. She'd enjoyed that. But did it give her deep happiness? Or had she been running from sadness? Those were two very different things.

Finally, Maren smiled and said with total surety, "The horses. The horses and this land. And maybe even cooking, lately. But definitely the horses."

Sybil smiled. "Yes, that's right."

***

The next morning before Sybil was up, Maren made cranberry and orange scones. She found that cooking was therapeutic, and she needed some food therapy after the disappointment of the night of the wedding. She put the kettle on and went to feed the horses and turn them out into the pasture. Then she went to the garden to see how her seeds and plants were doing. It was April and the Scottish spring weather, a constantly shifting mix of rain and sun, was doing wonders, and all the plants were thriving.

Walking back round to the front of the cottage, Maren saw a minivan pull up. She knew instantly who it was. She felt suddenly guilty. She'd meant to call them after she found the circle but then she'd been so busy she'd totally forgotten.

Isobel and her friends climbed out of the car and called over, "Yoohoo! Maren. We hope you dinnae mind us showing up again!"

"Not at all," Maren called back. "And I have news!"

Maren invited the women inside and found Sybil had come down while she was out. She introduced the Sisters of the Stones to her aunt, and there was instant chemistry between them.

"What a joy to meet women who understand the stones," she said, as Maren poured hot water into the teapot.

When everyone was seated with a cup of tea and a warm scone, Maren shared the news. "You will never believe it. But I found the standing stones. The circle!"

The women gasped, and Fiona clasped her hands. "I knew it! I knew it was here, I could just feel it!"

Sybil smiled at her enthusiasm.

"How did it go unseen for so long?" Fiona asked.

"It was hidden by a thick bramble. It was Sybil who helped me find it actually. She could feel it too. I'll take you there when you've finished your tea.

The excitement from the group of women was electric.

"Maren these scones are heavenly," Isobel said as she slathered butter on the last bite and popped it in her mouth. "That's the best scone I've ever had. Package them, dear. You'd make a fortune!"

Maren laughed, though the idea piqued her interest. She received a small stipend for her little horse rescue. And she had her shrinking savings. But it wasn't enough to live on and keep an old house from falling apart. Maybe there was something to Isobel's off-the-cuff suggestion.

But that was a thought for later. Maren had a tour to lead. The women all walked up the path on the hill behind the cottage, being sure not to walk so quickly that Sybil couldn't keep up. Sybil had the staff, and that helped her.

When they dipped down into the valley, the circle came into sight, and the women all stood stock still. It wasn't planned. It was the awe of the ancient, powerful stones that created the reverent silence.

"Oh, Maren. It's beautiful," Isobel almost whispered.

"It is," Maren agreed. "And the feeling inside the circle is beautiful too. Let's go."

As the women reached the huge monoliths, they stopped.

"We cannae walk straight in like it's a supermarket," Clara said. "We need to ask permission. Of the stones, and the energy."

Maren had felt this too when she had entered and had done a sort of halfhearted "May I?" as she entered. But this was different.

The women clasped hands, closed their eyes, and breathed deeply. They didn't say a word, but Maren felt they were communing somehow. With something. When they slowly opened their eyes, they smiled at one another and slowly entered the circle.

Fiona put both hands on the largest stone and leaned against it. She closed her eyes and Maren could swear she saw a slight glow emanating from the woman's body.

After a while, Sybil looked tired, and Maren said she was going to walk back with her aunt, but that the women should stay at the circle as long as they wanted.

Back at the cottage Maren made lunch. The Sisters of the Stones would be hungry after their long walk and time in the circle. She shredded chicken breasts she had boiled the night before and made a Greek yogurt curry sauce to mix it with. She toasted some sourdough bread she had baked the day before and added tiny arugula leaves, the first plant she'd been able to pick from her spring garden. She then layered the creamy chicken salad on top and sliced some apples for the side of each plate.

Just as she was finishing, the women returned full of stories of having felt the healing magic of the stones, of thinking they saw visions, and of being excited to come back. They all sat around the large wooden kitchen table and Maren served lunch.

"Maren, you have a gift," Phillipa said, biting into the sandwich and closing her eyes in pleasure as the layers of flavors mingled in her mouth.

"Thank you, Phillipa," she said. "I really do love to cook, it turns out."

"But it's not just the flavors. It's something else. Everything on Earth has an energy, from humans to spiders to stones. And your food, it has a special energy. A healing energy. Maybe because it's prepared just down the path from that powerful stone circle. Or maybe it's you and your energy and the love you put into it. But I can tell you, I feel it. And all that aside, it's just delicious."

Maren smiled proudly. Once again, the idea of making and selling her scones popped into her head.

Before the women left, they asked if they could return that weekend, and Maren said of course they could. Sybil was tired and she and Maren shared an early dinner of leftovers, then Sybil went to bed. Maren poured herself a glass of wine and sat by the fire. Mac jumped in her lap and purred.

Maren was going over the events of the day, wondering if she really *could* sell her baked goods for some extra income, when there was a knock at the door. She wasn't expecting anyone, and when she answered, she was surprised to see Alex.

"I was just driving home and thought I'd stop in and say hello. I know you moved your aunt in this week. I wondered how it was going."

"Come on in," Maren said. She led him to the living room and poured him a glass of wine. She was surprised, and touched, that he'd remembered Sybil. But she was also confused by him. Maybe he was just being a good neighbor.

"It's been wonderful. I love having her here. So far, I think she likes it too. And today a group of women showed up and wanted to see the stone circle on the farm, so we had an amazing time doing that. It's been busy around here," she said with a laugh.

"Excuse me? Stone circle?" Alex said.

"Yes," Maren said. "There's an ancient stone circle on the farm. I found it, with Sybil's help, hidden by a huge blackberry bramble, but I've cleared it out. It's the most amazing place, you can feel the energy of the stones… it's like…I don't know how to describe it. Like they buzz or vibrate or hum. Sybil says they're healing stones, and I believe it."

"That's incredible. I know there are a lot of stone circles in Scotland, but to find one on your own farm! Verra cool," he said. "Will ye show me some time?"

"I'd love to," she said. Then added, "I have to feed the horses their dinner. Want to help?"

He said he did, and they refilled their wine glasses and went out to the stables.

They each took scoops of feed and filled the horse's buckets. Then, Alex took the long hose and filled up their water buckets, while Maren sat on a bale of hay, drinking her wine. She loved to watch him move. His muscular build and confident, gentle way of being with the animals was both sexy and sweet.

When he finished filling the last bucket, he caught Maren staring at him with a smile on her face. He smiled back at her, that slightly mocking, half smile that made her breath catch.

Alex looked down the length of the stables. There were six horses in what was now, legally, Hidden Stone Horse Rescue. But the stables were huge. There were twelve stalls on either side of the flagstone central corridor.

"What are ye going to do with the rest of these? Bring in more horses?" Alex said, pointing at the empty stalls.

"I don't know," Maren replied. "I hadn't really thought about it. I guess I should do something with them. Yes, maybe more horses. They're so wonderful, but they're a lot of work, and the stipend I get barely covers their expenses. I don't know how much more time I can put into more horses. I need to start earning more money."

"What are ye thinking of doing?" Alex asked, sitting on the bale of hay next to Maren.

They leaned against the barn wall. "I don't know yet. Someone suggested maybe I sell my scones. I don't even know if they meant it, but it did get me thinking I might start baking. Or cooking, somehow, and selling some things."

"That's a great idea," Alex said enthusiastically. "There are so many shops that love to sell local products. And the tourists love that too."

Maren liked his instant business planning on her behalf.

"Yes, it is an idea for sure. I mean, I could still be home with my aunt a lot of the time while I did that," she said.

They sat in comfortable silence for a while, as Maren looked around the barn, now closed up for the night, clean, cozy, and peaceful. She was suddenly very tired. "I wish I could just curl up and sleep here tonight," she said. "It always makes me feel so safe and peaceful being around the horses, and in the barn."

"Well, why don't ye?" Alex asked with a smile.

Maren thought for a moment. "You know, maybe some time I will," she said, realizing there was no reason why she shouldn't.

Finally, Maren got up, knowing she would, in fact, fall asleep on that hay bale if she didn't get herself inside. Alex rose with her. Maren stopped at Laddie's stall to scratch his forehead and say, "Goodnight sweet boy," then to all the horses, "Goodnight, guys."

When she turned around, Alex stood inches in front of her. His smile was gone, and he looked at her intensely. Maren let out an almost inaudible little gasp and her heart started pounding.

Alex stepped forward, and Maren's breath caught as he placed his large hand on the side of her face, leaned down and kissed her.

In an instant, the butterflies disappeared, and there was just a feeling of joy in Maren's whole body. The kiss started off gently, as they tested each other's responses. But then it grew hungrier. Maren's mouth opened slightly, and she felt the flicker of his tongue on her lips. Alex took her face in both his hands now, as they kissed, passionately, moving their bodies until they were pressed against each other.

Maren ran her hands down Alex's back, feeling the taut muscles under his shirt.

Then, the kiss grew gentle again. Finally, they took a step back and both opened their eyes. They both grinned.

Alex sighed forcefully. "Okay, now I can think again. That's been the only thing in my mind since the night of the wedding."

Maren quietly said, "I thought you were going to kiss me that night." She immediately felt embarrassed for having said it.

"I wanted to. I thought that whole night about it. But it didnae seem right so soon after you'd been manhandled by that ass. It felt wrong."

Maren's heart melted. *That's why. He was being thoughtful.*

They walked back to the cottage holding hands. Each time Maren caught his eye, Alex was smiling as much as she was.

At the cottage door, Maren said, "I would invite you in for a nightcap, but, well, maybe another time." She didn't want to rush this. She always jumped in with both feet and then burned relationships out. She wanted to savor whatever this was.

"I can't say I'm not disappointed, but I ken yer right, lass. Can I take ye out one night soon? Maybe Friday night. We could go to my brother's restaurant in Inverness."

"I'd love that," Maren said, hoping she hadn't sounded as insanely excited as she felt.

Alex leaned in and kissed her again, a long, slow kiss. Then he squeezed her hand and said goodnight.

Maren walked into the living room, although it felt more like she floated in. She bit her bottom lip and wanted to yell, she was so excited. Instead, she poured another glass of wine, sat cross-legged on the floor in front of the fire and went over every detail of the evening in her mind. Grinning like a fool the whole time.

CHAPTER 13

That night, Maren had a dream. She was sleeping in a stall in the stables, but she was in a bed, with a quilt and a little light on a side table next to her. There was a rug on the stall floor, and she was cozy and happy and slept like a baby.

When she woke up, Maren went downstairs to make some crepes for breakfast. Some with strawberries and cream and the others with Nutella and banana. As she cooked, the image from the dream kept coming back to her. She really would love to spend the night in a stall, and there was no reason she couldn't put a bed in one and try it out. Just for fun.

She finished the crepes and went to look in the room full of boxes and storage upstairs. There'd been a bed under all those boxes years ago. And sure enough, it was still there.

Maren moved all the boxes aside and took off the mattress and dragged it out to the front yard and beat it with the carpet beater. Then, she easily took apart the bed frame, which just slid into slots to be assembled. She carried the pieces to the barn.

Never one for waiting, once she had an idea, she decided it would be fun to show Alex, whenever he came back, that she had acted on that late-night romantic suggestion of sleeping in the barn.

The back end of the stables was pristinely clean, as Maren had scrubbed every stall after all the horses were healthy and there was no more fear of mites or illness. She took the small rug from the boxes room and shook that out and put it on the floor, then put the bed frame back together and put the mattress on top. A side table and lamp from a closet upstairs and a pillow and sheets from the linen closet finished the project in less than an hour.

Maren stood looking at the little room and was elated. It was neat, tidy, cozy, and unique. There was nowhere to plug the lamp in, but she fixed that by running an extension cord from one of the outlets that were in the barn.

"What do you think, guys?" Maren asked the horses as she fed them and opened their stalls to let them out into the field.

Sultan leaned his head over the stall of her little room and sniffed. Then he walked outside, uninterested. The others did the same. Laddie was the only one who stayed and waited for Maren to come over and talk to him.

"It's my own stall. Just like a horse!" she said, laughing.

Laddie nuzzled her neck with his soft lips, then trotted off into the field.

Back at the house, Maren found Sisters of the Stones standing in the doorway, where Sybil had clearly just opened the door to them. What are they doing here again so soon?

"I'm so sorry we're back so soon," Isobel apologized. "Please don't think we're going to come every day. But we have two friends who have been verra sick. We just thought maybe we could take them to the circle and they could get some healing. We aren't expecting miracles, but even healing of the heart and soul is powerful. And, of course, miracles are never out of the question! Please don't feel you have to do anything for us. But, if it's all right, we'd love to take them to the stones."

Two women Maren hadn't seen before stepped out of the minivan. One was very thin and pale. The other was wheezing and clearly trying to catch her breath.

Maren leaned in closer to Isobel, speaking quietly, so the sick women couldn't hear. "I don't mind at all, but they don't look up for the walk over the hill to the stones. I don't know how you can get there." Then she had an idea. "Do they ride?"

Isobel looked confused. "Ride horses?"

"No, broomsticks." Maren laughed. "Yes, horses."

"I dinnae ken," she said. Then she called to the women by the van, "Alice, Eileen, do ye ride?"

"Aye," they both said. "Why?"

Maren walked over to introduce herself. "Hi, I'm Maren. I'm so glad you want to visit the stones. It's a bit of a hike, and I have some very gentle horses. I thought maybe you could ride to the stones."

"Och, I'd love that," said the wheezing woman. "I've no' ridden in a while."

"I'm no' so sure," the pale, thin woman replied nervously. "I haven't ridden in years. But I suppose, if you have a very, very slow horse, that would be a good way to get there, thank ye, lass."

Maren decided Eileen could ride Star, and Alice would ride Laddie.

"I've made breakfast if you'd all like some. As usual, I made far too much for just me and my aunt. Then we can go after that."

The women accepted with alacrity, and they all sat outdoors at the table in the garden as it was a beautiful warm day.

"Maren, I have to say I'm going to come here just for yer food, my dear," Fiona said.

Maren laughed, but it secretly delighted her.

After they ate, Sybil went inside, and Maren led the women to the stables. Fiona helped her put the tack and saddles on the horses, while the other women walked around, admiring the stables.

"Oh my goodness. What is this?" Clara stood in front of Maren's little bedroom stall.

"I just set that up this morning," Maren told her with a grin. "It was a dream I had last night, about how wonderful it would be to sleep in here sometimes."

Clara said, "Och, I want to sleep here, look at it! It's like out of a storybook. And with the horses nearby all night. Och, I'd pay good money to stay in your little stall, if ye'd ever consider letting me."

"Really?" Maren said, her interest piqued.

"Aye," Clara said. "I really would."

Isobel and Eileen came over and oohed and aahed over what a wonderful idea it was and how cozy the stall was and said they'd have to fight over it, as they all wanted to stay there too.

Maren helped Eileen and Alice mount their horses, using a mounting block that enabled them to walk up steps, stand on a platform and simply sit atop the horse, carefully placing one leg over once they were seated. Maren took the reins of Alice's horse, and Fiona volunteered to take those of Eileen's, to ensure a smooth ride.

The woman all headed single file out of the stables, on foot and horseback, up the hill toward the valley with the standing stones.

Sybil stood at the window of the living room facing out, sunlight streaming in and warming her face. She could hear the women talking and laughing, and in her mind's eye she could see them. These were the outliers that had existed since time began. The healers, the sick, the ones with second sight, and the teachers. Sybil was with her people. She didn't need to see with her eyes to know it. She felt it. And she knew that the land felt it too.

***

As the women's voices grew faint, Sybil heard a knock on the door. She used her staff to find her way to the front door, and when she opened it, no one said anything.

"Hello," Sybil said, hoping the visitor would identify themselves.

"Hello," a little voice said. It came from down low, so Sybil decided it must be a child. A little girl by the sounds of it.

"Can I help you?" Sybil asked.

"I don't think so," the little girl said. "I'm here to help you. I clean the stables. And stuff."

"Och, aye, you must be Sally!" Sybil said with a smile. Maren had told her about her little helper.

"Yes."

Maren had also told her that Sally was a girl of few words, but the words that she did use were always exactly what she meant.

Then Sybil heard another, older voice, speaking kindly.

"Hello, you must be Sybil. Maren has told me about you. I'm Gillian, Sally's mother. And this is Sally," she said.

"Hello, dears," Sybil said. "Would you like to come in for a cup of tea?"

"No. I want to see the horses," Sally said.

"No, *thank you*," Gillian corrected.

"No thank you," Sally said, before running off…in the direction of the barn, Sybil assumed.

"I'd love a cup of tea, if it isn't too much trouble," Gillian said. "I won't stay long. And I'll make the tea."

Sybil knew she was being kind, while also likely not wanting to imply the old blind woman should make her tea.

"I usually drop Sally and pick her up later, if that's okay. Is Maren around?"

"Maren took some lovely ladies on a walk up in the hills. And, aye, whatever you arranged with Maren is verra much okay," Sybil said.

She went into the kitchen, determined to make a pot of tea herself. By now, she knew where the electric kettle was, and it was easy enough to push the button down to set the water heating. Maren had led Sybil's hands when she arrived so she would feel that the teapot was next to the kettle and a jar with teabags and one with sugar were next to the teapot. And sure enough, a few minutes later, Sybil had a pot of tea, little bowl of sugar and the milk jug on the countertop.

"I think I'd better ask for help at this point, dear, if you dinnae mind," Sybil said. "I'm needing my hands to get around."

"Of course," Gillian said, and she jumped up to pour the tea and carry the things over to the table.

There was a knock at the door. Sybil started to rise, but Gillian laid a hand on her arm. "I'll get it."

"Oh, hallo," Sybil heard a man say.

"Hi," Gillian said. "Maren's out with some guests, but come on in. Charlie, this is Sybil, Maren's great-aunt. Sybil, this is Charlie, our town vet. Sybil and I are just having a brew. Would you like to join us?"

Sybil sensed Charlie hesitating in the doorway. "Please, join us, young man."

"Come on, Charlie," Gillian encouraged. "Maren made crepes."

"Well, in that case," Charlie said, and Sybil could hear the smile in his voice.

"Hallo, Sybil. How are ye today?" Charlie asked.

"I'm well, thank ye, Charlie," Sybil said.

With Sybil's permission, Gillian got out another mug and poured Charlie some tea.

Sybil sensed the young man might be watching the young mother with something like interest.

He cleared his throat, suddenly, as if he'd been caught doing something embarrassing. "I was driving by and thought I'd stop in ta see how the horses are getting on," he said.

"Oh, isn't that nice of you," Sybil said.

"Are you having a crepe, Sybil?" Charlie asked. When she said yes, he got up and fetched the plate and placed it in front of Sybil.

Sybil felt the energy in the air between the two young people, and thought, *Oh yes, that is just perfect.* But she didn't say a word.

***

At the stone circle, Maren realized she hadn't thought how Alice and Eileen would dismount. It wasn't as if either one were in shape to swing a leg over and jump down. And even if they were, how would they get back up for the ride home?

"I'm so sorry, I didn't think about getting you off the horses, or back on," Maren said, feeling foolish.

"Well, dear, we sprung this on you with no warning," Clara said. "It's our fault really. We just felt so much healing power here yesterday, we had to bring our friends."

Eileen had the perfect solution. "Let's let the horses carry us into the circle," she said.

Everyone agreed it was a wonderful idea. The women, Maren included, closed their eyes and asked the powers that be for permission to enter the circle. Then the horses, without any coaxing, walked in, as if they knew exactly what their job was. They led the sick women to two of the largest stones and got close enough that the women were able to place both hands on the stones. Alice closed her eyes. Eileen cried. The glow surrounded the women, and this time, Maren knew she wasn't imagining it.

"Do you see that?" Isobel whispered.

"I do," Maren said.

"That's the healing. That's the magic," Isobel said, and Maren knew she was right.

Half an hour later, the horses led the women out of the stones.

"I saw a woman," Eileen told them. "Dressed like it was a very, very long time ago. Long flowing robes. And she was holding a baby, in this very circle!"

Maren got chills and the hair on the back of her neck stood up. It sounded like the vision she had had too.

"You had a vision, Eileen!" Fiona said. "Aren't you lucky?"

Eileen agreed she was blessed.

As they headed back to the cottage, Maren noticed that Eileen was wheezing less, and Alice had a flush of color in her cheeks. Maybe it was just from the excitement and the fresh air. But she knew it wasn't.

When the women had all dismounted, cleaned up, and were ready to leave, Maren went to help Sally in the barn for a while before Gillian had arrived to pick her up. She and Maren made plans to go to the pub for a glass of wine later that week.

Sybil sat down in a chair by the window after Maren came in and flopped down on the couch.

"Something is brewing in your head, isn't it, dear?"

"How did you know?" Maren asked.

"I know. I don't know how. What is it?" she asked.

"I'm not really sure yet, Aunt Sybil," Maren admitted. "A few crazy ideas whirling around. But as soon as I make sense of them, I'll tell you."

"Och, crazy ideas are the best kind. Well, you tell me when you're ready. I think it's something good," she said, and Maren agreed.

The phone rang. It was Alex asking if Maren would like to have dinner at his brother's restaurant the following night. Maren said she'd love that. She got off the phone, head buzzing with ideas, and body buzzing with the excitement of seeing Alex.

***

The following day Maren took Sybil shopping. Sybil smiled constantly as they walked the busy streets of Inverness and went into various shops. In one window, Maren described some colorful clothes, and Sybil said that's where she'd like to go.

A little while later, they emerged with a beautiful, deep red tunic, flowing black trousers, and a sweater that was mustard yellow with navy blue trim. Clearly, her aunt liked color. Even if she could only see it in her mind.

They had lunch at a small bistro. When Maren looked out the restaurant window, she knew it was a sign. Right across the street was an art supply shop. She told Sybil, who clasped her hands and held them to her chest. She said she would love nothing more than to be able to paint again.

"Will you…I mean, will you be able to?" Maren asked, wondering how that would work now that she was blind.

"I dinnae ken, my dear. But I see such beautiful things, even without my eyes. I'd love to try and paint them," she said, beaming.

"Then it's settled. After lunch, we'll go and stock up on paints and canvases and whatever the things are that painters use!" Maren said.

"I've only my little pension," Sybil said. "I'll get that the first of the month, and of course, I'll give it all to you. You're taking such grand care of me. I wish I could do more," she said.

"You do, so much more than you know, Aunt Sybil, I promise," Maren said, and she meant it. But, at the same time, she worried she didn't have the money to just keep spending. Some of the ideas swirling around in her head were going to have to be put into action. Either that, or she'd have to find a waitressing job or something to make ends meet. She pushed the thought aside for now and just enjoyed her lunch.

That afternoon, the two women arrived back home. *Home.* Sybil had two new outfits, a winter coat that fit, and a bag of art supplies. Maren had treated herself to a new top to wear to dinner that night, and both women were satisfied and tired.

Sybil went upstairs to nap, and Maren fell asleep on the sofa with Mac curled up in her lap. When she woke, it was almost dark. She rushed upstairs and changed into black pants and the new pink blouse. She put on makeup and twirled her hair into the loose curls it naturally fell into with a little coaxing. She stepped into some black ankle boots, sprayed on some perfume, and went downstairs.

When Maren stepped into the living room, she gasped. There was Sybil. But a different Sybil. She was in the red tunic and black trousers, which flowed, and at the same time fitted her trim body. Sybil had worn her hair in a bun the whole time Maren had known her. But now it was in a long, silver braid down her back. She had on red lipstick and a turquoise necklace they had bought in one of the shops. She was stunning. Powerful. Changed.

"Aunt Sybil!" Maren said, throwing her arms around her. It was as if the person who had been imprisoned had been set free. This Sybil was whole, radiant, and glorious.

"My dear, I'll never be able to thank ye for what you've given me. I feel, right now, like myself in a way I have not since I was sixteen years old. You've given me my life back."

"And you've given me family back. Something I haven't had in…well, something I don't think I've ever really had. I will never be able to thank you, either." Both women started to cry.

"Dinnae fash, lass," Sybil finally said with a sniff. "You'll ruin your makeup. Are ye wearing makeup?"

"I am, and you're right." Maren carefully dabbed under her eyes as she laughed.

Maren threw a log on the fire, and they sat together, the news on the television, but neither of them listened to anything but the driveway, waiting for the sound of a car.

Maren was nervous to leave Sybil alone and go to dinner with Alex, so Alex's father, Hugh, had said he'd come over and have a glass of something and meet his newest neighbor. He said it would be a wonderful way to spend an evening. Maren could tell this was another example of Hugh's chivalrousness, acting like they were doing him a favor letting him come over, rather than the other way around. Maren had made a roast chicken with rosemary and sage and left it on the stove with a salad, a freshly baked loaf of crusty bread, and a bottle of wine.

When Alex arrived and greeted her at the door with a mischievous grin, she grinned back like an idiot.

Hugh broke their trance by saying. "Are ye letting me in or no?" They all laughed. Maren hugged Hugh and led them both into the living room.

Maren told Hugh and Sybil that dinner was on the stove, and wine and whisky were in the kitchen. Hugh told them to have a wonderful time. He said he and Sybil were going to have a grand evening. Sybil agreed.

Alex drove several yards away from the cottage, then stopped the car. He put it into park and leaned over and grabbed Maren's face, pulling her to him, kissing her while his hands moved from her face into her hair.

Maren opened her mouth in response and ran her hands up his solid chest and down his muscular arms. After a moment, they both ended the kiss softly, and sat back in their seats, grinning. Neither one said a word. They both knew they'd been thinking about that kiss since the other night, or at least Maren hoped that Alex had. She certainly had.

They drove the winding roads between hills that rose gently in some places, steeply in others. It was getting dark, but Maren could feel the mountains, their huge, silent presence a comfort. Solid. Still. Permanent. She exhaled and closed her eyes.

Alex looked over and smiled at her. "Penny fer your thoughts."

"Just happy," Maren said. Embarrassed, she added, "I mean, about everything. Happy I came to Scotland. And about the farm. And Sybil and everything."

He smiled his half smile and teased, "Nothing else?"

Maren laughed. "Oh yeah, and dinner with you, of course!"

Alex laughed.

Alex explained to Maren that his brother, Ian, owned The Black Drum. It was on the ground floor of one of a long row of buildings that were several hundred years old. A large plate glass window showed a row of neat tables, with white tablecloths and tartan napkins. The walls were a deep red color and black lantern-like light fixtures hung over the tables. It was both contemporary and classic at the same time.

"Alex!" a cheerful red-headed man called out with a big smile as they entered.

"Hi there, little brother," Alex said. He stepped aside, adding, "This is Maren Phillips. Remember Gordon McGlashan?"

"Aye," Ian said.

"Maren's his niece. Moved into his cottage a few months ago," Alex said.

"Wonderful to meet ye," Ian said, extending his hand.

"Nice to meet you, too," Maren said, immediately drawn to his warm, enthusiastic personality.

"Have a seat, and someone'll be right over to get you a drink. I've got to run. We're mad busy tonight." Ian quickly headed back to the kitchen.

"He seems nice," Maren said.

"Aye. He can be a pain in the arse, really, but he's not bad," Alex said with affection.

When Maren had a glass of wine and Alex a pint of beer, Maren said, "Your dad seems so sweet. A real old-fashioned gentleman. It was so nice of him to come to be with Sybil tonight."

"Aye," Alex said. "He's one of the good ones. I'm not sure they make them like that anymore. Never complaining, always positive, funny, solid. He's a good man. He raised me, Ian and Kate on his own."

"He did?" Maren said.

"Aye. My mother died when I was five, Ian was three. In a car accident. Some bastard ran right through a stop sign, here in Inverness. Killed while she sat right next to Dad in the car. I cannae imagine how he got through that." Alex's voice caught and he cleared his throat.

"Oh my gosh, that's awful!" Maren reached over and put her hand on Alex's.

"We were at school. I was just a wee lad, but I remember every minute of that day. Though, after that, life is a bit of a blur for a long time. Anaway, it was just the four of us after that. My dad never remarried. But he raised us well. We were young, so we missed her something fierce, but after a while, we were happy. It was a good childhood, running wild in the Highlands. Visiting my dad at his office. He was a doctor in Lochend. It was really like a storybook in a way, going on house calls with him, raising a few animals on our little farm. The village chipping in to help raise the wild Campbell bairns." As he spoke, he smiled, looking into the distance, as if he could see himself as a child doing all those things. "And what was it like growing up for you?"

Maren's dark humor took over. "Oh, it was a storybook too. Fields and dogs and love and neighbors." Then she laughed at the confusion on Alex's face. "No, sorry. I was kidding. It was...it was pretty awful if I'm honest." Over the next few minutes, Maren told Alex about the past, the neglect, her parents' drinking and their death when they'd driven, drunk, into a tree when she was eighteen. "My father was more mouse than man. My mother bossed him around and he wasn't much of a presence at all. He was a quiet man sober, and an angry man, drunk.

My mother didn't know how to be a mother. I think she wanted to. But she couldn't do it. I remember one day her coming home with a doll. I didn't have toys, there was never money for that, not after the booze and cigarettes. But she handed me a doll that day and I was so happy I burst into tears. Then I noticed it was dirty and it clearly wasn't new. At first, I wondered if she'd stolen it. Then I thought maybe she'd found it or gotten it at a thrift store. But I didn't care. It was my doll. I played with it for hours. I'd make little pretend dinners for it and brush its hair and dress it and clean it and play with it. I gave it all the things I didn't have but desperately wanted. One day my mom came over and took the doll and said, 'Let's play!' She'd never played with me before and I remember being confused. I think that's the hardest part about growing up like I did, as a child you always want to believe in your parents, no matter how much you know they'll let you down. You trust over and over. And get hurt over and over. Anyway, she took the doll from me and then just sort of looked at it like she had no idea what to do. Which she didn't. I mean she couldn't even raise her own real-life child, of course she didn't know how to play with a doll. She sort of bounced it up and down a few times, then looked angry and tossed it at me and went to the kitchen where I heard the familiar clink of ice in a glass and knew the day's drinking had started."

Maren paused and Alex looked at her with sympathy mixed with something, maybe protectiveness. She wasn't sure. "A few months later I think my mom thought she had come up with a way we could actually have fun together. Something she knew how to do. She gave me a beer. I was twelve. I took a sip and spit it out and it made her mad. Like everything did. I think she told me I was no fun or something like that. Later I spent a decade proving her wrong, doing nothing but having fun. Except in the end, it wasn't fun at all. It was the wrong kind of fun. Then a few years later, they crashed their car and died."

Maren paused and took a sip of her wine. She tried to remember if she had been devastated, as Alex's family had been by his mother's own accident. Looking back, she remembered only surprise. And then a strange sense of having been freed.

"So, I had a few relationships that didn't go too well. I ran my parent's little shop for a while. Then I realized that was not the life I wanted, and I took off. Closed the shop, rented the apartment out, eventually sold it, and then I spent years traveling. Living sometimes for quite a while in a place. But always moving on. Looking for something, I guess," she said.

Alex looked at her with a mix of sympathy and curiosity. "I'm so sorry, lass. That's no' a way a child should live. I'm sorry fer you. Explains a bit about you, though."

"What do you mean?" she asked.

"Independent. Fiercely, I would guess. You certainly seem it, moving to the Highlands, taking on a farm, starting a horse rescue, finding your aunt. My lord, you've done a lot in just a few months." He laughed.

Maren laughed, too, and realized she really had. "Yes, fiercely independent, that's probably accurate. And good at many things, master of none."

"And what was it, do ye think, that ye were looking for, with all that searching?" Alex asked.

Maren wasn't sure how to answer that. She preferred not to think about things like that too much.

But after a moment, she said, "I think I was searching for a home. Or more than that, I was searching for myself. Trying to figure out how to build a life when no one had shown me how to do that. Like a bird who doesn't know how to make a nest, flying around flinging twigs and leaves everywhere and just making a mess. That's what my life felt like. And then one day, in the hospital actually, I realized no one was going to parent me. That ship had sailed. The past was the past. And if I wanted a different life, it was up to me to make it. And in that moment, I knew that the only thing I wanted was to come here. That my uncle's farm was home. A starting place anyway. And a few weeks later, I was here."

"Amazing," Alex said. "You're bold, and no doubt." Then he asked, a note of hesitation in his voice, "And when the shine is off the apple here, will ye pick up and disappear one day from here too?"

Maren felt his energy retreat as he asked it.

"No," she reassured him. "I don't ever want to leave here."

But something flickered in the back of her mind, or maybe in the bottom of her heart, and she hoped she meant it.

Their dinner was served by a friendly waiter. Maren had a delicious shrimp, scallop, and asparagus linguini in a cream sauce, and Alex had ordered a traditional steak and kidney pie with fresh petit peas.

"Those are both mine," Alex said with pride, pointing at their plates as the waiter put them in front of them.

"What are?" Maren asked.

"The asparagus. And the peas. And a lot of the spring vegetables being served here tonight," he said, looking around at the other customers' plates.

"Really?" Maren said. "That is so cool!"

"Why, thank you!" Alex said puffing his chest out exaggeratedly. "Yes, I grow a lot of the veg for several others in the area too. Mostly in my greenhouse at this time of year. And I sell wool from the sheep, that's to a local Aran sweater shop. Mostly for tourists."

"Wow, that's awesome. You're really made the farm work for you. I'd love to learn more about growing here. It's so different from any other climate I've known. I've got my uncle's garden planted, but I don't really know what I'm doing."

"I'd be happy to come take a look and give you a few hard-learned tips. I had a couple of rough years to start, but I did learn some things I could teach you," he said. "Of course, at a price," he added with a wink.

Maren's heart flipped. "Why, sir, what do you mean?" she asked, trying to look coy.

"Well, I wilna say what I really mean, but I'll exchange for some of yer baking. I hear you make a fine scone," he said.

"That I do! Apparently. And it's a deal," she said, then she added, "Actually, speaking of scones, and the farm, I want to tell you my idea and see if you think I'm crazy."

Alex smiled and leaned back in his chair. "Tell me, lass."

Heat rushed through her body every time he called her that. Or smiled his half smile. Or basically was within a hundred feet of her. She shook it off so she could tell him her idea.

"Well, I need to make more money. I love having the horses and rehabilitating them. That's my passion. But it isn't enough to really support me, and the farm needs work here and there. And I've fallen in love with cooking, which is very surprising since I've never cooked much in my life before coming here. There's something special about the food growing here…" Maren trailed off. She decided the conversation about magic vegetables and color blindness was for another day. "And I've got the enormous, gorgeous stables, half empty. And then there's the stone circle."

Alex laughed. "That's a long list! I'm even more curious about this idea now."

"There were women visiting the stone circle a little while ago. Sisters of the Stones, they call themselves. They're a group that travels around to all the standing stones, monoliths, even to the ancient trees in Scotland. And there are loads of people drawn to stone circles. The circle on the farm has healing powers. I know that sounds crazy, but it does. I've felt it myself. And so did the women." Maren paused, waiting to see his reaction.

"Och, I dinnae think it's crazy. My aunt was a great one for the stones. There's lots here that still believe. And imagine what went into making those, thousands of years ago. There must have been something powerful to make them go to all that trouble with nothing but ropes and strong men to do it," he said.

Maren loved that this man—this brawny, fist-fighting Highlander—was also a believer in Highland magic. Only in Scotland.

"Yes!" she agreed. "Well, the women said they'd like to bring others to the farm. And they were saying my cooking is so good, and even healing, that I could sell it. And I set up a stall with a little bed in it, thinking it would be fun to sleep out there now and then with the horses, and they were practically begging me to let them stay there. So my idea is—" Maren paused for dramatic effect, "—I want to take the little money I have left and convert the front half of the stables into a bed and breakfast. It'll be like nothing else that I know of. Take down a couple of stall walls, and turn the stalls into little cozy bedrooms. I'd have to extend the stall walls up to the ceiling and add doors…and power. And then, every two or three stalls, I'd have a little bathroom with a shower. And in the middle, on the stone corridor, a really long wooden table where I'd serve my meals. Visitors could do healing work with the horses—I got trained in that back in Arizona. And then also visit the stone circle." She paused to let him take it in. "What do you think?" she asked, almost breathless with the excitement of hearing her plan out loud.

Alex said, "Lass, that is a brilliant idea. I'd never have thought of any o' that, but that is a braw idea! I think you'd be booked all the time. What a thing to think of!"

Maren beamed. "I'd have to find someone to do the work. I'm handy and can help, but obviously, I can't do all that myself," she said. "But if I can get that all done this spring, I can start hosting by the summer." She was suddenly so eager to get started she wanted to get up and walk out of the restaurant and start hammering nails right then.

"Ye do like an adventure, I can see that," Alex said.

Suddenly, Maren felt irritated. She'd noticed flashes of unexpected anger that were coming more frequently lately, and they scared her. They were like fissures in the Earth, with the lava of her past, her anger and fear, bubbling up and threatening to destroy things in their path. She wasn't really sure why she felt irritated. Maybe because he was right. Because she *was* trying to build a life here in Glenmuir, but she was creating adventure, and maybe even drama, with this idea, rather than settling down and living a quiet life.

Was she unable to live a quiet life? A sense of panic rose, where, just moments before, had been excitement and pride. Was she going to fail at building a solid life, a real home, like she had failed at all her other attempts at life? Failures hidden by the drama and chaos of constant moving? No one could really see that she didn't have any friends, or a career, or a partner, or a real life…not if she kept moving and calling it "adventure," instead of fleeing. Which, deep down, she knew it really was.

She brushed the thought away and scolded herself for feeling annoyed at Alex, who hadn't done anything but point out the truth.

"Are ye all right?" Alex asked, as if noticing she had suddenly become quiet.

"Yes, sorry," Maren said. "Just thinking." But the mood had shifted and now they sat in silence.

They eventually recovered from Maren's pulling away, and the conversation flowed again. At the end of the meal, they said goodbye to Alex's brother and walked, holding hands, through the streets of Inverness. It was dark out, and it had rained while they were at dinner. The light from the lampposts and shop windows made yellow reflections on the wet pavement. Alex put his arm around Maren when she shivered in the chilly air.

They strolled the city, looking in the windows of the shops. Maren commented on how it seemed like they were in a movie, men wandering the streets in kilts, ancient stone buildings. History practically oozing from the cobblestone streets. Alex agreed it was a special place, you could feel the history, and the pride, of Scotland here.

"I have somewhere I think you'll like. If you're up for a drink," Alex said.

"Definitely," Maren said.

Alex led them down a tiny alley between two old buildings, a "mere" he told her they had been called centuries back. These alleys connected different parts of the city. Halfway down the alley, they came to a tiny four hundred year-old pub, called The Lantern.

They ducked their heads to enter and stepped down three steps into the small, dimly lit pub. It consisted of one room, with a bar in the center, ancient wood beams on the ceiling, and a few wooden tables and chairs. Alex indicated it had been a poor man's public house hundreds of years ago.

Nothing fancy. A place where men could have a cheap drink after working or selling in the town market.

Maren could almost feel the presence of the men of the past, grubby, tired, sharing a drink, probably sometimes a fight. It was cozy, but the energy was a bit dangerous. Nothing having to do with the present. But Maren felt it. Maybe the danger of living in poverty with no safety net. The danger of being poor hundreds of years ago. She shuddered, grateful for her comfortable life.

"How did you find this place?" Maren asked when they were seated with a beer and a glass of wine.

"I had a little flat in this area, right after my divorce," Alex said.

"Oh," Maren said, unsure how to reply.

"I spent far too much time in here, I will admit," he said with a smile. "It was a rough time."

Maren felt she couldn't say *nothing*, but she didn't want to pry. "I'm sorry you went through that. It must have been hard."

"Aye. It was the worst time of my life. I mean, we didnae have children, though I wanted them. But I was glad there weren't children dragged through it. But, even so, it was awful. Ye don't get married thinking it's going to end. I felt like such a failure. Not able to make it work. And then it got nasty, though I tried everything I could to prevent it." He gazed into his beer with a look of regret.

"No. No one thinks that will happen to them, I'm sure," she said.

"When I looked back, years later, I think she was so angry because she was hurt. Even though it was she who ended it. She said she'd changed. But really, she'd had an affair. With a good friend of mine. And then she got mean, saying awful things. It's easier to be mad than feel grief," he said.

"She had an affair with your friend?" Maren asked, shocked.

"Aye. One of my best friends at the time. I dinnae ken which hurt me more, that my wife did it or that he did. It rattled me for, och, for a good year or two. Broke my heart, if I'm honest. Though, looking back, I now know it was a blessing. She was right, we were verra different. And she'd have hated the farm! She was a city girl through and through. She liked to live high. My farmer's salary would've been a problem. So, it was the right thing. But the way it happened, it was a terrible time. Then, one day, I decided to chuck it all in and buy the farm, and have my dad move in, and slowly, I recovered. Slowly, I remembered how to be happy. And now, I've never been happier in my life," he said with a crooked smile.

Maren was sure that had nothing to do with her. They had just met. But she hoped that maybe she would come to be part of the reason.

"I'm so glad you're happy now," Maren said. "You're such a good person. You deserve to be happy. We all do," Maren said, and he leaned across the table and kissed her.

They finished their drinks and walked back to the car holding hands. Maren felt even more tenderness for the big Highlander, knowing he'd had his heart broken.

Back in his car, Alex kissed her again. Softly, then more urgently. His hand went to the side of her stomach, then slowly rose till he felt the swell of her breast. He let out a sigh of pleasure. Maren ran her hands up his muscular chest and then found her way under his shirt, feeling the deep pleasure of his hot skin on her hands.

Realizing this could quickly get out of control, Maren pulled back. "Much as I might like to, I'm not going to…well, you know, go any further in a car." She laughed.

"Aye, yer right, lass," Alex said, taking a deep slow breath to regain his composure. "That's no' how I want it to be." The suggestion in the sentence sent a bolt of desire through Maren, and she was sure Alex had felt the same.

"I should get home and make sure Sybil is okay," Maren said, wishing it weren't true, but knowing it was. "I've been out for so long. And your father must be tired by now too. It's late."

"Aye. Let me get you home, and we'll go out again soon." He winked at her, and they drove off toward the cottage.

CHAPTER 14

The following week, Maren found a contractor to take a look at the stables and go over her idea. At first, he looked at her like she was crazy, wanting to turn horse stalls into a B&B. But as she described her vision, he ended up thinking it was brilliant. He'd never heard of anything like it and was sure, to the right person, it would be very appealing. He said he'd have to talk to a plumber and electrician, but that he'd get an estimate to her within the week.

Spring was in full swing now, with yellow daffodils popping their sunny heads out in any valleys or spots along stone walls or houses that held a bit of extra heat or got a bit of extra sun. They were the first promise of life and warmth returning, and Maren felt both excited and anxious, realizing she would have a lot to get done if she wanted to make this happen by summer.

Sybil was settling in wonderfully. She used her staff to get around the outside of the house and was now easily making tea, toast, and basics in the kitchen, and finding her way to the weathered old teak table in the sunny spot in the front of the house. Maren had come up with the idea of laying paths, so Sybil could find her way to the garden and to the stables. A woodchip path led to the stables, and a gravel one to the garden, so she could tell the difference. On sunny days, Sybil sat for hours outside at the table or in the garden, eyes closed, a look of bliss on her face. She told Maren she was talking to nature. Talking to the universe, spirit, energy. God. She said people had all different names for it. But it was the all-encompassing energy of the universe, and it was beautiful.

One day, she asked Maren to walk her to the little woods near the stone circle. Once there, she gave Maren a little lesson.

"Trees all have their own energy, did you know that?" Sybil asked.

"No, I didn't," Maren said. "What do you mean?"

"Each kind of tree has its own energy. And if you get verra still and connect your energy to the tree, ye can feel it." Sybil slowly walked over to a tree and held her hands, palms open, near to the bark, but not touching it. "It's stronger if ye touch the tree," she said, "but I want to show ye I'm not just feeling the bark to know the tree." With her unseeing eyes looking ahead, Sybil got very still, and after a few moments, she said, "This one is a birch."

Maren gasped. "How did you know that?"

"Ye feel it. Come try." She waved Maren toward her. "Put yer hands on the tree and talk to it. Get verra still and quiet inside and try and merge yer energy with the tree. It may take a while, yer new to it, but you'll feel it. I ken ye will," the old woman said.

Maren did as she was instructed, put her hands gently on the tree and closed her eyes. After two or three minutes, she felt something shift. She felt a melting away of the barrier between herself and the tree. She felt a new, clean-feeling energy enter her body.

"Oh my gosh, I feel it!" she exclaimed.

"Aye, ye do. What does it feel like?" Sybil asked, smiling.

Maren thought for a moment. "It feels like...clear. Like light. I see light," she said.

"You're strong with the vision, my dear. Yes, indeed. This is a birch, and in the ancient Celtic lore, its magic is lightness. It chases away bad energy. Chases away the shadows, both outside and inside the body. It's an energy that cleans. Yer feeling that," she said.

"Yes, I am. I mean, I really *am* feeling that," Maren said, astonished.

"Walk me to a different tree, my dear," Sybil said.

Maren led her a few yards away. Sybil again put her hands near the tree and was quiet for a full minute.

Then she said, "Och, this one is powerful. It's an oak, that is certain. The oak is the mightiest of trees. A chief among trees. Did ye ken that the word druid comes from the ancient word for oak, duir? Which is where the word door comes from, as they were often made of oak. It's mighty and was revered for its strength and usefulness, from acorns to wood. It's a strong spirit tree. Many of the oldest ones are considered verra sacred by those of us who practice the old ways. This one is quite old," she said.

Maren was amazed. It was an oak tree, enormous and knotted, it did, indeed, look very old.

Maren placed her hands on the oak and felt a deep pulse, much different from the flickering, light energy of the birch. This felt powerful and solid, rich and protective. She was amazed that, all her life, she had walked by trees, never realizing how different they each were.

"This is incredible, Aunt Sybil. Like a whole new world I didn't know was there! It's like when I started seeing color. Like a new language, an unspoken language," Maren said, the words tumbling out of her excitedly.

"Yer right, my dear. A whole other world many don't even know is there. Another day, I'll tell ye about second sight, if ye like. I have it. It caused me a lot of problems in my youth, but ye have it too. You're lucky, it's more accepted now, like it was before my day. But, for now, I think I need a cup of tea and a warm-up by the fire, if that's not too much, dear."

Maren led her home, lit the fire, and her aunt fell asleep in the big soft chair before Maren even had time to make the tea.

***

Maren woke bright and early. It was a clear day, colder than it had been, and windy. She was excited because the contractor was coming back to give her an estimate on her B&B idea. She'd find out that day if she could make her dream come true or not. She also had a dinner date with Alex that night. This time, Maren was going to take Sybil to Alex's house, where she could stay with Hugh for the evening. Everyone was looking forward to it. Alex and Maren were looking forward to it because they decided that the date would happen at the cottage. Maren planned to cook dinner for them, and then they'd have the place all to themselves for several hours. She had butterflies from the moment she woke up, just thinking about a whole evening alone with him.

Sybil was already downstairs, pot of tea steaming on the table. Maren thanked her and thought how wonderful it was to wake up and have family, and family that *felt* like family. Here was a woman, who was eighty-eight years old and blind, who made her tea and toast in the mornings…more than her own parents had ever done for her.

Sybil sat at the kitchen table, Mac purring loudly in her lap. Maren grabbed a piece of toast, buttered it, and stuck it in her mouth as she pulled on her coat and her rubber boots and headed outside. The horses all snickered and bobbed their heads as she slid the big door aside.

"Good morning, lovelies," Maren said. She filled their grain and water buckets, then opened the stall doors and let them out into the paddock.

Maren heard a car pull up and ran out of the stables, but it wasn't Dan, the contractor. It was Gillian and Sally. Maren had forgotten it was Sally's day to help out.

"Hi!" Maren called out.

"Hi, Maren!" Gillian called back.

"Hi," Sally said, looking happy that morning. "I brought the horses something," she said with a smile.

Maren hadn't seen Sally smile much. It was just the way she was, Gillian had said. And it was fine. But it was nice to see her smile.

"And what is that?" Maren asked, raising her eyebrows in exaggerated curiosity.

"Apples!" Sally said.

"Oh, they'll love that. That's so nice of you. Why don't you go on in and give them to them. Thank you!"

"Cup of tea?" Maren asked Gillian.

"I worked the breakfast shift this morning, so I've been up since four. I'd love a cup of tea!" Gillian said.

"Hi, Sybil," Gillian said, sitting down with a sigh at the table.

"Och, hello, my dear," Sybil said.

"I've made carrot muffins, Gillian," Maren said, gesturing to a tin on the table. "If you want one."

"Och, lovely," Gillian said.

Maren put down a cup of tea and watched her friend take a sip and close her eyes.

"Thank ye," she said.

There was a knock at the door, and Maren looked out the window to see Dan.

"This is the contractor. I have to go talk to him."

Gillian looked confused.

"I'll tell you later," Maren said, laughing as she went out to hear what Dan had to say, leaving Gillian and Sybil to drink their tea and chat.

Half an hour later, Maren came back inside, beaming. "It's going to happen! It's going to work!" she said. "I can't believe it. They're going to start work next week!" She sat down, breathless, and told Gillian all about the plan to build The Horse and Stone Bed & Breakfast.

Several hours later, Maren dropped Sybil off at Alex's farmhouse. Sybil was a little bit nervous being in a new setting, but Hugh was a gentleman, as always, and said she could sit by the fire, and he'd take care of everything. He was making the one dish he said he was an expert at, scrambled eggs and sausage. Sybil laughed and said that sounded like the perfect dinner.

Maren left while Alex was still out taking care of his sheep. The ewes were all heavily pregnant and any day now the lambing would start. And then all hell would break loose for several weeks, while his flock brought the next generation of adorable sheep into the world. Maren went home to change and get the meal ready, so she wouldn't have to spend the whole evening cooking. She was making a lemon and parmesan risotto with haddock seared in butter and served with parsley. There was a small salad, picked proudly from her own garden, to go on the side, with a Dijon balsamic vinaigrette she had shaken up in a jar the night before so the flavors could mix.

When the risotto was done and ready just to be reheated, the salad made, and haddock ready for the pan, Maren headed upstairs. She took a long hot bath, with lavender oil, luxuriating in the quiet, and allowing herself to relish the anticipation of pleasures to come. She washed her hair and then dressed in form-fitting jeans and a black button-down blouse. She blow-dried her hair, a rare event for Maren, and wore it straight. She put on a bit more eyeliner, mascara, and blush than usual, and when she stood back and looked at herself in the mirror, she thought didn't look half bad.

Downstairs, she lit the fire and wondered if lighting candles would be over the top, like she was trying too hard to seduce him. Deciding that candles were never a bad idea, she lit them and poured herself a glass of red wine.

At six on the dot, there was a knock at the door, and even though she had been expecting him, Maren jumped. Her nerves were on edge hoping tonight would go well, so she downed the rest of her wine in one gulp and went to open the door.

Alex walked in, ducking his head to get under the low doorway. When he stood up, he looked at Maren with undisguised desire.

"Wow," was all he said. His eyes swept her head to toe. Then a moment later, he said, voice raspy, "You look gorgeous." He didn't ask, he didn't hesitate, he just grabbed her, pulled her to him, and kissed her.

Lightheaded, Maren let herself melt into the kiss. When he stood back, it was her turn to take him in. He was in a pair of jeans, boots, and a crisp blue shirt that fitted well enough that Maren could see his muscular arms through the fabric.

She took a deep breath. "Can I get you a drink?" She felt herself flush at the unexpected desire in her voice.

With eyes fixed on her, Alex said he'd love a whisky, and she went and poured him two fingers of Oban and brought it to him in the living room.

"Any news on your big idea?" Alex asked as he sat on the sofa and took a sip from his glass. "Och, you got the good stuff!" He beamed, clearly recognizing the smooth feel of a good whisky.

"I did," Maren said with a flirtatious smile. "I need to impress my neighbors when they stop by. And yes, I did hear back. It's a go! Dan McKenna and his crew are going to start work next week. I'm so excited!" Maren explained the plans, the little rooms with beds and lamps and tiny chests of drawers, bathrooms every two rooms.

"Amazing," Alex said. "It'll be the talk of the Highlands. I mean that! Well, maybe not for your five-star hotel people, but for who yer aiming for, you'll be booked solid. What a great idea!"

Maren loved his unbridled enthusiasm. It almost matched her own.

"I can help," he offered. "I do all the building and repairs on my farm. I can help with the building if they need a hand. And can provide vegetables and fresh lamb if you decide to serve that."

"That would be great!" Maren imagined gardening and harvesting and cooking with Alex. And then imagined Alex shirtless, with a tool belt on, building her little guest house. The last image made her smile guiltily.

"I'm calling it The Horse and Stone," Maren said.

"I love it!" Alex said. "Do ye ken what yer surname, Phillips, means?"

"No," Maren said, wondering what that had to do with anything.

"Phillips means 'one who loves horses'," Alex said.

"No way!" Maren said. "That's crazy, I didn't know that!" She thought for a moment and then said, "It must be in my blood. I mean for real. Since people got their last names based on what they did—Miller, Carter, Smith—so one of my ancestors must have loved horses. I love it. It all feels like coming home. All of it. Being here. The history. Finding my own history. It's what I feel like has been missing my whole life. Belonging. Does that sound pathetic?" she added, suddenly embarrassed at being so vulnerable when she hadn't planned to.

"Lass, that's not pathetic at all. That's beautiful. I love that you're finding that here. To me, there's nowhere on Earth like the Scottish Highlands for knowing who ye are. Fer connecting to a place. I'm just sorry ye didn't have it before now. But that's behind ye. Look what you're building here now," he said. He leaned over and put his big hand softly on the side of her face.

Maren felt like she might cry. She wanted to change the subject before she did.

"What about you? You lived in California for a while. Did you always know you'd come back?" she asked.

"Aye, I did," he said. He moved his hand now, so it rested on Maren's. "I did. I'm a Highlander and couldna stay away long. After the divorce, I decided to follow my own dream and buy the farm. Slowly, the more I worked the earth, got my hands dirty, worked with the sheep, I felt better. It took years, to be honest. But, eventually, one day, I realized I wasn't just okay, I was happy again. That was a good day," he said. He looked up, as if remembering where he was, and smiled.

"Well, I'm glad you found your way back to being happy," Maren said.

"Aye. Me too. I guess we both found our ways to happiness. On farms next to one another. Funny that," he said.

Maren got up to refill their glasses and realized she was tipsy, and she'd better get dinner going before she was drunk. Alex followed her into the kitchen and sat at the table as she seared the haddock and let it cook, warmed the risotto, and served the salad.

After they'd eaten, Alex pushed his chair back and declared it delicious. He cleared the plates. Maren helped and reached around him to put the salad bowls in the sink. Alex took the bowls and put them down, then took her hand and turned her to him. He turned and pushed Maren gently up against the counter and kissed her. She tasted the whisky on his breath and felt her heart quicken. Alex held her hands at her sides as he kissed her, then pushed his fingers into her hair as their kiss grew passionate. Maren's mouth opened, and she let out a little moan as he gently bit her lower lip.

In an instant, he lifted her up and set her on the countertop. He stood in front of her, both of them now hungrily kissing one another. Maren unbuttoned Alex's shirt, her breath catching at the sight of his muscular chest, as she pushed the shirt down his arms. Alex didn't have the patience for buttons and lifted Maren's shirt over her head in one swift motion. Their bodies pressed against one another with the blissful feeling of skin on skin.

When Alex's phone rang, they ignored it. Eventually, it stopped.

A few seconds later, it rang again.

Alex groaned loudly and pulled away from Maren, looking at her questioningly. Maren nodded. Hugh was alone with Sybil, and someone was clearly trying to get in touch with Alex. He had to at least look.

He walked to the table and picked up his phone. It was his father. Alex tapped the phone and lifted it to his ear.

Maren took the opportunity to drink in his shirtless body before she heard him say, "Dad, what's wrong?"

Suddenly, the spell was broken. Concerned, Maren hopped down from the countertop.

Alex just listened for a minute. "Okay, I'll be right there. Can you call Charlie and have him come out?"

Maren exhaled. It wasn't Sybil. If he was calling Charlie, it was one of his animals.

Alex got off the phone and said, "I could murder that ewe myself, her timing! Two of my sheep have starting lambing, and one's not doing well, bleeding and looking poorly. I don't want to lose her. I'm so sorry, Maren, but I've got to go."

He picked his shirt up off the floor and started putting it back on. Suddenly embarrassed, Maren reached for her own shirt and pulled it over her head.

"It's okay," she said, hiding how frustrated she really was.

As Alex was pulling on his shoes, he said, "Hey, want to see something amazing?"

"Okay." Really she just wanted to go collect Sybil and come home and feel sorry for herself.

"Get a warm sweater, nothing nice, and yer wellies. You can see a lamb being born, if ye want to come with me," he said.

Maren perked up. That sounded wonderful!

She followed Alex in her own car, knowing she'd return later with Sybil, and in a few minutes, they were both pulling into the courtyard of Alex's farm. Hugh waited in the doorway, calm as could be. Maren had worked herself up on the drive over, worrying about the bleeding ewe. But just seeing the handsome older man smiling, hands deep in the pockets of his corduroy trousers, unconcerned, made her calm down. Alex seemed a bit more anxious, but not alarmed.

Maren went into the kitchen and found Sybil by the fire, listening to the radio.

"Hi, Aunt Sybil," Maren said, and the old woman turned her head toward the door.

"Oh, hello, dear." Sybil stood and walked toward the door. Her long gray hair flowed in waves past her shoulders. She was flushed from the fire, or maybe from whisky, Maren thought with a smile. She was beautiful.

"If it's alright, I'm going to watch this lamb be born. I'd love to see that. Are you alright here for a bit longer?"

"Aye, dear, I am happy as can be," she said. And she looked it.

Hugh stepped inside. "We're having a grand time. You go with Alex. We're fine," he said. He took Sybil gently by the elbow and led her back inside, to the warmth of the fireside.

In the barn it was cold. The stones held onto the winter chill and hadn't warmed up yet with the spring sun. Alex found the struggling ewe right away, in a pen with several other sheep, standing upright, staring straight ahead and panting.

Alex deftly moved the other sheep into an adjoining pen and then spoke to the ewe softly to calm her. The ewe strained and strained, but there was no sign of a lamb. Each time she strained, she bled. Maren was worried, having no idea what a normal lambing looked like. But she could tell Alex was concerned.

Charlie arrived a few minutes later, greeting Maren and Alex before examining the sheep. He then washed his hands and put on a huge plastic glove that went up to his shoulder. He gently reached inside the ewe and felt around, looking ahead, but clearly seeing what was going on inside with his fingers.

Finally, he withdrew his hand. "It's a muckle lamb, Alex."

Maren wondered what that meant.

"It's stuck tight," he added, and Maren deduced muckle must mean big.

Charlie slid his hand back inside the ewe, and after lots of straining and pulling, a little black hoof appeared, and then another. Then, in one fell swoop, a slimy white pile landed on the straw.

The mother sheep bleated and turned around, pulling the amniotic sac off the tiny lamb, which she began to lick clean. A little white head lifted shakily off the straw and looked up at its mother. It was beautiful.

Maren found she had tears streaming down her face. Alex grabbed a handful of straw and wiped the lamb down. He looked over at Maren, her cheeks stained with tears, her eyes shining brightly and a smile on her face.

"It doesnae get old. Every time's a miracle," he said.

She laughed and wiped her cheeks in awe of having seen life enter this world. And in awe of being in a barn in the Highlands in middle of the night with a gorgeous farmer. How was this her life? *How did I get this lucky?*

Within half an hour, the little lamb was standing, staggering a few shaky steps, and nudging under its mother to nurse. Another ewe had been lambing at the same time, and she, too, delivered a tiny wriggly white ball of fluff into the world in a nearby pen. Charlie had left, as the other ewe wasn't having any problems with her delivery.

By the time Maren and Alex walked back into the kitchen, there was only Hugh at the fireside. He looked up and raised his eyebrows in question.

"Two healthy lambs, one boy, one girl," Alex said like a proud father.

"Braw!" said Hugh. "And now it starts."

"Aye, and now it starts," Alex said. Looking at Maren, he added, "Lambing season is a wild ride. I'll no' sleep now for a month. But I love it."

"Sybil was knackered," Hugh said. "So, I took her to the spare room and let her lie down."

"Oh, thank you for doing that, Hugh," Maren said. "I totally lost track of time out there. If you point me in her direction, I'll go get her."

Hugh led Maren to the spare room off the kitchen. Sybil was on a bed, under a blanket, sound asleep. Her long gray hair spread around her.

Hugh said, "Why wake her? It's so late. She can stay the night. Ye both can, if ye like."

Alex agreed, insisting Maren stay in his room. He'd sleep on the sofa in the study. Within the hour, everyone was sound asleep in the farmhouse, and the sheep in the barn and out in the field were, one by one, getting ready to have their babies.

In the morning, Maren cooked everyone a hearty breakfast of fried potatoes, eggs, and bacon, while Alex made coffee and checked on the sheep. They stole a moment alone by the sink and agreed it was the strangest, and best, date either of them had ever had.

"But I'd like to try that being alone in the cottage thing again soon," Alex added with a wink.

***

Sybil had started painting. Maren set up an easel and several large canvases. She arranged the colors of the acrylic paints according to the rainbow, so Sybil would know what was where. Even though she was blind, Sybil said she'd like the easel set up in front of a window with good light. She said she could feel the sun, and even feel the view, so Maren put the setup in the window of Sybil's room, which faced east and looked out over the hills.

Maren spent her time working with the horses, planting her garden, including a huge herb garden. She decided she would grow herbs, both for cooking and for healing, and which she would sell at her B&B. She experimented with recipes, trying to come up with a menu for when she started getting guests. The chicks were growing quickly, their delicate yellow feathers being replaced by darker brown ones. They were old enough to wander the garden now and she loved their cheerful company as she gardened. Luckily Mac and the chickens seemed to consider themselves one flock and they didn't bother one another. Instead, Mac joined the hens following Maren around the garden while she worked.

One night Maren made so much coq au vin, she decided to take a big pot of it over to Alex's house. He was out with the sheep most of the night and in his greenhouse most of the day. When she dropped it off, she found Hugh looking pale and tired. Lambing season appeared to be hard on him, too, as he took on the running of the house on his own. He was grateful for the meal and called the next day to ask what magic she'd put in the stew, as he felt much better after eating it. Maren told him the magic ingredient was love, but, really, she had a growing suspicion that the herbs and plants from her garden really did have some sort of magic in them. The ground itself seemed to heal, the grass the horses ate, the stones. There was a sparkly energy Maren was beginning to be able to see, not just feel.

And for her, it was healing her heart.

One day, as Maren poured wine for her aunt and herself, before going back to chop fresh chives for a new recipe, Sybil said she'd finished a painting and asked if Maren would like to see it.

"I'd love to, Aunt Sybil!"

Maren followed her aunt upstairs. Maren was stunned by what she saw. Bold red, blue, green, and purple created a rich, layered painting of the Highlands. It was almost impressionistic in its choppy brush strokes, but it captured the wild energy of the Highlands perfectly…the hills, the heather, the rivers…all beautiful and perfectly placed on the canvas.

"How did you do that?" Maren asked in awe.

"I keep telling you, dear, that eyes are only one way to see. The much more powerful way to see is by looking inside.

By looking with the soul. By seeing what the universe wants to show you, not just what lays on the ground at your feet," her aunt said with a smile.

Maren suddenly had an idea. "Aunt Sybil, can we hang your paintings in the B&B when it's done, in the rooms? They would be perfect!"

"If ye like, dear. Would be nice to have someone see my paintings. I painted in the hospital fer years, but I never knew what they did with them. Threw them out, I assume. Humoring a crazy woman by letting me paint. But, aye, I'd love to hang them, thank ye, dear," she said.

That week, Dan and his team arrived and started work on the stables. The spring was warm, and Maren put the horses out in the pasture, so the banging of the builders wouldn't stress them. She spent long hours riding, grooming, or just sitting and being with the horses, all of whom were now healthy and friendly and seemed to know that Maren had saved them, they were so gentle with her. Even Sultan had quieted down, though he would always have a wild streak—it was just who he was.

Maren could barely sleep for the next two weeks as she saw her dream slowly becoming a reality. She hadn't seen Alex even once. He was right, between lambing season and his gardens, he was barely sleeping and had no time for anything other than the farm. But he did call and say he'd try to get to her stables and help on the build soon.

The crew took out the wall between a few of the stalls to create rooms big enough for a queen-sized bed. They left the rest of them as they were, which would accommodate a single bed and a small dresser. After power washing every part of the front of the stables with a bleach solution and letting it dry, they nailed up pine boards over the existing stable walls. They framed up the space to the ceiling, and eventually, hung drywall so the walls had a cozy wooden bottom half and a clean, white, upper half, on which Maren would hang her aunt's paintings as she finished them.

A month went by, with Maren and Sybil—and twice a week Sally—getting into a routine of gardening, painting, horses, chickens, and the occasional evening in the pub. Alex and Maren spoke often. The lambing was over, and life returned to normal on his farm. He finally found time to come see how things were progressing on the barn. After that, Alex was there most days, at least for a while, helping frame, drywall, and later lay the wood floors in the rooms.

Maren loved to watch him work, swinging a hammer, working the table saw, laughing with the other workers. At her request, the men had built a huge, rustic, wooden table, twelve feet long, and Maren went to estate sales and charity shops and bought twelve mismatched, old wooden chairs to put around it.

At midday each day, Maren brought a big lunch out to Alex and the workers: pasta dishes, roast chicken with rosemary, salmon fresh from local rivers, all the while slowly creating what would be her menu. The workers had never been fed so well and said, if she kept it up, they might start slowing down their work so they didn't finish the job. They didn't want to go back to cold ham sandwiches from the shop.

One day, as Alex was heading home to take care of things on his own farm, he said, "I know life has gotten busy, but how about we try that date again?"

Maren's heart jumped. She'd been so consumed by work on the stables she hadn't thought of much else. Except at night. And at night, she thought of Alex, and not much else.

"I would like that," she said, slightly breathless at the thought.

Alex gave his half smile and kissed her until the workers saw them and started hooting and catcalling. Alex and Maren burst into laughter.

Two days later, Maren dropped Sybil back at Alex's farm, along with a platter of chicken and mushroom crepes and a salad. She met Alex back at her cottage and put water on to boil for rice. Alex arrived with a bottle of whisky.

"Smells delicious," he said, walking toward Maren, his eyes fixed on her jeans and tight sweater.

"I haven't started cooking anything," she said with a laugh, turning to face him.

But he wasn't smiling. He slowly placed the bottle on the table and came to Maren, took the dishtowel out of her hand, and put it on the counter. He placed his hands either side of her face and kissed her. Maren leaned toward him and enjoyed the slow tease of the gentle kiss, knowing they were alone and had time to savor this.

As the kiss grew more passionate, Maren felt her body heat up and her heart quicken. Alex pressed the full length of his body against hers, and Maren had to strain her neck to reach up to kiss him. He moved his lips to the side of her neck, and Maren let out an involuntary moan of pleasure.

Then he turned off the stove, took a step back, took her hand in his, and wordlessly led her upstairs.

In Maren's room, Alex reached under Maren's sweater and felt the smooth warmth of the skin on her belly, her back, and then her breasts. Maren let out a tiny gasp of pleasure and reached to unbuckle Alex's belt. Alex lifted the sweater over Maren's head and stood back and drank her in.

"My God, you're gorgeous," he said, his voice raspy with desire. He pulled his own shirt over his head, and Maren itched to touch him.

She ran her hands up his muscular arms and down his back. He pushed her against the wall, and they kissed with a deep need. Maren walked to the bed, slipped off her jeans and lay back. Alex pulled off his own jeans, lowered himself over Maren and kissed her belly, working his way up her body to her mouth, their bodies moving as one.

***

It was pitch black out when a buzzing woke Maren from a deep sleep. Confused for a moment, she looked over and saw Alex asleep next to her. She smiled and snuggled against him, then heard the buzzing again. It was her phone. Caller ID showed it was the phone at Alex's farm.

The clock beside the bed said eleven p.m. She'd left Sybil at the farm much later than she'd meant to! Although Hugh and Sybil had said to take their time, both with a sly smile, and that Sybil could spend the night in the spare room if they had too much whisky and decided not to drive back. Alex and Maren had laughed, knowing that "having too much whisky" was a code for ending up in bed together.

Maren answered the phone. "I'm so sorry, we lost track of time."

"Maren, you and Alex must come quickly." Sybil sounded calm, but serious. "It's Hugh. I can't see what has happened, but he's gone silent.

He's not talking to me, and I just went to touch him to see if he was asleep and...he's not moving."

"We'll be right there!" Maren hung up the phone. "Alex, wake up!"

Alex slowly opened his eyes and smiled at her.

"What's going on?" he asked sleepily.

Maren said, "It's your dad."

CHAPTER 15

Alex rushed in the door of his farmhouse to find Sybil standing next to Hugh, who was in his chair by the fire, head fallen forward onto his chest. Sybil quietly stepped aside as she heard Alex and Maren enter.

Alex knelt before his father and touched his shoulder. "Dad?"

But it was obvious. Hugh was gone. Alex dropped his head, and Maren gently put her hand on his shoulder. Alex reached up and held onto her hand, then looked up with an expression of shock and pain, tears on his cheeks. Her heart ached for him. "Oh my God," was all he said.

Alex turned to Sybil. "I'm so sorry you had to be here on your own Sybil. Do you know what happened?" he asked, choking on tears.

"I don't, my dear," she replied gently. "He and I were having a lovely chat. We were both tired. He went quiet and I thought he'd fallen asleep Eventually, I tried to wake him and couldn't. Whatever happened it was very peaceful. And he wasn't alone."

"No. Thank you for that, Sybil. I feel terrible I wasna here though," he said, his face pained.

"Do you want me to call Ian and Kate?" Maren asked gently.

Maren could tell Alex's head was spinning. How was any of this happening? It was all too fast.

He sank into a chair, in shocked silence for a few moments. Then he stood up, and said, "Thank ye, but no. I'll call them myself." He squeezed her hand and walked back to the car to get his phone.

An hour later, Ian and Kate arrived. Ian and Alex gently lifted their beloved father out of his chair and laid him on his bed. He was in his pajamas and bathrobe, and the siblings knew that their father would never want to be taken away, or buried, like that. Hugh had worn a shirt and tie almost every day of his life. Certainly, every time he left the farm. *You never know who ye might see*, he would say.

Maren watched in awe at this heartbroken act of gentleness and love, as Alex, Ian, and Kate undressed their father, then dressed him in his favorite outfit, corduroy trousers, leather shoes, checked shirt, and tie. They softly brushed his hair, which Maren thought was the most beautiful and heartbreaking thing she'd ever seen. Then they sat next to him well into the night.

At one point, Ian said, "Let's play him some music. Dad loved his music."

"Aye, he did," Alex agreed. "Good idea Ian."

The brothers put on Scottish pipe and drum music, the bagpipes wailing passionate, moving music that filled the old farmhouse. The three of them sat and cried.

Maren helped Sybil to bed in the spare room at about two in the morning. As Sybil was pulling the comforter up, she sat up and reached her hands out to Maren, who walked over and took them in hers.

"Dinnae fash yerself, Maren. Hugh is here, sure as he ever was. He's here and he's gone, both. But he's pure light now. Pure joy. Pure love. He just dropped the veil of his body, that's all that happened."

"I know. I do believe that. And I do actually feel that," Maren said. "But it's still so sad. It still hurts."

"Aye. That it does, my dear," she agreed, and she lay down and closed her eyes.

**

Doctors determined that Hugh had had a massive heart attack, death would have been almost instant. He hadn't suffered, which was a blessing.

Hugh's casket was brought to the funeral home and lay there for three days so people could visit. The wake was held at the farmhouse the day before the funeral. There had been many tears and much to do, practical things that suddenly everyone had to become adept at in the midst of their heartbreak: funeral planning, estate documents, travel for relatives from afar.

But the wake was a time for family and close friends to get together and celebrate Hugh's life. Whisky flowed like water, and people told stories, laughed, and cried all afternoon. Hugh had had a wonderful sense of humor, and there was no shortage of stories to be told. Like how he and his mates got drunk and went swimming in the sea in nothing but their tam o' shanters. The police found them and gave them a stern warning. Or how, at boarding school, he had put frogs in one of the professor's lunch bags and got hit with a cane for it in front of the whole class, back in the days when you could whip a child for bad behavior.

It was the loss of a good man from a different time. Alex and his family's hearts hurt as they also celebrated and laughed.

The funeral was the next day, on a Sunday. The small stone church in Glenmuir was packed. People stood against the back wall to pay their respects to the man, and the family, they had known so well. Alex, Ian, Kate, and some of their extended family sat in the front row. Maren sat with Sybil, Gillian, and Sally a few rows back. Each of Hugh's three children got up and spoke. Eloquently, lovingly, of the father they adored, who had raised them on his own and who had been their role model of how to live a good life. How to be honorable. And how to be happy.

And then the door to the church opened, and a high-pitched sound made everyone turn. There, in the doorway, was a bagpiper in full regalia—kilt, huge black feather hat, sporran and sgian dubh. The sound turned into a slow, mournful playing of "Amazing Grace." Now there wasn't a dry eye in the church. Alex, Ian, and six other strapping young men who were close friends of the family, all also dressed in kilts, each in the tartan of their own clans, gently lifted the casket atop their shoulders, linked arms, and slowly marched down the aisle of the little church. Their kilts swayed side to side as they stepped solemnly in synch out the door.

Many of the crowd stayed behind, but close friends and family slowly left the church, walking behind the men, casket held shoulder high, all led by the bagpiper, who played stirring, plaintive music as the group slowly walked up the hill from the church to the graveyard.

Maren couldn't stop crying, and she wasn't even sure why. She had known Hugh and grown to love him, but she hadn't known him long. She felt like a lifetime of pent-up sadness was welling up and spilling out. Maybe it was feeling the deep love of this family for one another and feeling, in some tiny way, a part of it all. Maybe Hugh had felt like the father she'd never had. Maybe it was the slow, sacred procession, walking single file up a narrow path, bagpipe music pulling at all their hearts. Maybe it was watching the man she was falling in love with walk with care and strength, carrying his own father to his grave, an act of such honor and love that it moved her deeply and made her feel proud.

Maybe all those things were pouring out of her at once as she made her way to the graveside atop the hill, overlooking the majesty of the Scottish Highlands.

The vicar spoke some words, and then the piper piped Hugh into the ground, playing as the pallbearers slowly lowered his coffin down. Each person took a handful of dirt and tossed it in. And then, as slowly as they had walked up the hill with the beloved old man, they all now walked away without him.

***

Maren and Sybil went home, and Sybil went to take a nap. It had been a long day for her. Maren lit the fire, for company and comfort more than anything, poured a glass of wine and sat and stared at the flames. She startled when her phone rang. It was Alex.

"Hi, Alex," Maren said gently. She had seen him briefly as everyone had walked back to their cars at the church, given him a hug, but there had been so many people wanting to give their condolences, she didn't want to be in the way.

"Hi," he said, sounding very sad.

"Are you okay?" Maren asked, then she said, "I mean, of course, you're not okay. How are you?"

"I'm all right. Sort of," he said. "We are going to the pub, Ian, Kate, and I, and Charlie and a bunch of others. Just doesnae feel right to sit here on our own. Do ye want to meet me there?" he asked.

Maren was touched, and honored, to be asked. She hadn't been sure how involved she should be at this incredibly hard time. They were lovers, but new lovers.

"I'd love to," she said.

She told him she'd be there in half an hour. First, she asked Sybil if she felt comfortable staying there alone. There was a landline, and Sybil knew where it was, and knew Maren's number. She said she would call her if she needed anything, and she had her cellphone, but she would listen to some television and go to bed early. She knew her way around the cottage well by now and had no trouble doing things for herself.

So Maren changed out of her funeral clothes into jeans and a sweater, went and fed the horses for the night, and left. The spring evening was chilly, and it was drizzling, making the evening outside match the feeling of the day, sad, dreary, dark. But as soon as Maren opened the door to the pub, she smiled and felt a sense of relief. Golden light and warmth greeted her. A fire danced in the stone fireplace, next to which a big white dog lay sound asleep. The pub was full. People were talking and drinking, and Maren felt she'd walked from death back into life. Back into her life.

Alex and his siblings and friends were sitting at several tables pushed together, and he stood and smiled when he saw her and waved her over. He greeted her with a kiss on the lips, which raised a few eyebrows. There had been talk that Alex was seeing the American, but now there was no doubt.

He pulled out the chair next to him and Maren sat. Under the table, Alex reached over and held her hand, resting it on his solid knee. She smiled. More stories of Hugh flowed, and stories of childhoods in the village, times gone by, fishing trips, munro walks, fist fights, and a few lost loves—all the highlights of lives well lived. The whisky also flowed, and after a few stories of Hugh as a single dad, dedicated to his children, always lending a hand to help anyone in need, and generally one of the best men anyone had ever known, Ian got up, and everyone in the pub went quiet. He began to sing.

"Of all the money that ere I had, I spent it in good company. And all the harm I've ever done, alas it was to none but me." He paused and Alex stood, whisky glass in hand, and joined his brother. "And all I've done, for want of wit, to memory now I can't recall, so fill to me the parting glass, goodnight and joy be to you all."

At that point, the entire pub joined in, and the walls almost shook with the sound of the familiar Scottish song. "So fill to me the parting glass, and drink a health whate'er befalls, then gently rise and softly call, goodnight and joy be to you all. Of all the comrades that ere I had they're sorry for my going away. And all the sweethearts that ere I had they'd wish me one more day to stay. But since it fell into my lot, that I should rise and you should not, I gently rise and softly call, goodnight and joy be to you all. Hail to me the parting glass, and drink a health whate'er befalls, and gently rise and softly call goodnight and joy be to you all."

By the time they were done, tears streamed down Maren's cheeks.

When the singing stopped, Alex raised his glass. "To my dad!" and the entire pub raised their glasses and said, "To Hugh!" and everyone took a long pull at their drinks.

Alex sat back down and gave Maren a sad smile, taking her hand again as if holding it was helping him survive the end of this long sad day. She gave his hand a squeeze under the table and smiled back.

***

The next day, Gillian brought Sally over to help with the horses. Gillian looked tired, and Maren asked if she'd like to stay for a cup of tea. She did. Maren put warm scones, butter, and jam on the table out front. The sun was hot for the first time, and it felt blissful on their skin.

She poured the tea, and Gillian said, "I think I'm losing my house."

"What do you mean?" Maren asked, worried. "Losing it how?"

"My landlord told me he's raising the rent. I only get a tiny bit from Sally's dad, and my waitress money is just enough to live on, but I also have to be home for Sally a lot. I barely get by. He's raising it, and I won' be able to pay it. I just don't know what I'm going to do." She started to cry.

"Oh, Gillian, I'm so sorry!" Maren cried.

Gillian had friends in the village. But no family. Maren hoped maybe one of her friends would know of somewhere less expensive.

As if she read Maren's mind. she said, "There are no' a lot of places ta move if I want to keep Sally in the village school, not ones less expensive than ours. I will ask around, but I dinnae ken what to do. I'm already at my wits end most days, working and raising Sally mostly on my own. What an arse he is to raise rent on a single mum. He's a rich man in Edinburgh, doesnae ken any of us."

"That's terrible," Maren said. "I don't know a lot of people, but I will definitely keep my ear out for somewhere. I'm so sorry."

They drank their tea and ate and sat in the sun for a while longer, then Gillian said she had things to do, and she'd be back to pick up Sally in an hour, as usual. Maren gave her friend a hug and went to say hi to Sally in the stables.

Dan and his crew had been hard at work, and the bed and breakfast was almost done. As with most construction projects, in the end, it had cost more than they'd expected. Maren was running out of money. She needed to start getting guests in. And as it neared completion, she was also second-guessing herself. Would people want to stay in her crazy horse inn? She spent many nights tossing and turning, hoping she wasn't being an idiot.

But it was too late now, she'd sunk her life savings into it. So, as the workers put the finishing touches on, painting the drywall, and nailing trim around the bottom of each room, the plumber added the sinks, toilets, and showers to the bathrooms, Maren made flyers and a website and started getting the word out about the Horse and Stone.

She needn't have bothered. When the Sisters of the Stones heard about Maren's idea, they couldn't get a reservation fast enough. Just from their group alone, the B&B was sold out for its opening weekend.

***

A few weeks later, opening night arrived. Maren and Alex had seen each other a few times, but they hadn't seen each other nearly as much as they'd wanted to. And with Hugh's death, there had been so much grief that Alex had needed time alone.

Maren had been busy scouring yard sales and charity shops and had found some charming furniture, headboards, side tables, lamps, and rugs. Then she'd had to spend money on things like new towels, bed linens, and pillows.

Alex decided there needed to be some fanfare to the opening, so that day he brought over a bottle of good champagne.

Sybil had decided the same thing, but her contribution was more unusual. She pulled Maren aside. "Come sit with me, dear. I want to show you how to do something."

Sybil walked outside, using her wooden staff as support. She went behind the cottage, near the herb garden, to an area free of vegetation and trees. She asked Maren to light a small fire, which she did. Then she asked her to pick some nettles.

"Sit, my dear," Sybil said.

Maren lowered herself to the ground next to her aunt. Sybil then produced a beautiful smooth stone that was oval in shape and a light gray color.

"Stones are powerful healing tools," she started. "They are used as talismans, for protection. But they can also be used for healing. We—" she smiled and said, "—meaning those of us who practice the old ways, say the stone should come to you. You'll find it unexpectedly when it wants to work with you. But for a healing stone, you can go and look for it. This one came to me when I was digging in the herb garden. Stones have been used for hundreds of years.

In fact, did you know there is a sacred Scottish stone under the throne on which all the kings and queens of England are coronated, including Queen Elizabeth II? Even King Charles III. It is called the Stone of Scone or the Stone of Destiny. It was used for the coronation of Scottish monarchs for centuries until the English seized it in the 1200s and brought it to London, where it was kept after that. Now it's been returned to Scotland when it's not being used in coronations. But it's still returned to England and placed under the throne at every coronation. How's that for belief in the power of a sacred stone?"

"That's amazing!" Maren said. "I've never heard of that."

"Many haven't," Sybil said. "Many of the old ways still exist, but we just don't hear about them. Anaway, I want to charge this stone with healing energy for the stables. For your guests. For the horses. For yourself. So here is what you do. Ye start by washing the stone in a river and letting it dry in the sun. I have done that already, in the little burn out back. Then you throw the nettles on the fire for clearing the energy."

Following her aunt's instructions, Maren tossed the green plants onto the flames, where they smoked.

"Good. Now place your hands on either side of the stone, flat on the ground," her aunt instructed.

Maren scooted over to the stone and placed her hands alongside it. Sybil then felt around and placed hers on the other side of the stone. "Now, close yer eyes, and connect yer energy to the earth, my dear. Just breathe, see yer hands on the earth, feel the energy of the earth pulsing. Take yer time."

Maren sat, at first not feeling anything and starting to berate herself for doing it wrong. But when she quieted her mind, she did start to feel something. A throbbing, almost like a breath, from the earth, rising in and out of the palms of her hands.

"There ye go," Sybil said, and Maren opened her eyes in surprise. Sybil must have had felt the moment Maren made the connection.

Maren quickly closed her eyes again.

"Now ye ask the earth to fill the stone with its healing and protecting energy," she said, and Maren did so.

They sat a while longer, both charging the stone, until Maren felt the energy start to ebb.

"There. Ye can feel we're done. Now ye thank the earth, and thank the stone, and open yer eyes."

Maren opened her eyes and smiled. She felt grounded and calm, which she hadn't in weeks with the frenzy and expense of the construction. Sybil told her she should place the stone somewhere in the stables, and that, if she got very quiet, the stone would suggest where it wanted to be.

Maren picked up the stone and felt a warmth, a buzzing energy coming from it. She almost dropped it in surprise. Sybil laughed, and Maren knew her aunt was seeing everything.

Maren walked into the stables and wandered down the corridor. In the back, in the tack room, which Maren had converted into an office to welcome and check in guests and run the business of the inn, the stone seemed to want to be placed on the ground, in the corner near the door. Maren placed it there, and somehow, she did feel more protected. She certainly felt a serenity she couldn't explain.

She went back outside and thanked her aunt, who was sitting in the sun, long gray hair blowing in the wind, face up to the sky and a smile on her face. She looked like a thing of both beauty and wildness, and Maren realized that she loved the old woman deeply.

***

At noon, Alex arrived with the champagne. He hadn't been to the stables in the few days, and he wanted a tour. They stood looking up at the large sign over the sliding door that Maren had had made. It was a simple white sign, and in black letters it said, "The Horse And Stone B&B" and in smaller block letters underneath that, "Eat, Heal and Be Merry."

Alex held two champagne flutes, and as he popped the bottle he said, "I've never met anyone like you, lass. Look at this place. How'd ye turn an old barn into a hotel? I mean, I dinnae ken how you even thought of it!" He poured the champagne and toasted, "To the Horse and Stone!"

"To the Horse and Stone!" Maren agreed, and they sipped the crisp, bubbly champagne as Maren pulled open the door.

Alex's mouth fell open. "Good lord, lass, this is incredible!"

Little white lights were strung from the exposed beams of the barn. At the far end of the guest quarters were several soft armchairs tucked on either side of the door separating the horses from the guests. The central corridor of the stables was scrubbed clean, with a long Persian runner rug down the center. On it, a sturdy wooden farm table, large enough to seat twenty people stretched toward the far end. Old wooden chairs lined the sides of the table. In the center were candles, which, on closer inspection, Alex saw were electric candles. Very realistic and safer than an open flame in a barn.

There was a dark red runner down the middle of the table, and white dinner and bread plates, wine and water glasses, and rustic linen napkins tied with twine, placed on the center of each dinner plate. Simple silverware laid beside the plates completed the charming, elegant, earthy, and clean place settings.

Maren led Alex to one of the rooms, which, along with the table, were in the front half of the stables. She opened the door to a stall, which now had floor-to-ceiling walls, and a beautiful wood door, to reveal a bedroom. It held a queen-sized bed, dressed with a white comforter, a tartan blanket folded across the foot of the bed, and new fluffy pillows. Two towels and washcloths were folded neatly on a wooden chair in the corner. There was a small dresser with a lamp on it, and each room had a small heater that looked like a wood stove. The heaters were electric and efficient and cozy. There was a mirror over the dresser, a window on the outside wall, and on the wall across from the bed, one of Sybil's paintings: large, bold, and colorful. Evocative of the power and beauty of the land around them.

Maren then showed him a twin room, furnished the same, just smaller and finally one of the bathrooms, white, clean, and cheerful. At the end of the corridor of rooms, Maren had had a wall framed and drywalled, and a large sliding door installed. That way she, or the guests, could close off the back half of the stables, where the horses were, if they wanted to. Or they could open it and have a good view of them if they preferred that. The horses were in their stalls that day, ready to greet the inaugural guests in just a few hours.

Alex refilled their glasses, and they sat together at the big dining table. Alex said it was all absolutely perfect. And she agreed.

***

Dinner was optional at Maren's B&B. Guests could order their evening meals at the time they made the reservation, to give Maren enough time to plan the menu and get the ingredients. The Sisters, having tasted Maren's delicious, magical meals, wanted dinner both nights of their weekend stay, so Maren's kitchen was full, and she was excited to serve her first meal in the stables. Alex left to give Maren time to get ready, and after she'd showered and dressed, she went to tend to the horses, to calm her nerves as much as anything. She walked down the hall of the barn and could hardly believe it was real. It was cozy, textured, rich, magical, and peaceful all at once. It matched exactly the image she had had in her head, and her eyes welled with tears. She had not only made a *home*—now she was offering a taste of home to travelers too. She had done it. She was inside a life she loved, no longer outside looking in the window of someone else's life.

"What do you think, guys?" Maren asked the horses as she scratched Bang's forehead. The horses looked interested. They had settled down from the commotion of the construction, and they seemed to be used to the change in the stables. But they could also feel Maren's excited energy, maybe even the energy of the visitors set to arrive any minute, and they all had their heads over their stall doors, ears forward, curious to see what was happening.

Maren heard car tires on the gravel, and she felt panic grip her stomach. It was the Sisters. Her first guests, paying good money to stay at the B&B. She had sunk her life savings into this idea. It had to be a success!

She walked out of the barn just as Fiona, Isobel, and the others were getting out of the minivan. She greeted them with a huge smile, as excited as she was nervous.

"Oh, Maren, look at this!" Isobel said, clasping her hands and looking at the B&B sign and the big red potted geraniums Maren had placed on either side of the stable's door.

"Hello! Welcome!" Maren said. "Let me show you to your rooms." She loved the way the words sounded.

Maren slid open the stable door and as the women stepped inside, they gasped.

"Oh, Maren. This is pure magic!" Fiona cried. "How ever did you do this? It's gorgeous!"

Maren smiled and told them about the vision that had just appeared in her head. All she had done was tell the builders what she saw. The Sisters all agreed that that was how the very best ideas always arrived—suddenly, clearly, meant to be.

Sybil followed the woodchip path to the stables. She stood framed by the doorway, long staff in her hand, her red tunic and her long gray hair billowing around her.

The Sisters saw her, and said, "Sybil, how lovely to see you."

Sybil said the same in return.

Maren showed the women—there were six that night in total—to their rooms. She showed them that there was a sideboard against the wall at the foot of the table with a large glass pitcher of filtered water with a few slices of cucumber for freshness and some nuts and dried fruit, in case they needed a little snack. It was two p.m., and Maren said that she would let them settle in and be back in half an hour and help them plan their stay.

When she returned, she asked them, "What would you like to do this afternoon?"

"Seeing the stones would be lovely," Isobel said, speaking for the group. "We thought we would wander up there and have a wee meditation there this afternoon. And then tomorrow, perhaps, we could work with the horses. We've no' done that before. I know you said you do energy work with horses, and we'd love to try that. Other than that, I think we hope to rest and write and read and just be on yer magical bit of land here."

"That sounds wonderful," Maren said. "Would you like me to walk you to the stones?"

"Thank you, dear, but we know how to find them. We are all set for this afternoon."

The women wandered up the path toward the stones, laughing and talking, and Maren went to the kitchen to start prepping for dinner.

At five, Maren went to the stables and put out several bottles of red and white wine on the sideboard, and on the table she placed round slabs of wood she had cut from a felled tree on the farm. She had sanded and rubbed them with olive oil, and now they made beautiful serving boards for appetizers. On one, she laid out several local cheeses, with sprigs of rosemary from her garden tucked around them. There were black and green olives and a mound of fig jam. On another wood plate, she placed crackers and thin slices of homemade crusty bread.

She placed them on the long table and turned on the electric candles. It looked like something out of a storybook.

The women arrived back from their time at the stones a short while later, excited and animated. Maren poured them each a glass of wine, and they sat at the table and in the armchairs and told her about their meditation in the stone circle—powerful, healing, full of visions to interpret and take back into their lives. It was pure magic.

Maren left them to wash up and enjoy their wine and cheese and told them dinner would be served in an hour.

As with any new venture, Maren had already hit some snags. If this were going to work, she was going to need help. At least if people all wanted dinner at the B&B. It was one thing to cook an amazing meal, but to do so while also serving, and making sure guests had everything they needed, checking in on them, running back and forth from cottage to stables—it was going to get tricky. But she would figure it all out as she went. She was good at that.

At six, Maren walked carefully out to the stables carrying an enormous platter. On it were plates, each with perfectly cooked medallions of filet mignon, served atop puréed potatoes with wild mushrooms and a side of crispy Brussel sprouts sautéed in balsamic vinegar. The food arrived to oohs and ahhs from all the women. Maren refilled their wine glasses and then went and sat at the little front office, in case they needed anything during their meal. She loved hearing the women laugh and talk and eat.

For dessert, Maren brought out individual small glass jars filled with Cranachan, the traditional Scottish dessert of oats, raspberries, whisky, honey, and cream. There was actual applause at that. The women loved that Maren had created something truly Scottish to end the meal. When she had cleared all the plates, she left a platter of homemade shortbread biscuits beside the kettle and tea station on the sideboard, placed a glass jar of milk and some glasses out, and left the women for the night, sitting in the soft chairs near the door to the horse stalls, recounting the adventures of the day.

When Maren had cleaned the kitchen and gotten organized for breakfast the next day, she went into the living room and collapsed on the sofa.

Sybil said, "How was it, my dear?"

"Wonderful!" Maren grinned. "They loved it—the rooms, the day, the dinner. It was wonderful. But, boy, I'm beat," she said.

"Yes, help is coming. I feel that. You'll have help soon," Sybil said.

Maren wondered what she meant but knew by now just to trust information that showed up like that. Out of the ethers.

"Well, that's good," she said. She said goodnight and went to bed while Sybil finished listening to the news by the fire.

***

The next day, Maren woke early to start breakfast and realized she needed another frying pan to make the full Scottish breakfast offered with the B&B. She panicked until it occurred to her to check the old cottage behind the oak trees. It had apparently been built by the farmer's son in the early 1900s, to house his new family while he stayed and worked the land with his father. Maren's uncle had occasionally used it if he had visitors, but mostly it had been sitting empty for years.

Obviously, there was a kitchen, so there must be pots and pans. Maren let herself in the cottage, which was dusty and musty smelling, but perfectly intact. She hadn't been in there since the night she'd found Mac inside. The cottage consisted of a living room and a large eat-in kitchen downstairs, with a small bedroom right off the living room that had a small fireplace, which shared a chimney with the living room. There was a bathroom off the bedroom, and then two bedrooms and a bathroom upstairs. Maren walked to the kitchen and went through the cabinets, thrilled to find wonderful old copper pots and pans. She took several back to her cottage, scrubbed them, and got to work on breakfast.

Maren cooked eggs, fried tomatoes, fried mushrooms, baked beans, sausage, black pudding, and toast, and took it out to the stables on a big tray. The women were all up and having coffee they'd made in the pot on the sideboard.

"Look at that scran! Well done, Maren!" Phillipa said as they all sat down to tuck in.

Maren heard a car pull up and left the women to eat while she went to see who it was. It was Gillian. As she often did, Maren had forgotten this was a day for Sally to come by.

"Hi there!" she called out, walking toward their car.

Gillian got out and saw through the open stable door, the women sitting eating at the big table.

"Oh my gosh, Maren, how amazing! You've done a wee bit of work since I've been here." She laughed. "I'm sorry. I didnae ken you'd have guests already. Shall I take Sally home?"

"No, it's great actually," she said, meaning it. "I'm so swamped, I haven't even fed the horses yet." Maren turned to Sally. "Do you think you could feed and water them today all by yourself?"

Sally puffed out her chest. "Yes. I know I can." She trotted off to the stables.

Maren watched Sally fill the feed buckets, while the guests all called out encouragement to her and told her what a good job she was doing.

"Come on inside. I have a few minutes while they're eating," Maren said, and a few minutes later, she and Gillian sat at the kitchen table with a cup of coffee.

"How's things?" Maren asked.

Gillian started to cry. "Not good," she said. "The arse that owns the house said rent is still going up next month, and if I cannae pay, I have to get out. Who puts a single mum out like that? I've looked, but there's nothing in the village I can afford. I found a small flat above a shop in Inverness. But I dinnae want to live in the city, and Sally doesnae ken anyone there. It's a right mess," she said, looking into her coffee dejectedly.

"I'm so sorry, Gillian. I wish there was something I could do. How can your landlord…" Maren trailed off.

Her mind flickered to the back cottage she had just been raiding for pots and pans. It was a perfectly habitable cottage, right there on her farm. Far enough from the main cottage that they wouldn't be under each other' feet. But did Maren want that?

She reined in her normal impulsivity. *Practice being an adult, Maren.* That was a big thing to offer, to have people living on the land with her. But she loved Sally. As Sally had gotten more comfortable there, she ha become a cheerful, gentle helper. And the thought of Gillian moving to a dingy flat away from everyone she knew was more than Maren could bear. She couldn't let Gillian and Sally live like that when she had a cottage sitting empty right on the farm.

Then she had another thought—Gillian was a waitress. Maybe, just maybe, if things really took off, Gillian could help her with running the B&B. That was as much thought as Maren was willing to do. She trusted her body much more than her mind at this point, and her body was giving her a resounding "Yes!" to the idea.

"Gillian, I have an idea."

Gillian burst into tears at Maren's suggestion, then jumped up and hugged her friend hard. She accepted on the spot and said it was like a dream come true. Sybil came in and put the kettle on, as the women told her about the plan. Sybil agreed it was wonderful. They called Sally into the house and told her, and she jumped up and down, cheering, and asked if she could see the cottage right away. Maren said she had to get back to her guests, but that they could wander over and have a look if they liked, and plan on what they'd need to do to get it ready. A deep clean was needed for sure. But it would need furniture and other basics too.

Gillian and Sally went off with springs in their steps toward the cluster of oak trees and the cottage, while Maren went back to the stables.

After breakfast had been cleared away, the women all met in the training ring beside the big pasture. Maren led Laddie into the ring. He was the gentlest and most patient horse Maren had ever met, and Sybil told Maren he was her "familiar." He was an animal spirit, who had a special connection to her. She knew that was right.

The women all stood around as Maren talked about energy work and horses as teachers.

"Horses reflect our energy state back to us. They teach us how to get profoundly grounded and present. And how to trust. The first exercise we're going to do is to have someone come pick the horse's hoof. I'll show you what I mean."

Maren walked slowly beside Laddie and ran her hand calmly down his flank, then down his back leg and in the same unbroken gentle motion, she lifted his hoof and placed it on her bent knee.

"Once you have the hoof up, you'll use the hoof pick to get out the mud and any rocks in there. It feels good to the horses, and it's good for their feet. Who wants to try?"

"I do," a woman named Flora said.

Maren had her come over to Laddie and greet him. Flora was a tall, thin woman, with quick, nervous energy. She was cheerful and enthusiastic, but as soon as she got near Laddie, the horse started to move, taking a few steps to the side. Maren held him gently by a lead rope and calmed him.

Flora dove right in and ran her hand down Laddie and to his leg and tried to lift his foot. It stayed where it was. She tried again, but his foot was firmly planted on the ground. Flora tried flat-out pulling and yanking on the horse's leg, but his foot wouldn't budge. It quickly became apparent that a hundred-and-twenty-pound woman would not be able to force a two-thousand-pound horse's foot off the ground.

Flora growled in irritation. "There's something wrong with him. Why won't he lift it? What's the trick?"

"There's no trick," Maren said. "A horse won't lift his leg unless he wants to. Unless your calm energy matches his calm energy."

"Well, that doesn't seem to be true. I'm calm and he won't lift it," Flora insisted, tugging on Laddie's fetlock again.

"Okay, this is perfect," Maren said. Flora didn't look like she agreed. "Let's step away from Laddie for a minute."

Flora let go of the horse and stepped aside.

"Flora, how do you go about things in your life? Things you want to accomplish."

Flora thought for a minute, then she said, "I decide what I want to do, and I do it. I'm a doer. I don't let anything stand in my way."

"Okay. And let me ask, when things don't go your way, then what do you do?" Maren asked.

Flora had to think longer this time. "I make them go my way, I guess," she said. "I just get more determined, and I don't stop till I get what I want."

"And that has probably been very helpful in a lot of ways in your life, I imagine," Maren said.

"Aye. It has," Flora agreed. "I've built a successful accounting practice in Inverness that way."

"But, here, that isn't working, is it?" Maren said. "With the horse, you can't force. You have to *allow*. And that's so important in life too. Many of us want to *make* everything happen. But it's just as important to be in the flow. To *allow* things to happen. Laddie here is showing you that. Now, let's all of us close our eyes and take a slow deep breath in for a count of three. Hold the breath for a count of three and then exhale for a count of five."

The women did the exercise, and the heightened energy of just a moment before instantly slowed and calmed.

"Let's do it again," Maren said and they did. "Now, picture your bare feet on the earth. Feel the soft earth under them. And picture energy flowing effortlessly from your body into the earth, where the earth cleanses it of any anxiety, and stress, anything negative. And then pure clean energy flows back up into you from the earth."

There was silence for several minutes as the women did this exercise.

Maren then said, "And whenever you are done, you can slowly open your eyes."

When the women opened their eyes, they were all smiling. The energy was totally calm, grounded, and peaceful.

Flora's energy had changed completely. She smiled.

"Okay," Maren said, "Now, if you're willing, let's try the hoof again, Flora."

Flora walked slowly over to Laddie, laid a hand softly on his flank and ran it down to his leg and to his hoof, which she effortlessly lifted and placed on her bent knee. She looked over at Maren and the other women with a huge, surprised smile.

Maren gave her the pick and she cleaned Laddie's hoof, before gently letting go. He put his foot back down.

"I can't believe it! It worked!" Flora said.

"It always does." Maren smiled. "How does your energy feel right now?"

"Calm," Flora said. "Happy."

"That's the gift of the horse. They teach us how to stay in this calm, easy energy. And when we do, life is so much easier. Things that are meant to be for us, show up, and we don't have to bang our heads against a wall to make them happen. Horses live their whole lives in the flow. And they teach us how to remember how to do it. Children do it naturally, but most of us have it 'taught' out of us. But we can relearn it. It's easy really. Once you know how it feels, it gets easier and easier to return to that state."

The women were thrilled at the lesson, and one by one, they all did the hoof exercise, with different horses. Then they did an exercise where one woman at a time got very grounded and very quiet and connected her energy to the horse. Slowly, the horse would follow her around the ring, in whatever direction she walked. As she moved about the circle, the horse, calmly and slowly, walked with no rope, just an energetic connection, everywhere the woman went.

The women all said they felt excited and enlightened by getting even more in touch with their own energy and power.

Energy work was tiring, so the women all had cold sandwiches for lunch and decided to read or nap afterward. In the afternoon, they wandered the garden, and then, eventually, made their way back to the stone circle for a sunset ceremony.

For dinner, Maren served locally caught salmon with dill and lemon, risotto and asparagus, with chocolate brownies and ice cream for dessert. The next day, there were scones for breakfast, and soon it was time for the women to leave. They all hugged, and there were even some tears, as the Sisters of the Stone said it was one of the most magical weekends of their lives.

CHAPTER 16

As Summer wore on, word about the Horse and Stone spread—the healing stone circle, the horses, the magical land, the delicious meals, and the unusual bed and breakfast. Maren suddenly found that she was booked solid for the next month. Gillian and Maren spent hours scrubbing the back cottage clean, and Gillian had hired movers to move her and Sally's things in. Soon the two were settled in at the cottage, thrilled to have endless room for Sally to play and explore, thrilled to have the horses nearby, and thrilled to have a home they didn't have to be scared they were going to lose. Gillian had given notice and went to part-time at the restaurant where she waitressed, and had begun helping Maren with serving the food, helping the guests, and cleaning between visitors. Gillian told Maren it was the happiest she had been in many years.

Maren's garden was a thing to behold. Rows of lettuce, kale, beans, peppers, tomatoes, potatoes, onion, carrots, and all sorts of other vegetable filled the tidy garden. The large circular herb garden she had planted was flourishing too. Sage, rosemary, thyme, lavender, dill, parsley, mint, chamomile, and others grew abundantly. Later in the summer, Maren planned to pick and dry the herbs and sell them in little muslin bags to guests.

Alex's farm was also in full swing, with the hills on his farm dotted with sheep, half of them sweet lambs, quickly growing. And his vegetable were impressive. His wasn't a garden, but a farm. Fields of vegetable grew in long rows, and Alex didn't tend them with a hoe, like Maren, but with a tractor. It was a busy time of year, and they were all loving it. Alex and Maren saw each other as often as they could. But it wasn't often enough for either of them.

One afternoon, Maren was feeding the chickens, having just spent the morning weeding the garden. She was covered in mud, surrounded by chickens, and happy as she'd ever been. She heard car tires on the gravel, but wasn't expecting any guests, so she went to see who it was. There in the driveway was Alex, dressed not like a farmer, but in nice blue trousers, a button-down shirt, and light jacket. He still managed to look rugged, even in more formal clothes, and Maren felt the now-familiar flutter in her heart, and warmth in her body she felt every time she saw him.

Wiping her hands on her jeans, Maren said, "Hi! I didn't expect to see you today." She crossed the yard to kiss him, careful not to touch him and get him dirty.

"I know you didnae. Now go inside and pack a weekend bag," he said with his crooked smile.

"What?" Maren said, confused.

"It's been so busy, and I ken I've been distracted since my father died. And we've no had more than a few hours together here and there, so I planned this with Sybil. She said you've no guests for two days, so I'm taking you away."

Maren was thrilled. Adventure! The unknown. She realized suddenly how much she had missed those things in her lovely, but steady, life in Scotland. Plus, it was so romantic.

She was about to throw her arms around him, but remembered the dirt and stopped. They both laughed and settled for another quick kiss.

"Okay, oh my gosh, this is so exciting. Thank you, Alex!" Maren said.

She ran inside to quickly shower and pack a bag. As she was packing, she felt a sort of panic rising. Anxiety. It was such a terrible feeling. It had been her constant companion growing up, and she had managed to escape it for years by having a life so exciting and chaotic that there wasn't room for anxiety. But now, calm, safe and about to go away for a wonderful weekend with a man she loved, she felt it. The tightening in her chest, the shallow breathing, the feeling of dread that she couldn't put a finger on. Then the anxiety made her irritable. She didn't want to feel any of these things, and she thought for a minute she wasn't going to go.

She zipped up her little suitcase and sat on the bed. Why was she suddenly feeling this?

It didn't take long for her to answer her own question. It was because life was so good. It was because she was falling in love. It was because she had so much to lose. All the years she had run from city to city, without a home, without lasting relationships…there was a safety in it. An empty safety, but a safety nonetheless. No one could hurt her if she wasn't attached to anyone or anywhere. Now she was attached in a hundred ways— to the farm, to her business, to Sybil, Gillian and Sally, and of course, to Alex. There was such vulnerability in trying. In loving. It terrified her. It made her want to take her suitcase and run away from her whole life.

Instead, she took some deep breaths and told herself that she was right. She cared so much about her life now that she *could* get hurt. There was no way of knowing what might happen. But she also told herself that she would be okay. That safety might not actually come from never risking her heart. It might come from knowing that no matter what happened, she would be okay. She knew it was true, and she hoped that her heart would believe it and stop flopping around in her chest like a fish out of water.

Half an hour later, she went downstairs, where she found Alex, Sybil, and Gillian at the kitchen table having tea. They all smiled as she walked in.

"You all knew about this?" Maren said, laughing.

"We did!" Gillian said. She and Sybil looked very satisfied at having helped pull off the surprise.

"Thank you!" Maren said and she hugged each of them.

Maren hadn't even thought of it when Gillian and Sally moved onto the farm, but it did also mean Maren could leave now and then and not have to worry about Sybil. It was a wonderful setup for everyone. Sybil had become like a mother figure to Gillian, and she and Sally had a special relationship.

Sally was very drawn to the quiet but powerful old woman. Maybe because she was a quiet but powerful little girl.

Alex and Maren said their goodbyes, and Alex carried Maren's little suitcase to his car and they drove off.

"Do I get to know where we are going?" Maren said, giddy as a child.

"Edinburgh," Alex said.

"Oh my gosh, no way! I've never been there. I've always wanted to go!" Maren said.

"I found somewhere ye've never been?" Alex said, joking. "Mission accomplished!

They drove in comfortable silence for a while, and Maren suddenly asked, "Who's taking care of the farm?"

"Charlie," Alex said. "He's staying at the farm for two days for me. He's a good friend." Alex suddenly looked sad. "My dad was old, he wasna up all night with the sheep or breaking his back in the fields, but I didnae realize how much I relied on him till he was gone."

Now it was Maren's turn to reach over and hold Alex's hand. "I'm so sorry."

Alex turned quickly and smiled a sad smile.

Maren continued, "You must miss him terribly. I know I didn't know him long, but I absolutely loved your father. He was special. I don't think there are many men like him left. Well, I guess there are. There are you and Ian. I see him in you both so much." Maren realized for the first time that she did. That one of the things she was growing to love about Alex was that he was both a slightly wild-feeling Highlander, as well as a total gentleman she knew she could trust. It was a completely intoxicating mix of traits. "And Charlie. He's a good one too," she added with a smile.

"Thank ye, lass," Alex said. "That makes me verra happy to hear. I can only hope to remind people of my dad. You're right, he was a special man. The farm isna the same without him. It feels very big, and very empty. Even though he didnae talk much, he was always there."

Maren didn't know what else to say, so she just squeezed his hand. Alex raised her hand to his lips and kissed it. They drove on in silence.

Edinburgh was pure magic. As soon as they parked the car and got out, Maren could feel it. The buildings were all stone, some dark with age and soot and smoke. Others were painted bright colors, a vibrant pink or a bright blue, which she hadn't expected. She still wasn't used to seeing in color. She was surprised to find that color actually affected her mood. These bright pinks and blues made her happy, almost giddy. It was an unexpected effect of the gift of seeing color. Other buildings were clean and gray and stately, like the elegant Georgian row house in front of which they were parked. The house had once been a private home, a three-story building with two windows on each floor, exactly the same as the other houses in the long row of attached homes on this upscale street. Now it was a boutique hotel.

Alex got their bags out of the trunk then went to Maren's side and whispered, "Look." He pointed over her shoulder.

When she turned around, she gasped. There was a clear view, high on a hill, of Edinburgh Castle. Dark, powerful, and so dripping in history Maren could actually feel the stories, the ghosts, the history pulsing from it. The castle looked like it grew right out of the enormous rock on top of which it sat, watching over Edinburgh and the Pentland Hills and all the land below.

"Oh, Alex, thank you for this!" Maren threw her arms around him and kissed him.

Alex laughed and carried the suitcases up the front steps and into the hotel.

A cheerful, round-faced woman checked them in, and they carried their bags up two flights of stairs to their rooms. There was a large bedroom with king sized bed, a luxurious tiled bathroom with a clawfoot tub and separate waterfall shower, and then a living area with a huge window overlooking the street below, and, in the distance, the castle.

As Maren stood at the window, Alex came over and stood behind her, putting his arms around her waist and kissing her neck.

"Beautiful," is all Maren could say, enchanted by the ancient city.

"Aye, ye are, lass," Alex said, and Maren smiled.

There was a moment where the electricity that pulsed through them sparked, and Maren turned and kissed Alex. The kiss was growing hungry when Maren, using all her inner strength, pulled away. "Can we go explore? And later…" She smiled suggestively.

Alex groaned but agreed. The summer evening was warm, and they held hands and wandered with no particular destination. Tomorrow, they'd visit the castle. Tonight was for exploring. They walked to the Royal Mile.

"Do ye ken why it's called the Royal Mile?" Alex asked.

"No idea," Maren said.

"It's the distance from Edinburgh Castle to Holyroodhouse, the royal palace at the bottom of the hill. That's how the mile came to be. It's this distance here, castle to palace."

"That's fascinating, I had no idea!" Maren said.

They walked the long street. There were plenty of tourist gift shops, but there were also tiny winding alleys, medieval buildings set crookedly atop others, and side streets that fell away from the Royal Mile and twisted like serpents away from the straight, bright castle road. Maren wanted to explore the side streets, and as soon as they stepped off the bustling Royal Mile, they were nearly alone on a side street, and the feeling immediately shifted. Magic.

On this quiet side street, they came across a shop that had beautiful and mystical things in the bowed bay window. Amulets and crystals and old books.

"Ooh, let's go in there!" Maren said.

Inside were runes, the ancient Norse alphabet used to divine the future. There were healing stones and pouches of herbs and books on Scottish witchcraft and much more. Half an hour later, they walked out, Maren carrying a bag full of treasures and gifts for everyone back on the farm.

"Okay, now I want to show you somewhere," Alex said.

He led her back over the Royal Mile and down some long, steep stone stairs, as if they were descending into another Edinburgh. At the foot of the hill on which the castle sat, they emerged into a large, open, cobblestone square. It was closed to traffic and felt like the town center of another time. The square was surrounded by little shops and pubs, and children ran around in the evening sunlight. It was a hidden little city within the city.

"This is Grassmarket," Alex said. "It was a huge market way back in the 1500s. For centuries it was a horse and cattle market, presumably with grassy areas for them to graze on, hence the name. But all sorts of things were sold here. That street is called Candlemaker Row, that one is Cowgate," he said pointing.

In the evening light it was beautiful. Ancient, inviting, and vibrant.

"Let's get a wee dram," he suggested, and they walked along the square, trying to choose from the many wonderful-looking pubs and restaurants.

They decided on a pub called The Last Drop. They got a table in front of the pub, set out on the sidewalk, and with a stunning view of Edinburgh Castle, which they could see in the gap between two streets, rising way above them, ominous and powerful. The sun was just setting, and the sky was a mellow orange. Maren was trying to take a mental photo of this moment to save forever. A photo that included the smells of the city and sounds of people talking and eating and children laughing and running; the slight, warm breeze on her face; the colors of the sky behind the castle; and Alex. Alex looking at her with love and amusement as he watched her childlike enthusiasm for this city, as she had for most things. She wanted to save the moment forever.

They both ordered whisky—good whisky—and Alex ordered haggis and neeps, mashed turnips. The traditional Scottish meal that most non-Scots found horrendous, but in which Scots took great pride.

"What exactly is it?" Maren asked.

"Well, I want you to try it, so I'm not sure I should tell ye," he said, smiling.

Maren turned to the waiter. "Okay, I'll take the haggis and neeps, too, thank you."

The waiter walked away, as Alex exclaimed, "Braw, lass!"

Maren laughed out loud. "Okay, now spill the beans. What am I about to eat?"

"Haggis is sheep's heart, liver, and lungs, ground up and mixed with oats, onion, and spices, and then stuffed in the sheep's stomach and boiled," he told her. "Though now they usually use a manmade casing to boil it. It's the traditional Scottish scran!" He beamed with pride after describing the most disgusting dish Maren had ever heard of.

"Oh my God, I think I need to change my order." She laughed through her grimace.

"Och, nae. Too late now, lass!" he said, and he raised his glass, "Sláinte!" he said. They both downed their whisky and ordered more.

The haggis was surprising. It had a strong taste, but not a bad one. The spices and onion helped. And not thinking about what it was actually made of helped too. But Maren declared she actually liked it, and Alex seemed proud of her for it.

After dinner, the pair walked back to the hotel, holding hands, through the dark streets of Edinburgh. Full, slightly drunk, and happy. In the hotel, Maren took a hot bath. It had been a long day, and it felt delicious to soak away the travel and the city.

When she came out, wrapped in the thick terry hotel robe, she found Alex on the sofa in the sitting room, head back, sound asleep. Maren was disappointed, but she laughed anyway.

He was so handsome and looked so sweet asleep like that. She went to put a throw blanket on him, and the slight movement woke him. He looked up at Maren, holding the blanket over him, and smiled with a mix of affection and desire.

He took the blanket out of her hand and put it down, then pulled her onto his lap, put his hands on either side of her face and kissed her. Softly. Teasingly. His tongue flickering, then disappearing, until Maren was hungry for more.

Then the teasing stopped, as Alex, too, wanted more. The playfulness disappeared as his kiss grew forceful. Maren straddled him, and they kissed again, her hair falling over his face until, in one swift move, he lifted her, stood and carried her to the bedroom.

He laid Maren gently on the bed and kneeled over her, unbuttoning and taking off his shirt. Maren's breath caught as she took in his gorgeous, muscular chest, flat belly, and thick, strong arms. He unbuckled his belt then lowered himself onto her. Her mouth opened and met his greedily. He slowly untied Maren's robe and pushed it open. His rough farmer's hand ran up Maren's body, finding her breast and cupping it. The feeling of his hand on her body took her breath away.

Alex kissed the side of Maren's neck and she let out a small moan. His lips moved down from her neck and slowly, exquisitely, moved down her body.

***

They awoke in the morning to the sun streaming through the window. They were naked, satiated, and hungry. After a long, sleepy kiss good morning, they both took showers and headed out to see the castle.

They walked the steep, uneven cobblestones to the entrance of the castle. Images of people in medieval dress wandering outside the castle, of soldiers armed and alert in the castle, of prisoners hidden in the bowels of the building all appeared unbidden in Maren's mind's eye, like quick reels in a movie.

"It dates from the 1100s," Alex said. "Though people have lived here since the Iron Age. The history is thick here."

Maren felt it physically, the thickness, the history. They walked to the top of the castle, to the cannons still pointed from inside the walls, as they had sat for centuries. There were ancient stairs worn down in the middle of each step by feet walking them for over a thousand years. Maren liked to imagine the people, the feet, the things that must have been around them as they shuffled up the stairs, century after century.

At the top of the castle, near the cannons, Alex stopped. "I'll tell you one more witch story, and then I'll stop."

"No, don't stop!" Maren said. "I love these stories."

"Alright, well, most people havenae heard of Agnes Sampson," he paused as if expecting a response.

"I haven't heard of her," Maren said, shaking her head.

"She lived in the 1500s. She was a midwife and an herbal healer. And she used the old ways, stones for protection, amulets. But mostly, she was a midwife and herbalist. And a Christian. She was smart enough to know that you wouldna survive if you weren't Christian. And she probably did believe. But, like most cultures, back then, the Scots combined their ancient pagan ways with Christianity. Well, she became more and more powerful, and the men in the church didn't like it. And so, one day, she was accused of witchcraft. She denied it passionately, but they did awful things to her. I won't even tell ye what they did to try and get a witch to confess." Alex shuddered.

"Thank you. I don't think I want those images in my head," Maren said.

"Of course, after enough pain, people will say anything. So to get it all to stop, she said that she was a witch, and she told a story of hundreds of witches performing dark magic and conjuring storms, one that almost killed the king of Scotland, who was at sea when it hit. Agnes's case, and the story she told, is what sparked the whole witch frenzy that led to thousands of women being burned at the stake in Scotland, England, and even in Salem, Massachusetts, near your hometown. They burned her at the stake, right here atop the castle on the 28th of January 1591."

Maren shuddered. The horrors that history held were unthinkable. "My gosh, the things women endured," was all Maren could say, and again, her mind went to her aunt, who had suffered a modern-day equivalent of this witch trial and imprisonment.

They shook off the dark mood by wandering the winding castle, visiting a tiny graveyard, just for the dogs of the soldiers who had lived there—which Maren thought was wonderful—and soaking up the more cheerful stories of the castle.

The two finally made their way back down from Castle Rock, along the Royal Mile, for lunch and a bottle of wine. They went back to the hotel after lunch and made love again, fell asleep, then woke in time to go out for a wonderful dinner at an upscale restaurant near Princes Street, the main shopping street in Edinburgh. Maren and Alex both wanted to taste some new dishes, get ideas for their farm and B&B, and to enjoy a good meal.

After dinner, they wandered the streets, enjoying the gray magic of Edinburgh. That night, their lovemaking felt different. It was passionate, but there was a depth and tenderness that had not been there before. Maybe it was from having spent two whole days and nights alone together. That time having taken them to a new level of intimacy. But that night, as they made love slowly, looking into each other's eyes, Maren knew something had shifted. She knew she loved him. It made her almost weep with happiness. And it terrified her.

When Alex and Maren arrived back at the cottage the next day, Gillian and Sybil wanted to hear all about the trip. Alex had to get back to his farm, to relieve Charlie and check on everything, so he said his goodbyes and left Maren to fill them in on the details.

As he drove away, Gillian said, "You look different. The pair of you."

Maren grinned. "Yes, it feels different." She linked arms with her friend and went to tell her all about it.

***

Life moved on in a beautiful rhythm. Days were spent feeding chickens, gardening, taking care of the horses, and running the B&B which, after an Instagram post, had gone viral and now had a long waiting list of people wanting to visit from as near as Inverness and as far as California. Maren had no idea how it was possible she now owned such a wildly successful inn and restaurant, but Sybil told her it was because she was doing what she was meant to. When we did that, things flowed in a way that could seem almost miraculous, she explained, and Maren knew she was right.

One evening, before a new round of guests was due to arrive the next day, Alex came over for dinner. Maren served them all warm goat cheese and beet salad on arugula to start, followed by duck confit. Alex had pulled the big kitchen table out into the garden, as it was a beautiful, warm, sunny evening. The table was laid with a white cotton tablecloth and there was a pitcher filled with flowers in the center. There were candles on the table and half-empty glasses of wine. Sally ran around the garden with Mac chasing her. The horses were in the field, peacefully grazing. Maren looked down the long table at Sybil, Gillian, and Alex, all talking and laughing. Dirty plates with the crumbs of a sumptuous meal and empty bottles of wine and whisky sat atop the table, with Sally and Mac running circles around them and Maren's heart felt so full she thought it might burst. This motley crew of abandoned horses, a lost relative, a single mum, a happy little girl, and a gorgeous Highland lover, were all hers. This unlikely group of people, this found family, the farm nestled in the hills of Scotland, the flourishing business, she couldn't believe how lucky she was to be right there, in that moment, with these people.

I did it. I made a life. One that was quirky and magical and beautiful. Exactly as it should be. She felt tears well in her eyes.

Sybil reached over and squeezed Maren's hand. Unable to see her emotion, but able to feel it, clear as day. Maren squeezed the bony, beautiful hand back.

***

Summer was going by quickly. It was so busy that the days began to blur together. Alex was in high farm production, with all the work involved in growing organic vegetables of a quality and quantity that top restaurants demanded. And now with the sheep shearer on his farm, expertly cutting the hot fleeces off the sheep ready to be processed and turned into Highland wool.

Maren was busy with her home and garden and bed and breakfast. Sybil had been busy painting, and now she sometimes also accompanied guests to the stone circle and gave little talks about Highland magic, pagan ways, rituals and myths and legends. She was becoming known for these little sacred tours, and she loved being able to share the magic she'd had to hide for so many years.

As Maren got used to running the inn and the farm, things settled down and became routine. And as soon as that started to happen, Maren felt the stirring inside that scared her. She woke a few times, in her perfect life she had so painstakingly built, feeling frustrated. Irritated. Making breakfast for guests…again. Some days she didn't feel like doing it and it seemed a chore.

With alarm, she recognized the feeling. She wanted her freedom. She longingly remembered quitting a job and hopping on a plane to a new life any time she felt like it. The thrill of arriving in a new city and not knowing a thing or a soul there. The possibilities. The potential. It was always about the potential.

But now that the potential had been made real, Maren felt itchy. Almost like she was trapped.

And the more she cared about Alex, the more she found herself finding reasons to be angry with him. Over nothing. She knew it was over nothing. She knew it was really that she was terrified to be so in love with someone, to be so vulnerable.

But still, she felt restless and irritated. She told herself this was ridiculous. She reminded herself that many of the days and nights she'd been traveling, she had been lonely. She'd felt lost. She had hated that she had no real life. She wanted children, a home, community.

But the siren song of no responsibilities began to sing to her. And it made her very nervous.

CHAPTER 17

Maren and Alex were spending several nights a week together now, sometimes at the cottage, often at his farm, with Gillian keeping an eye on Sybil. One evening, they were in Alex's kitchen, and Alex was cooking dinner.

"You shouldn't heat the oil up that much. It ruins the meat," Maren chided, hearing the nasty tone in her voice and hating herself for it.

"Oh," Alex said, turning to her, surprised. "Okay, no worries. I'll turn it down."

"It's too late, you've already put the meat in. I mean, we can eat it, but it's not the way to cook meat. It'll be like a leather boot."

"It'll be fine. I have actually cooked before, ye know," he said, smiling, clearly trying to shift the energy.

"I'm just saying, you do things so fast and furious, you make more mistakes. I mean, it's like when you were talking to that guy who wanted to buy the fleeces off the sheep this summer. You were so overly talkative, you totally turned him off."

Now Alex turned off the stove and turned around to face Maren, frowning. "What are you talking about?"

"That guy. I mean, I know you don't want my advice, but he clearly just wanted to make a deal with you, and you were talking his ear off for, like, an hour." She huffed out a frustrated breath. "He was getting annoyed, and you didn't even see it. I mean, did he even want to buy the fleeces after that?"

"I dinnae ken why you're saying this. First of all, yes, he did buy the fleeces, and he said he had a grand time visiting the farm. Second, I know how to cook a steak. Lass, you're wonderful, but ye do this all the time lately," he said, now sounding annoyed himself. "I've no' said anything before, because I think you mean well, but you're constantly telling me what to do or telling me I'm doing something wrong.

I did manage to survive, and be verra successful, for a long time before you came along, ye ken," he said.

"Fine, do what you want," Maren said. "You can never take criticism. You're so defensive."

Then feeling anger boiling up, unsure why she was this upset about something as stupid as a steak, she stood up. "I'm going to go home. I have an early start tomorrow."

She grabbed her bag and drove home.

***

Alex called Maren the next day, but she didn't answer. He texted her saying he was sorry if he had seemed mad the night before, but also asking what was going on, why she had been so angry. Maren didn't reply. She was busy with guests, who seemed very high maintenance, wanting snacks or fresh towels constantly. She snapped at one of the guests once and found herself in a terrible mood the whole two days of their stay.

Finally, when the guests had left, Sybil said, "Maren, my dear, come sit with me."

Maren followed her to the garden, where they sat with glasses of wine.

"What's going on my dear?" Sybil finally asked.

"Nothing," Maren said curtly. Then she felt guilty talking to her aunt like that, so she added, "I'm just tired."

"Well, I dinnae believe you, dear. What's really going on?"

Maren sat in silence for a long time, trying to figure out what *was* going on. Why, lately, she was irritated by the guests fulfilling her dream, by Alex whom she loved, by the life that meant everything to her. She knew the answer, she just didn't want to feel it.

Finally, she said, "It's who I am. I don't like to need people. I don't like to risk my heart. I don't want to get hurt. And I don't want to do things I don't want to do. I want my freedom. That's all. I'm trapped, and I hate it."

Now it was Sybil's turn to sit in silence. After a long while, she smiled lovingly. "Ahh. I see."

Maren blew out a frustrated breath. "What does that mean?" She'd expected her aunt to tell her she was wrong or give her some sage advice.

"It means, I think yer right. I do think yer trapped. But, no' by the farm, or Alex. I think you're trapped by your little heart that you never took the time to heal, my dear. Until you heal it, yer right, you are trapped. You'll destroy anything you love, because yer broken heart tells you to do so."

These were the words of wisdom Maren thought she'd wanted. But she didn't like them. Because they were true.

"I have to go," Maren said. She got up and walked down the garden path.

There it was. Walking away. Walking away from anything that didn't feel good. Like a child.

She walked to the stone circle and sat for a long time, until it grew dark. But all she could hear were her own thoughts of all these people relying on her, everyone demanding things from her, Alex annoying her. She'd hoped for a miraculous healing, but her own dedication to her angry thoughts had made that impossible.

Back at the cottage, Sybil had gone to bed. Maren sat in the living room and checked her social media accounts. The guests who had just left the B&B had left a bad review.

"The B&B is adorable, and the stone circle amazing, but the owner seemed short-tempered, and we felt uncomfortable asking for things from her, which, in the end, ruined the weekend for us."

Her first bad review. Who the hell were those boring old ladies to be publicly criticizing her? They could go to hell. Everyone could go to hell and leave her alone!

Maren drank too much wine and fell asleep on the sofa.

At midnight, her phone rang.

"Maaaaren!" she heard a woman yelling into the phone, the background incredibly noisy with what sounded like music and a crowd.

"Hello?" Maren said.

"It's Maddy!" the voice yelled. "From New Orleans!"

Maren had to think for a minute. Then she remembered her birthday Maddy had been her dancing, drinking, and general mayhem partner.

"Oh my gosh, Maddy, how are you?" Maren said, sitting up.

"I'm awesome. I cannot believe you are living in the middle of no where in Scotland, I heard through the grapevine you were living in the Highlands! I found your number by Googling you. You have a hotel That's nuts! Want to meet in London?" she asked.

"Meet in London? When?" Maren said, feeling suddenly excited. Why not? She deserved a break. Gillian could run the inn for a few days.

"Next week. I'm in Berlin right now, and I'm coming to London for a few days, then heading to Turkey. Want to go to Turkey too!?"

Now she had Maren's full attention. Turkey. Exotic, adventurous, unknown. Yes, she wanted in on this plan! No more scrubbing dishes and being criticized by Alex and B&B guests.

"Wow, maybe. That sounds amazing!" Maren said.

"Okay, well it's super loud in this nightclub," Maddy said, laughing. "I'll call you in a few days, and we'll make a plan!"

"Okay. I mean I'm not totally sure I can get away but call me. It sounds great," Maren said.

They got off the phone, and Maren was buzzing. The call of the wild, she laughed to herself. She hadn't made anyone here any promises. Well, maybe to Sybil, she had. But Gillian loved living on the farm, Maren could disappear for a week. Or a month. Or a year. They'd be fine without her.

And she desperately wanted to *feel* like she'd be fine without them.

There were no guests expected for the next two days. Mondays and Tuesdays the B&B was closed, Maren had quickly found she needed the days off to restock, clean, and also have a moment to rest. Maren spent all Monday in the stables, giving the rooms a deep clean. After a few hours, she was exhausted.

She turned on the old electric kettle in the stable's little front office to make tea and slumped down on the floor near the horses' stalls. Star slowly clomped in from the field and bent her enormous head down to snuffle Maren's hair. Maren smiled and reached up to rub the horse's nose. Star didn't leave. She stayed standing next to Maren, relaxed, head hanging down like she was half asleep. Horses knew when their people needed company.

"I don't know what to do," she said to the horse. "Why do I feel so restless? I mean…Turkey? I've always wanted to go to Turkey."

Star simply reached into the open stall next to her and pulled a mouthful of hay out of the string bag and chomped contentedly. Maren found the horse's disinterest soothing.

Eventually, Maren got up and walked back to the cottage, ready for a shower and to change out of her cleaning clothes. When she got out of the shower, Maren looked out the little bathroom window and screamed.

"Fire!" She pulled on her dirty clothes from the bathroom floor and ran downstairs yelling, "Fire! The stables are on fire!"

Maren grabbed her phone and dialed 999.

As she raced to the stables she screamed again, and Gillian came out of her cottage. "Oh my God!"

"I called 999, the firefighters are on their way!" Maren yelled as she instinctively ran to make sure the horses were out of the building.

"I'll call Alex!" Gillian said.

The horses were all safely on the far edge of the field, their instincts making them run as far as possible from the flames.

Maren got to the front of the stables. Her office was engulfed in flames. She got the hose and turned it on full blast, aiming it at the base of the flames, but the fire was spreading quickly. Gillian retrieved a bucket of water and ran and threw it toward the flames, but it was so hot she couldn't get close enough and it landed on the grass.

"Throw water on the parts of the barn not near the flames, to stop the spread!" Maren yelled, and Gillian raced back to the spigot and filled another bucket and went into the stables from the horse's end, which was untouched by the fire so far. She threw the water onto the ground there, dampening it. She did this over and over again, wetting the walls of the horse stalls as best she could.

A few minutes later Alex came roaring up the driveway and leaped out of his car. Maren was coughing from the smoke, and Alex took the hose from her and told her to take a break. Soon, the fire department arrived with a huge tank truck filled with water. The men unwound a thick canvas hose and blasted water at the stables.

Alex stood back out of the way and pulled a now-sobbing Maren to him and wrapped his arms tightly around her. She buried her head in his shoulder and cried.

Thankfully, the firefighters were able to put the fire out quickly. But it had taken a while for them to arrive at the remote farm, and the damage was substantial. No one was allowed inside just then, but Maren could see the front of the stables had been burned, black timbers visible. The walls were gone, burned to ash, the office, entryway, the first part of the corridor, and the first one of the B&B rooms were destroyed. Maren was sure there would be smoke damage to the rest of the place.

A firefighter came out of the wrecked barn. "Looks like it started with the electric kettle. A short circuit, or old wire, maybe."

"What?" Maren remembered she had put the kettle on, then forgotten about it, going inside to shower. "But it was automatic, it was supposed to shut itself off after the water boiled," she protested.

"They can malfunction and not shut off. Or the cord can get frayed. It does happen, I'm afraid," he said to her matter-of-factly.

The firefighters coiled their hoses, collected their things and, after Maren and everyone else thanked them profusely, they left.

Maren, Alex, Gillian, Sally, and Sybil remained, staring in shock at the blackened stables.

Maren started to cry again. "What am I going to do? I sunk my life savings into this. I can't fix it."

"Your insurance will cover it, lass," Alex said gently.

"I don't have insurance. I was going to get some this fall, when I had the money," Maren sobbed, furious with herself for, once again, expecting the best and not planning for any other possibility.

"You don't have insurance?" Alex asked, clearly now deeply worried.

"No. I just said I didn't. I really don't need you making me feel like an idiot right now," she said, then stormed off into the house and to her room.

Maren stayed in her room that night, though everyone tried to convince her to come downstairs. Sybil finally said that she clearly just needed some

time to be alone. So, late that evening, after tending to the horses and trying to calm them by feeding and watering them on schedule, Alex went
back to his farm, and Gillian and Sally to their cottage.

The next morning Maren was gone.

***

In London, Maren met Maddy at a packed bar. She had brought some of
the clothes from her old life, tight tops and high heels. She did her hair and
put on makeup, and it felt nice. She thought back on the night of the fire.
She had called Gillian and told her she was leaving. Gillian had agreed to
look after things there, including Sybil. There wouldn't be any guests now,
obviously. She asked Gillian to tell Sybil she was sorry. And Alex…Alex.
She had simply texted him. That she had lost everything and she was going away. She didn't say if it was for a week, or a month. Or forever. She
knew it was cruel. She knew she was dismissing what they had like it had
meant nothing. And suddenly her mind flashed back to the last life-chang-
ing event, the motorcycle crash. And how Trey had so easily walked away.
What she had with Alex was worlds different than that. She loved Alex.
But it all felt like a mess. She cried as she thought about everyone on the
farm, and she felt shame at her childish recklessness. But she pushed those
thoughts away. What good did those thoughts do? Instead, she headed out
for the night to dance and drink. And not think. And most of all, not feel.

Maren and Maddy greeted each other with squeals and hugs and proceeded to drink several cocktails too many and then go out dancing. They
ended up back in Maddy's hotel room, falling asleep at three a.m. and
waking the next day with headaches but ready for a new adventure.

Maren loved not knowing what would happen that day. Not being be-
holden to anyone or anything. They had a full English breakfast, the milky

tea and greasy meal reviving them. Then they wandered to the Tate Gallery to see an exhibit, and later decided to go to a new popular neighborhood near Greenwich Park, where they had dinner and then went to another bar.

Maddy ended up disappearing into the night with a handsome man they'd met at the bar, leaving Maren to take a cab back to the hotel. Maren climbed in bed and felt lonely. Her mind flickered back to the horses. Were they ok? Did they notice she'd gone? What would Sybil be thinking about her, having run off. Maren shut her mind off, refusing to feel the sadness and anxiety reaching for her. She turned on her side and hugged her pillow and fell asleep.

The next day, Maren and Maddy boarded a plane to Turkey. Maren had saved some money from the B&B, but it was disappearing quickly. She'd need to land a job somewhere. She'd wait tables, or if she was lucky, teach English for a while. But Maddy would need to do the same, so that wouldn't be a problem. That's how travelers survived.

Maren knew she was being supremely irresponsible and even ridiculous. But thoughts of the destroyed stables, like a huge tangible sign of her failure, along with the shame she felt, and now the fear when she thought about Alex and how much she cared for him, all made her push thoughts of Scotland aside and rush around without pause, like she had done for so many years.

The first few days in Turkey were exciting. They visited the Hagia Sophia, Blue Mosque, and the huge bazaar. They drank sweet mint tea at sidewalk cafés and ate at street stalls. It was pure freedom.

But very quickly, Maren felt the thrill wearing off. She knew this drill. She knew what came next, and she realized that, in a way, this was just as predictable as being on the farm. The excitement, new job, new people… then the boredom, irritation, and abandoning it all to start the exact same pattern again.

She heard Sybil's words…that she would be trapped until she healed her heart.

Sybil had been right. This was a trap, too, this false sense of elation and freedom.

Maren didn't say any of this to Maddy. She didn't think she'd understand, or maybe it was that she wouldn't care. She enjoyed the adventure as best she could, but with each day that passed, she thought more and more about the farm. Sybil. Alex, the horses, the B&B.

One night, over dinner at a noisy café, Maren told her friend she was going home. As she said it, she burst into tears. It *was* home. She had a home. Finally.

The heartache of her childhood was no longer her story. She had rewritten her story. Her story now was one of love and a home and joy and friends and family.

She felt the decades-old crack in her heart start to heal. Yes, the stable had burned. But she was resourceful. She would wait tables and save her money and rebuild. It was only the front of the stables that had burned after all.

Most of all, she missed Alex and Sybil. She missed her life. She just hoped she hadn't burned those relationships to the ground too.

***

It was summer and the Highlands were green and warm. Pink roses were in full bloom in front of the cottage, the lawn was a deep green, and heather was starting to bloom in huge seas of purple over the Highlands.

Maren pulled her car into the driveway on the farm in the dusk of late evening. She had called ahead, so she didn't startle Sybil.

When she got out of the car, they were all there, Sybil, Gillian, Sally… and Alex.

Gillian and Sally ran over and wrapped their arms around her. Sybil followed them slowly and joined them. They all laughed and cried. They were happy she had come back.

Maren apologized and told them she was embarrassed at how childish she had been, but they all reassured her she didn't need to be embarrassed. They knew her past. They understood.

When they stood back, Maren looked at Alex. He smiled just slightly, and without planning it, she ran straight toward him and threw herself into his arms. He embraced her and kissed her.

"I'm so sorry," she whispered.

He whispered back, "I know."

"I was being an idiot. A child. It was my old wounds rearing their ugly head. But this is my home. And I love you, and I don't want to be anywhere else on Earth. But it's terrifying too," she said, her head against his shoulder.

"I love ye, too, Maren," he whispered into her ear. "I don't know what the future holds. None of us do. And life gets messy. But that's just life. If you stay, even in the mess, it just gets better and better." He lifted her chin and kissed her.

They all went inside and had a glass of wine, while Sally sat on the floor, brushing the long suffering cat's hair like he was a doll. They talked and talked, and Maren got the strange feeling they were all smiling at something she didn't understand.

Eventually, Sybil and Gillian and Sally all went to bed, and Maren went home with Alex to his farm, where they made love until they were spent and fell asleep, limbs entwined, smiling.

In the morning, Alex cooked them breakfast and jokingly asked Maren if he was doing it right. She laughed and said it was just fine. Then he drove her back to Hidden Stone Farm.

"Close yer eyes," Alex told her, as they neared the driveway.

She shot him a confused glance. "What?"

"Just do it," he said with a chuckle.

With a laugh, she shut her eyes.

When he parked, he came around to her car door to open it and led her down the drive.

As she slowly made her way, holding Alex's arm, Maren heard lots of noise and banging.

Finally, Alex said, "Okay, open yer eyes, lass."

Maren opened her eyes and gasped.

There in front of her were Charlie, Ian, and several others, standing around smiling at her. The burned wood of the B&B had all been removed, and they were fixing the barn!

She couldn't take in what she was seeing at first. She turned to Alex. "I-I don't understand."

"It's for you, lass. You've loads of people here who love ye. Who've seen ye work your fingers ta the bone to create this gorgeous thing, to help these poor horses. Ta help Gillian and Sally. Ta help Sybil. This is what happens when you've got a community. When ye put down roots. I put the word out about the stables, and people poured in ta help. I have led the crew, by the way, so I get credit." He laughed, and Maren threw her arms around his neck.

"But the money…I can't repay you," Maren said.

"Dinnae fash yerself. All donated. Farmers always have loads of lumber lying around. The village donated a bit. There was a collection, and we bought some things. It's all paid for, lass," he said.

She stood back and said to all the people working, "Thank you! Thank you so much. I don't know how I can ever repay you!"

Ian yelled back, "It's great to see ye, Maren! You're welcome. And we know how ye can repay us," he said, and the others all laughed.

And she did repay them in just the way Ian and the others wanted, by cooking them gorgeous dinners and serving wine and whisky and three-course meals at the long table in the barn each night after they were done.

Maren had just enough money left to replace all the bed linens, which had gotten damaged by the smoke. And soon, the stables were repaired, a new sign was made for the front, and Maren was ready to reopen.

Maren contacted the guests she'd had to cancel, and almost every group rebooked. Soon, she was fully booked again through the fall, the highlight of which was going to be a huge celebration in the stone circle on October 31st, to celebrate the sacred pagan holiday of Samhain.

The night before reopening, Alex came over, and he and Sybil called Maren outside.

"We've something for you, dear," Sybil said, and she pointed toward the barn door. About thirty feet in front of the door was a tiny tree that hadn't been there before.

"It's a rowan tree, dear. The rowan tree is a protector. This will keep you and your guests safe," Sybil said.

Touched, Maren's eyes filled. She had also taken out a good insurance policy and installed better smoke detectors, that would keep them all safe, too, she thought with a smile. But she loved the idea of this little sapling, growing, putting down roots, and protecting her.

"Thank you, Aunt Sybil," Maren said, hugging her tightly.

Sybil went back inside, leaving them alone.

"And I have something for you too," Alex said, and he handed her a package wrapped in pretty green paper.

"Ooh, a present, thank you!" Maren carefully opened the wrapping. When she saw it, she burst into tears. It was a beautiful big scarf in the McGlashan tartan.

"You can wear it as a scarf or wrap it around yourself if it's cold. It's your tartan Maren," he said.

She was thrilled to be able to see the colors, the vibrant red, yellow, gray all woven together. "I love it so much, Alex. It's the most thoughtful gift I've ever been given." She wiped her tears. "My family's tartan," she said out loud.

***

One morning in September, as the first chill was in the air and the hint of frost was on the tips of the grass, Maren woke early, lit the fire in the living room, wrapped her tartan scarf around her shoulders, and sat with her coffee in a big soft chair next to the fire. Mac jumped into her lap, and Maren got out her notebook and pen to plan the menu for the day. The current guests were having a wonderful time, and they wanted dinner each night. Maren, now known by all the local farmers, had some wonderful locally sourced meals in mind for their stay.

Alex would be coming over that evening after she'd served dinner, so they could go out to the pub for dinner on their own. And tomorrow, the farrier was coming to reshoe the horses.

But for now, it was almost time to go to the kitchen to make scones for breakfast, and then it would be time to lead the group to the stone circle. And then to cook dinner.

And soon she'd need to start planning. She was throwing an enormous Samhain celebration on October 31st. It was to be the largest pagan celeoration the area had seen in decades. There were a thousand things to do. And she couldn't wait to start…

The End

Epilogue

Highland Magic was inspired by the tragic, true story of my great Aunt Sybil Campbell. Sybil was locked in an insane asylum in Scotland in her twenties and her family never spoke of her again. None of us knew she existed for over seventy years. My father did not know his own mother had a third sister until 1998 when the two other sisters moved to a nursing home and we went through boxes of very old photos and uncovered pictures with a fourth little girl in them. Luckily, we found the photos before those great aunts passed away and they, reluctantly, told us that Sybil had been a painter, and a bit eccentric. But the only story we were able to get out of my other great aunts when we asked why she had been committed was that one time Sybil decided she didn't like any of her paintings and she burned them all in a big metal drum. In those days, you could have a woman committed for anything from "melancholy" to being pregnant out of wedlock. To me, the fact that her family never again spoke of her and pretended she didn't exist is almost as heartbreaking as locking her up in the first place. Amazingly, when we discovered her and contacted the asylum, which was by then called a hospital, she was still alive! She was 95 years old and, at that point, living in a nursing home.

I quickly traveled to my aunt's house in England, then took the train to Scotland and a bus to the nursing home. And there she was, a beautiful, frail old woman sitting in a big chair, holding a cup of tea. She was completely blind, but she was very alert. She knew the date and day, where she was, and she remembered details about her sisters from decades before. I sat and held her hands since she could not see me. And I said I was so sorry for not having come sooner, but that I hadn't known she was here. We talked for about an hour, I told her I loved her, kissed her cheek and a nurse took the only existing photo of her since her youth. I left the nursing home and returned to the United States. My parents flew to England shortly after, with the sole purpose of visiting her, but while they were en route, Sybil died. I will forever be grateful that I was able to meet her in the tiny window between finding out about her, and her passing. It was almost as if she had been waiting for someone to come find her before leaving this earth. As a ward of the state, Sybil was going to be buried in a graveyard near the nursing home, and near the asylum which had been her prison most of her life but I said absolutely not and had my parents quickly contact the nursing home and have her cremated. She is now buried in Maine, right next to my mother and father, in a beautiful cemetery overlooking the sea. I wrote this book because I love Scotland and it's magic and history. But also to re-write Sybil's story and set her free.

Heather

About The Author

 Heather Morrison-Tapley, author of *The Herbalist*, is a nationally licensed acupuncturist and Chinese herbalist. She also has a master's degree from the University of Chicago in Social Science and an undergraduate degree in Anthropology. Heather was born in New York City and grew up just outside the city. She is a dual US/UK citizen and spent her summers in the UK with her family, part of the time in London and part of the time in sixteenth-century thatched cottage in a small village. She lives with her husband, children, dogs, cat, and chickens in coastal southern Maine.

Printed in Great Britain
by Amazon